Targets of Treachery

TARGETS

OF

TREACHERY

GRIFF HOSKER

LUME BOOKS

LUME BOOKS

Published in 2021 by Lume Books
30 Great Guildford Street,
Borough, SE1 0HS

ISBN 978-1-83901-283-9

Typeset using Atomik ePublisher from Easypress Technologies

www.lumebooks.co.uk

Dedicated to Alice Rees, my first editor and a lovely lady.
I shall miss working with you!

List of Historical Characters in this Novel

King Edward 1 of England
Queen Eleanor of England
Prince Edmund (the king's brother)
William de Beauchamp (Earl of Warwick)
Sir Roger, 1st Baron Mortimer
Lady Maud (his wife)
Edmund Mortimer (his heir)
Roger Mortimer (his second son)
Otto de Grandson (Savoyard knight serving King Edward)
John de Vesci (a northern knight serving King Edward)
Prince Llywelyn ap Gruffydd (Prince of Wales)
Owain ap Gruffydd (Llywelyn's brother and a prisoner of
King Edward)
Dafydd ap Gruffydd (Llywelyn's brother)
Gruffydd ap Gwenwynwyn (a Welsh lord from Powys)
Lady Hawise (his wife)
Gilbert de Clare, 7th Earl of Gloucester
John Giffard (an English soldier)
Stephen de Frankton (an English soldier)

Map of Northern Wales, 1277

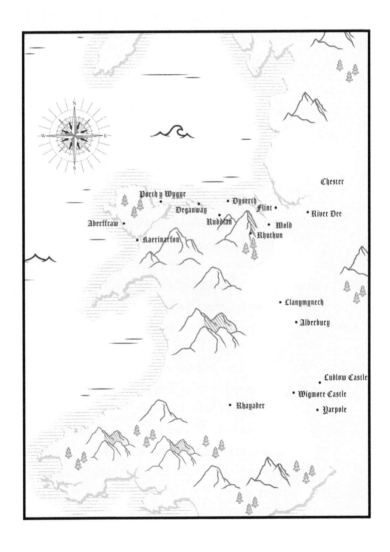

Chapter 1

England, 1274

It was January and when I returned to England, with the woman who would be my wife and my men from the Crusades, I could not know that the new King of England, my master, Edward, and his wife, Eleanor, would take two years to return to England. In contrast to our new king, my men and I could not wait to get home, for we had invested our money wisely in silks and spices. We hoped that when we reached England, we would make ten times the price we had paid for them in the Holy Land. Due to many events beyond our control, we made even more, for we returned to a land that was more lawless than when we had left.

Robert Burnell, who had been left in charge of the country when King Henry became ill, was a fine administrator, but he was not a ruthless man and that was what was needed. As a result, we feared for our safety on the roads of England.

We stayed in London for just three days, but it was necessary, for we had goods to sell and items to buy. We hired a carter to take out purchases and our belongings with us. We rode through our homeland, heading for my village of Yarpole, as though we were going to war. My men were protective of Mary, the slave I had rescued from the Turks, as well as me, their paymaster. I had earned two wounds in the war, one in my back and one in my leg. Neither had threatened my life and would not impair me as an archer, but my men were concerned that I should not suffer another before I reached home.

Sarah, my housekeeper, and her son, James, my steward, were delighted to see me but Father Paul, my priest, was overjoyed when he saw I had brought a bride-to-be, for he had long thought that I should not be a bachelor.

The object of my affections, Mary, was overawed by it all; it was as warm a welcome as she could have hoped, and it contrasted with the weather. Although the weather in England was clement for the time of year, she had been brought up in hot climes and she found it almost bone-chillingly cold. That first evening, as we sat in my hall, having enjoyed a hastily prepared but nonetheless delightful meal, we two spoke. Sarah and James were preparing a chamber for her. My priest had made it quite clear that Mary had to be alone before we wed.

"I am so lucky, Gerald. I have a home for the first time in my life and it is a magnificent home. You are surrounded by the best of people, but yet I fear that I will let you down."

"How can you do that? All you have to do is to be yourself."

"You are a great lord. You told me that you were an archer, but I should have known from the way the queen spoke of you that you are more than that. You are close to the man who rules this land and I know that I will have to meet great ladies. They will see that I was a slave, and it will reflect badly upon you."

I took her hand and kissed it. "I told you on the voyage home of my life. There are no secrets between us. I am a humble archer

2

who has now been made a gentleman. I have done things which might have seen me hanged if events turned out differently. All that you endured was no fault of yours! No more talk of letting me down." I waved a hand around the room. "While the banns are being read and we prepare for the wedding, give thought to how you would like to decorate our hall. I am a man who has neither the experience nor the eye to furnish a hall. In a day or two, we will ride to Wigmore and I will introduce you to Baron Mortimer and Lady Maud. He is the lord of the manor, but Lady Maud is the one who runs it! I think that you should meet. You will get on!"

I was proved correct. I knew not why, but Lady Maud had great affection for me, and it was not just because I had done great service for her. I believe she saw me as another child. She took to Mary immediately and as soon as she heard our news, she whisked her off to meet her ladies and to hear the details of our romance. Lady Maud ruled this part of the Marches because she knew all that was going on. The lords of the land told their wives their innermost thoughts and none could keep that information from Lady Maud.

I was left with Roger Mortimer, the baron. I had been away some time and now I saw that he had aged. He was an old man. Now I knew why he had not gone on crusade with us, for he was close to the king, both now and when he had been the prince, Lord Edward. I had given him a gift of wine and we drank it.

"Lord Edward, sorry, *King* Edward, although he has not yet been crowned, asked me to stay on the borders, for although the Treaty of Monmouth was signed, he did not completely trust the Welsh. It was good that I did, for Prince Llywelyn ap Gruffydd, their leader, has begun to take advantage of a sick king in King Henry and an absent warlord in Lord Edward. He has angered de Bohun and de Clare. He forbade de Clare to build his new castle at Caerphilly. Robert Burnell knows how to count and to tax but that is all. The sooner King Edward comes back to be crowned, the better."

"He planned on travelling to Rome and I had the impression that he was in no hurry to return. He knows nothing of these matters, my lord. When we headed north, we heard of great restlessness in the land and we travelled armed."

"You were wise to do so, my friend. Our only hope is that the brother of Prince Llywelyn, Dafydd ap Gruffydd, seeks to undermine him. He is an ambitious brother. I shall invite him to dine here before Easter, when the roads are better, so that you may meet with him."

I shook my head. "Baron, I am an archer who is now elevated to be a gentleman. The politics of this land is far above my station."

He poured us some more of my wine. "Did you think, when Lord Edward gave you Yarpole, that it was on a whim?" I nodded, for I had thought the land had just become vacant. "Then you are wrong, for he wants you here on this border. You have skills, Gerald Warbow; you are not only a good archer, possibly the best I have ever seen, but you are also a warlord, a leader of men. I know my own limitations. I am a fair swordsman, and I am brave enough, but you are like your master; you have a mind for war. You are well named." He smiled. "And I am old. My bones ache these days. My sons, Roger and Edmund, will have to rule this border, but they are not yet ready. Until they are, I fear that you will need to be vigilant. But you are just recently returned home. You have a wedding to plan and lands to manage."

"Aye, lord, and I need to know what my obligations to you are as Lord of the Manor."

He shook his head. "I wish that all of those who owed me fealty were as keen to please. So long as you pay the taxes to my reeve when they are due and give me or the king forty days' service, then I shall be a happy baron!"

"As the king has yet to return, I do not think that it is likely he will require service, and you say that there is a sort of peace along the borders, my lord?"

He shook his head. "There is anything but peace. The Welsh raid our farms with impunity and when we complain, Prince Llywelyn flourishes the treaty in our faces. So far no noble has died, but when they do…"

I said nothing but I knew that there had been deaths. The men and women who had died or been taken off to be slaves would not have been nobles. They would have been servants or tenants. They might have been a hired sword or even an archer.

"And what is my obligation, Sir Roger?"

"Six archers under your command."

"And if I have more?"

He gave me a quizzical look. "Most tenants would rid themselves of extra mouths to feed and warriors to pay. Yarpole is not a rich manor, Gerald; make sure you can afford them."

"I know not where you get that idea, my lord. Sarah and James have increased the yield from the land and reduced the burden on those who are tenanted to me. The village is a happy and harmonious place compared with what it was. We make a profit. Am I allowed to hire men at arms?"

He burst out laughing. "You are, but why should you? They are more expensive to maintain and you are an archer and a captain of archers."

"And I have seen the merit of having a warrior with a sword, shield and spear close by. I have none in mind, but I believe that I could afford one."

"If you do not object to giving me an answer, where will you find the coins to pay for your warband?"

"King Edward rewarded me for my services, and I did not waste it. We also took some treasure when we were in the Holy Land, and we invested all wisely. The spices, fine cloth and jewels we fetched back were sold at a great profit in London. My men do not require full wages, and each of them has a plot of land at Yarpole which they farm. They are content."

"And you, my young friend, are lucky! Perhaps I should have gone on crusade too, and then I would be rich and could hire men at arms!"

I said nothing, for the rewards had come at great cost. King Edward had almost died! He would be a changed man when the crown was placed upon his head.

The ladies returned an hour after they had departed. To be truthful, I was eager to be away. I had much to plan and Sir Roger's conversation was not particularly interesting. He was like most lords and too concerned with power and perceived slights from other nobles. I had thought Sir John Malton, who had been Lord Edward's squire when I had first met him, was different, but he had shown me on the way back from the land of the Mongols that he was changing. I suppose the knight with whom I had the most in common was Sir Hamo l'Estrange, and I would never see him again, for he was married to a lady who was a virtual queen in her own land. His new elevated status would not change Hamo. Sir John, however, was another matter.

Lady Maud beamed. She always seemed to have a soft spot for me. Perhaps that was because it was I who had brought back the head of Simon de Montfort for her. "You have a most interesting and beautiful bride-to-be, Gerald, for a humble archer. I know of ladies who are noble-born but not as refined as Mary here, and to think she served Good Queen Eleanor! You are blessed, but then again, she could have done worse!" Lady Maud never minded about the sensibilities of others and I wondered if this jibe was at the expense of her husband.

"We shall see you at the wedding, of course. Make sure that we can attend, Gerald!"

That was a warning if ever I heard one. "Of course, Lady Maud."

"And of course, Sir Roger will give a generous gift for the most renowned of his tenants. The man who saved the life of the king should have been rewarded more than you have, Gerald."

With that, we were dismissed, and we rode home. I had taken six of my archers with me as an escort that was not for my protection, as I never feared brigands, but for Mary. She was unmarried and I wished her reputation to remain unsullied. Robin, son of Richard of Culcheth, led the five others who acted as bodyguards for Mary's honour. He was tanned, for he had been to the Holy Land with me. Roger of Barnsley and William of Matlac, in contrast, appeared almost white. As the crusade grew more distant, the dark skin would fade.

I spoke to Mary as we rode. "Well, what did you think of Lady Maud?"

"She is the most terrifying woman I have ever met, and I would not like to get on the wrong side of her, but you are right. She has a soft spot in her heart for you and I think that there is no more well-meaning soul in Christendom, but when she hates…"

"Did she show you de Montfort's pickled head?"

"I know she hated him, but she has…?"

I nodded. "I brought it from the field of battle to her. The only surviving offspring of that rebel is Eleanor de Montfort and she is in France. If she were any closer, then Lady Maud would seek some way of hurting her."

We rode in silence for a mile or two. Mary was well wrapped in furs, and the clear blue skies allowed her to see the beautiful but potentially deadly borderlands. Her breath appeared before her fur lined hood. Darkness would soon come, but by then, we would be safe in my hall before a roaring fire with the finest of foods prepared by Sarah and the servants.

"Do you mind having to set the date of our marriage on the whim of Lady Maud?"

"Do not forget that I was a slave for most of my life until I met you. For me, living my life by the orders of others is normal. I care not when we are wed, just that we are, for I would put my past behind me and live in this future with you. I like your home, if not the climate!"

I laughed. "We can always wrap up against the cold."

Even though a lord and lady would be in attendance, we determined to make those two the only wedding guests from outside the manor. I knew not if Sir John Malton had returned yet, but I would not invite him, even though he had been there when I had met Mary, for he lived on the other side of the country. However, the sheer numbers involved meant that we had to buy more platters and goblets, as well as a set of good knives with which to cut meat. The food was easy; my archers and I would hunt in the wood which came with the manor. We would act as husbandmen and ensure that whatever animals we took would be those likely to die before winter was out. As Sarah said, there were ways to cook any meat and make it delicious. Mary spent a great deal of time with Sarah, for she had much to learn. Cooking and cleaning had not been part of her duties. She had been a slave but a specialised one.

I stood, one day, in the corner of the kitchen as Sarah taught Mary how to make that most basic of foods after bread: pottage. I had grown up eating this on a daily basis. It usually began life on Monday when whatever the meal had been on the holy day, Sunday, was recooked. We were luckier than most people, for we had access to rabbits, ham and venison. When the goats we used for milking dried up, then they might be butchered. To whatever leftover meat there was, a stock would be added with the bones of the animal and then whatever vegetables were available.

Mary asked questions all the time as Sarah gave her a lesson. "What are skirrets, Sarah?"

"Why, my lovely, they are like parsnips but a little smaller!"

My soon-to-be wife was a quick learner and, to be truthful, I quite enjoyed her mistakes! I could not help but smile, one Friday, as Sarah prepared our meal. It was the law that no meat was to be eaten on Fridays and Sarah had managed to acquire a beaver. The delicacy of the tail would be served to us whilst the workers would enjoy the rest.

Mary turned to me. "But Gerald, this is not a fish! It has fur!"

Sarah nodded and said firmly, "It swims and lives in the water. It is a fish!"

Every day was a learning experience for Mary. Her lessons allowed me to ride my lands and visit my village. I had grown up poor, and I appreciated not only the life I had but the responsibility I owed to those who lived under my care. I had experienced the worst of masters and whilst I was not yet a lord, I knew my duty. I rode with James and he re-introduced me to the village and my tenants. The previous owner had been not only a supporter of de Montfort but also a bad landlord. In the time I had been landlord, many people who had left had since returned. That was largely down to James and his mother. Yarpole was their home.

And so, the days before my wedding were filled from dawn until dusk and often beyond. My archers practised without me, and our experiences meant that the practice was extended to include swordplay. We had brought weapons back from the east and my men were taught to use them.

John of Nottingham and Jack of Lincoln were the leaders of my men, but I doubted that they would travel to war. Both had married and had children; I had given them smallholdings on my land. Each was the size of the home my father had built. I gave them permission to enlarge them if they needed to.

Alan, too, had married, and he and his wife lived beyond my walls with their two sons. He was a hunter and lived close to the woods.

The others, who were single, lived in a small hall which was attached to the Great Hall. The previous owner had used it for his half dozen men at arms. The only other exception was Richard of Culcheth, who shared a small house with his son, Robin, son of Richard, and Mags, the woman he had married.

The night before our wedding, Mary and I went to the church to speak with Father Paul. We would both be shriven and the ceremony explained. With no father to give away Mary, that part would be omitted.

For Mary, this was all new. She was a Christian, but she had been brought up in the Eastern Church and for most of her life she had lived amongst non-Christians. She wished everything to be done correctly. On our way back from the crusade she had insisted upon visiting the churches in each town we passed. As she observed to me, she had been forced to be away from them for so long that she had to visit them as often as she could.

For myself, I knew that this was a momentous time in my life. It was not just a wife I was taking on; hopefully, there would be children, and it was as we walked back to my hall, wrapped in furs against the wicked wind which blew in from the Welsh mountains in the west, that she expressed her fears to me. I think she chose that moment for we were alone, and she wished none to overhear her words.

"Gerald, I am not sure if I will be able to have children."

I said nothing, for the thought had crossed my mind.

"Since first I became a woman, someone who was used by men at court, I have taken those drugs and potions which prevent a child from being conceived. Since we decided to wed, I have not taken them, but I know not what effect it will have had upon my body."

I nodded. "I wish for children as you do, but I also want to spend my life with you and that is more important. What

11

will be shall be. If you cannot bear children of your own, there are many orphans in this land who need someone to care for them. Let us not speak of that. Tomorrow we wed, and you are anticipating that which may never come to fruition."

She squeezed my arm as James opened the front door and we saw the warm glow from within. "You are a good man, and I am lucky. I thank God for the day you were sent to rescue me!"

As much as I wished to be married, the day itself was something of an ordeal. I could not relax because of Lady Maud's brooding presence. She made a gift of a fine table and chairs as well as ten golden marks, but I would have preferred that she was not there. All the rest were my people and, with them, I was both at ease and more confident. Mercifully, Lady Maud and Sir Roger did not stay beyond the baron giving a toast to his most loyal gentleman, Gerald Warbow of Yarpole. His age meant he did not like to be out late.

After they left us to make the journey home in daylight, I relaxed more and could play the host to my men and their families. We celebrated! When all had departed and I took Mary to our bed, I was nervous. I had almost no experience with women and in my twenty-odd years on this earth, I had yet to lie with one. Mary was gentle with me and that, in many ways, was surprising, for she had been ill-treated, certainly by the last warrior who had abused her. I had expected, at worst, tears, and at best, nervousness. Yet there was neither, and it was she who led me into the joys and pleasures of marital coupling. I was unsure if I had done things right and I dared not ask, yet when I cradled her head in the crook of my arm, she gave a contented sigh and said, "I have a good man and a gentleman. God has been kind to me!"

Life on the manor began to become hectic as spring approached. I had yet to see a full year at Yarpole, and while King Edward remained abroad, that was likely to continue. I placed myself in the hands of James who was patient with me. Mary was busy learning to be the lady of the manor as well as a homemaker. Sarah was patient with her too.

As early summer approached, two things happened. Firstly, in the middle of April, we discovered that Mary was with child. She and Sarah were so close that it was my housekeeper who saw the first signs, and they were confirmed by the village midwife, Anne of Yarpole. I was filled with happiness and Mary even more so, for all of her fears seemed to be groundless. We celebrated by broaching a new barrel of ale.

The second event was also important, but I did not see it at the time. It happened the night of the barrel-broaching. Robin, son of Richard, had been restless since our return from the Holy Land. Added to that, he lived with his father. Richard of Culcheth had remarried a widow, Mags, and they shared a bed. It was a small house and I think that began the discord. It was aggravated by the fact that Richard still thought he could tell his son what to do and, having been a crusader, Robin objected. It came to a head when I was woken in the middle of the night by the noise of brawling. Grabbing my sword, I raced outside and found Richard and his son fighting. Robin was winning! John of Nottingham and Jack of Lincoln were on hand to pull them apart. Father and son were bleeding heavily, for while they had not used weapons, archers are strong men and when they punch, they break skin and bones.

"What is going on? My wife and I have been disturbed!"

"I will not be told to be quiet in my own home by a stripling of a boy!"

Robin spat out a tooth. "And I will not endure a fat old man heaving the night away with a slattern!"

"I will—"

"Enough! Richard, go back to your bed. Robin, you shall sleep in my hall this night and when, tomorrow, heads are clear of drink, we shall sit, and we shall talk!" The voice I used was that of a captain of archers. The two were used to obeying it, and they nodded and headed off in different directions.

My wife had been listening and Mary, who had grown close to Robin on the journey home, led him to the chamber next to ours. There was a straw-filled mattress on the floor. When my child was born it would be their room.

"Thank you, Captain." There was no door, just a curtain, and he closed it.

I lay with Mary and she said, "This is not like Robin. He is normally placid. I do not know his father. Is he normally a bully?"

I shook my head. "Richard is no bully. There is more to this than noisy lovemaking. I will speak with Robin in the morning." I smiled in the dark. "I suppose that everything else has gone smoothly, and it is natural to expect some sort of payment for my joy!"

I did not sleep well, for my mind was filled with strange thoughts. Would I have such arguments with my child when he or she was older? I had never been close to my own father, and how would I ensure that my child and I were different? I also worried that I had, somehow, created this problem. Should I have given Robin his own dwelling?

The result was that I was well awake before the first cock crow and even beat Sarah to the kitchen. I put on the pot of porridge, which was our staple breakfast, as I began to bring the bread oven up to temperature. There was little bread left from the previous day, but the pieces which were left could be toasted on the fire and served with Sarah's butter. I drank a beaker of beer and stirred the porridge.

Robin arrived shortly after Sarah. As I expected, Sarah was less than happy at my intrusion. The kitchen was her domain, although she would share it with Mary. "Get yourself back to bed, Captain! There is naught for you to do here!"

"I am awake, and I used to make porridge for my father. I can still do it!"

She nodded and went to the covered dough which had been left proving. Made with the left-over dregs of beer from the bottom of the jug, it was well risen and the little bubbles over the top showed that it would have a good crust. She began to shape the loaves. Robin arrived as she began to round them.

"Another one who cannot sleep! Is there some animal in the beds I should know about?"

We would periodically allow smoke to fill the bedrooms to eliminate any insect life from the beds. The cats we kept would rid the rooms of any vermin such as mice or rats.

Robin knew Sarah and smiled. "No, Gammer, but I heard the captain speaking and I need to talk with him. It does not do to let things fester."

She saw the bruised face and knuckles. Perhaps she had forgotten the fight, for she would surely have heard it. She nodded. "My ears are closed, Robin, and you speak in here as though I was a priest."

I poured him some ale. "It was not like you nor your father to fight so. If it is my fault for putting you in the same house, then I am sorry, and you can move into the warrior hall."

He shook his head. "No, Captain, the row last night was bound to happen, for it is my father and me. He still sees me as a boy he can order around, but you know I am a warrior and a good one. I did not let you down on crusade, did I?"

"No, Robin, you were a beacon for others to follow and I could not fault you."

He nodded. "It is clear that we both cannot stay here, and I cannot expect you to rid yourself of my father and his woman. Do not misunderstand me, Captain; I would rather stay here and serve you, but we both know that this company needs to be of one mind, and if it is not then we cannot fight for you as well as we might. My father and I will be like pebbles in a boot. We will upset the others. I will seek service with another lord, for I am a good archer, and the Marcher lords seek such bows as mine."

My heart sank; only Will Yew Tree had left my service and he had returned quite quickly. Robin had come to me as a boy with his father, but he was right. We could not have dissension and it made more sense for the son to leave, but he was the better archer and would be missed more than his father.

"Perhaps some time apart might help."

He shook his head. "It is the parting of the ways, but I am sorry that I am leaving you. I would go now, Captain, before the others are awake. I do not like goodbyes, and I do not wish to make your company choose between my father and me."

I could understand those reasons. He was young and he was doing that which I had done when my father had been murdered.

"Take your horse. He is a gift. And take this too." I reached into my purse and took out ten marks. It was the money Lady Maud had given us. Mary would wish Robin to have it. "This will keep you fed until you find employment."

"There is no need, Captain. You have paid me well; better, in fact, than other archers."

"Nonetheless you will take it."

I saw that Sarah was crying quietly. She had heard the words and knew that Robin meant well, but she was a parent and knew the distress it would cause Richard. She said quietly, "And I will pack you some food. We have a spare ale skin, sir; can I give it to him?"

"Of course, Sarah, and anything else that he needs."

All of my men had good war gear and they all kept it to hand. Robin had collected his and saddled his horse before anyone else had risen. It was still dark when I clasped his arm and Sarah handed him his bundle.

"Where will you go?"

"Powys, I think. I have heard that Lord de Clare and Lord de Bohun seek men to fight for them against the Welsh."

"Farewell, Robin, and if this does not work out, then return. Do not let pride keep you away from us!"

His horse clip-clopped across the stones of the yard and Sarah sighed. "Families! Both father and son have stiff necks! Had I known there was a problem, then I would have spoken to Mags. She could have handled them. Too late now." Shaking her head, she said, "I had better get the bread into the oven. That will wake the hall."

She was right. There was nothing better to wake to than the aroma of freshly baking bread.

Mary was in the kitchen when we returned. She said simply, "Robin has gone?"

I nodded. "He wants a new start, but his father will be hurt. These are the problems of the manor, my love. They must seem petty after life at the Mongol court."

"Believe me, husband, the nobles around the khan had similar arguments, but I feel sorry for both of them. Suppose they never see each other again? Robin has left without a goodbye."

"I do not think he meant to hurt his father, rather the opposite, but I know Richard and it will hurt."

I was right and I had never seen my archer so distraught. "I had had too much to drink, Captain, and he could be so obstinate. I just wanted the best for him."

I nodded. "And I think he knew that, but I have trodden the same path as he has chosen, and I have ended here. Fate has a way of levelling out our lives. I lost my father and found service with Lord Edward. Robin has not yet lost you, but he has lost a home. Who knows what he might find?" I saw that sinking in. "I told him that he will always have a home here and he can return at any time but, if he does, Richard, then I want no repetition of last night."

"I am sorry for that, Captain. You gave us a home and you do not deserve it. I will work twice as hard from now on."

Chapter 2

Robin's departure was the talk of the manor and the village for a fortnight, and then we found other things to occupy our minds.

The manor needed all of us to work. Even I found myself stripped to the waist and toiling in the fields. There were new animals born and to be marked, as well as fields to be ploughed and sown.

Life was far more hectic for a farmer than an archer, though we still maintained our practice and I made a weekly competition when we were at the butts. I asked the men of the village to join us, for they could all use a bow, and Baron Mortimer and the king were entitled to ask for service at any time. Each week I gave a prize of silver to the best archer. The men of the village vied for the four pennies I offered. The result was keen competition, and men ensured that their bows and their arrows were of the highest quality.

We had passed the longest day; July was almost upon us, and my wife was becoming noticeably pregnant. While I worried about her, Sarah and the other women on the manor told me, politely, that this was women's work and all was well. I did not argue, for I was as far out of my depth as I had ever been. I understood neither women nor their world.

We were at peace but that did not mean that we were not vigilant, for we were soldiers, and being vigilant was second nature to us. June had ended and I was already anticipating harvesting some of the early crops. I smiled to myself – a few years ago I would not have even dreamt of such things. Farms were simply places I might raid to find food.

My thoughts were interrupted by a whistle from Martin, who pointed up the road. A man was walking down the road and while one arm was bandaged, the other held a spear which he used as an aid to walk. By his clothes, he was a warrior, for he still wore a leather brigandine.

I put down the pitchfork I had been using to turn the horse muck and walked towards my sword, which hung from a gate-post. One man did not worry me, but I had used a trick like this once before. He could be a scout or even a decoy. I nodded to John and Jack who went back towards the hall. They would arm themselves.

The closer he came, the less threatening he appeared. He had no sword, and the spear was an old one with a hastily repaired head. His buskins were well worn. This was a warrior who was down on his luck and I wondered if he sought shelter. If so then I would grant it, for it was not only a Christian thing to do, but I also had an affinity for all those who wandered the roads of the realm. I had done so when I had been younger.

He was not a young man, for I saw streaks and flashes of silver in his hair. Now that he was drawing closer, I saw that his left hand was bloodily bandaged. It was a recent wound, and yet I had heard of no battles that were nearby. The man had passed my village and was heading for my hall. Father Paul would have offered him comfort so why was he seeking me?

I took the ale skin from its hook and the wooden beaker from the top of the post. I poured a beakerful. "Welcome, friend. It is a hot day and I dare say you could use a drink!"

He leaned his spear against the fence, which also allayed any remaining doubts I might have harboured. "Thank you, master." He addressed me thus because of my sword. He drank the ale down in one and I waited. He had sought out my hall. "I am looking for a Richard of Culcheth."

I turned, for Richard was repairing the fence around the sheep pen we would be using to mark the new sheep.

He heard his name and looked up. "I am Richard of Culcheth. Do I know you, my friend? From your dress, you are a soldier but not an archer. How do I know you?"

"You don't, but I know your son, Robin; that is to say that I *knew* your son."

My heart almost stopped, and I saw the look of terror on Richard's face. This must be the worst fear for any parent and my yard was not the place to hear news which sounded bad. "Let us retire within the hall. Robin of Barnsley, continue with the work."

"Aye, Captain. I am sorry, Richard."

Like the rest of us, Robin of Barnsley assumed that this was bad news. If I had learned anything on my travels it was to assume the worst and then you were rarely disappointed. I thought, from what the stranger had said, that Robin, son of Richard, was dead, and I wondered what this would do to Richard, who had been a shadow of his former self since his son had gone.

John and Jack had alerted Sarah and my wife. Even as we arrived there were chairs ready for us in the hall we used for dining. There were questions in their eyes, but their voices were silent. I sat next to Richard and I noticed that John and Jack stood behind him. Sarah disappeared and I knew that she would bring in food.

I patted the other seat next to me. "Sit, wife, for this man has news of Robin, son of Richard here."

The man said, "My name, lord, is Peter of Beverley."

"I am not a lord. My title is that of captain. Tell your tale, John. Sarah, refill his beaker, for he is thirsty."

"Thank you. Robin mentioned a captain of archers, but he did not tell me your name. In truth, I barely knew him, but I knew you would need news.

"I will begin at the start of my story. I am a spearman by trade and have been for my whole life. My wife and son were taken from me by the pestilence ten years since, and I served Lord Jasper of Alberbury. Robin arrived a few weeks ago and, being an archer, was taken on immediately, for there was a need for good archers. Lord Jasper hated the Welsh and was aggrieved by the Treaty of Monmouth. Hearing that King Edward was on his way back to England, he decided to take a raiding party into Wales while he still could, for it is rumoured that King Edward will not try to regain the lands and castles his father lost."

I was not sure about that, for the man who had left England on his crusade was not the same one who would return, but I said nothing. I wondered how close to England were the new king and queen.

Peter of Beverley shook his head. "It was a disaster, for the Welsh were waiting for us just after we crossed the bridge at

Crewgreen. Your son tried to warn Lord Jasper and begged him to let him ride as a scout, but Lord Jasper, well, he was Lord Jasper and called him foolish. It was a mistake, for Lord Jasper was the first to die. He had no helmet upon his head and the Welsh arrows threw him from his horse. Most of our men were killed. I almost died." He held up his left hand. "A Welshman with an axe hacked through my shield and almost took my arm. When the handful of us who survived were taken, they took my hand and sealed the stump with fire. I suppose I was lucky."

Mary put her hand to her mouth. "Lucky? You poor man!"

He smiled. "I am alive, and I am free. The Welsh took the other four survivors as prisoners and they were taken to the silver mines at Llanymynech. Robin was one of them. Prince Llywelyn uses the silver to fund his ambitions. I was sent with a message for Lady Gwendoline. I was told to tell her that if there was any retribution, then Prince Llywelyn would wreak havoc in her lands."

Jack of Lincoln said, "But there is peace! The Treaty of Monmouth!"

Peter shook his head. "And that means nothing, my friend. Who can enforce it when King Henry signed away so many rights? I returned to Lady Gwendoline and after she heard the news, she turned me out."

Silence descended. Sarah came in with a platter of food. I saw Peter's eyes widen in anticipation and I said, "Eat. John, have a bed made for him in the warrior hall. You shall stay the night, Peter of Beverley. Continue with your tale when your appetite is sated."

He began to eat and the five warriors in the room exchanged looks. We knew what this meant. Life as a slave in a mine was

23

measured in weeks, not months. But by my reckoning, Robin, even if he had been captured soon after he left us, would only have been a slave for a couple of weeks. We had a chance. He was not dead, and so long as he lived, then there was hope. I saw in Richard's eyes that no matter what I did or said, he would seek his son.

Mary squeezed my hand. She, of all people, understood what it was to be a slave and without a word, I knew that she would wish me to rescue the young archer with whom she had been so close on the journey west.

Peter finished his food, and I saw that Richard was leaning forward in his chair as though wishing to drag information from the wounded warrior. Had I not been there, then he might have already asked questions.

As it was, he had to let me do the speaking. "The four men taken – were they hurt?"

"You mean like me?" I nodded. "They had no use for a cripple and let me go. The others had minor hurts." He gestured with his half-empty beaker to the men in the room. "You are all warriors and know that even in victory there are hurts. Your son was whole, but they took his weapons and his horse."

"And why come here?" There was suspicion in my voice, for there were four captives and I did not know why he had chosen to act as Robin's herald.

"That is simple, Captain. Robin was the only one I knew to have family, and he spoke often of his father and his regret that he had left with such ill feeling. When we prayed, the night before we left Alberbury, he said that if anything happened to him and I survived, then I was to tell his father that he regretted speaking the way he did and to beg his forgiveness. He did not

24

want to die with bad feeling." He smiled. "And now I have done my duty, I will be on my way."

I restrained him. "And where will you go?"

His face became sad. "I know not. Where do cripples such as me end up? The gutter. Perhaps I—"

Mary suddenly burst out, "You will not leave my home! God has sent you here for a purpose. Husband, we can find a place for this man! There are jobs he can do." Her eyes pleaded with me and I saw them welling with tears.

I nodded. "Of course you shall stay, for, Peter of Beverley, there is more we need to know. Richard, take Peter and help him to wash. John, you are good with wounds. Clean up his hand and give him some clean clothes from the slop chest." We had a war chest and a slop chest; one with weapons and one with clothes.

"Thank you, Captain, and I will work. I know not what at, but I will do all that I can." He shook his head. "I served Lord Jasper and his father for fifteen years and this was my reward."

Left with Jack and my wife, I could speak openly. "Richard will want to find his son."

Jack said, "All of the men will wish that, Captain. Robin was popular and he sought forgiveness. Isn't there a story in the Bible about a prodigal son? Mistress Mary is right; God has sent this man for a purpose."

"But it is not as simple as that, Jack. Firstly, we know not how many men we face and, secondly, probably more importantly, we risk the ire of King Edward, for if we go then we invite retribution from the Welsh and censure from the king!"

There was silence, but I knew that even if I did not agree to it, my men would head north and west to rescue the prodigal son.

Mary said, "Queen Eleanor would wish you to rescue him."

I smiled. "Aye she would, but Lord Edward, the king? He can be a cold and ruthless man. All of my service to him might have been as nothing if I disobeyed him. I need to ask more questions and to sleep on this. Llanymynech, if memory serves, is less than fifty miles from here. That is just two days of hard riding, and we cannot leave tonight, for we have not all the information we need."

Richard and John came back with a much cleaner looking spearman. His bandage was no longer blood-soaked. Richard gave me a sad smile. "We had to clean the wound with vinegar and apply more honey. It does not smell bad, but I shall find some maggots in case it turns out to be so."

I nodded. We had learned that if you put maggots in an infected wound, they eat the dead and infected flesh and leave the healthy. When they die the wound is clean.

"So, Peter, tell me about the others who were taken and why you did not visit with their families."

"Stephen de Frankton is a man at arms, and he comes from Shropshire but hates the Welsh like no man I have ever met, for they slew his whole family – mother, father and young brothers – who lived on the border. He only survived as he was fighting in Gascony when his family fell. He returned not long before Robin arrived and sought, like he, to fight, but in his case, it was not an accident that he served Sir Jasper. Stephen wanted to fight the Welsh. He and your son, Richard of Culcheth, are close. The other two, Jacques and Henry, are Breton crossbowmen. I would not even know how to get in touch with their families." He gave me a sad smile. "Robin did not get on with them!"

"He is an archer and they are crossbowmen! My son would spit on their shadow!"

"I have heard of Llanymynech, but I know not what to expect," I said. I saw Richard's eyes widen and the hint of a smile appear on his lips. "Aye, Richard, we know you wish to rescue him, but we do not do so like the wild men from north of the wall. Do you understand? If we do this then I command, and you obey."

"Yes, Captain!"

"So, what can I expect?"

"It is a silver mine, Captain Warbow. They have a hall for the twenty or so warriors who guard the miners and the silver. There is a slave hall. The slaves are shackled with fetters around their ankles. When they are marched to the mine, they are chained one to another."

"And the guards? Mailed?"

"There are three men at arms who wear brigandines and looked to be handy. The rest are just hired swords and archers. They looked to me more like bandits than warriors."

Jack said suddenly, "When did this capture happen?"

"Three weeks since. I was held there for a couple of days and it took me a week to get back to Alberbury. The rest of the time I was heading south. People are not as kind as I remember."

He needed to say no more; I could picture his journey. Eating from the hedgerow and drinking water from streams used by animals and humans as a toilet was not conducive to a fast pace.

Mary took Peter's good hand. "Well, now, Peter of Beverley, you have a home, and you shall be fed. When you are healed," she tapped his head gently, "here as well as your hand, we will find work that you can do."

I had married well, for there was no kinder woman than Mary.

Later, Peter, along with Richard and Mags, were invited to dine with us. It was Mary who invited Mags, and I knew why. Since Robin had left us there had been an unhappy atmosphere in the home Mags and Richard shared. Mary hated discord. It was cleverly done, for Peter's sad story – and the more we heard of his tale the sadder it became – seemed to draw Mags and Richard closer.

"Who will you take, Captain?"

Richard waited until we had finished the dessert, which was a concoction of stewed early summer fruits topped with oats and rye, mixed with a little honey.

I wiped my mouth. "I will not take all of my men, Richard, for I now have a family here." He nodded. "John and Jack would come as they are both experienced, but they have families of their own. You will be the one with experience. It goes without saying that I will take David the Welshman. Robin of Barnsley regretted my decision not to take him on crusade and he was close to your son. Martin; William of Matlac; Tom, John's son and Will Yew Tree will be sufficient."

Mary looked at me and her mouth dropped open.

Peter looked at her and said, "Captain, did you not hear me? There are three good warriors and seventeen others!"

"From what you told me, the seventeen will be like bandits and we have fought such men before. It seems to me that night-time is the best time to attack them. Were all twenty on watch, all night?"

"No, Captain. While I was there one of the better warriors would watch at night with three others. There were twenty miners, but they do not live long. Four guards at a time can manage them."

"Then we have enough men to deal with four warriors, even if one of them does wear a brigandine. As soon as the miners are freed, then we shall have twenty-seven men and they will have just sixteen. Those odds I like."

Peter nodded. "It is still a risk, for you have seven miles yet to go to reach the border."

"We both know that there is no border there. Shrewsbury is England and that is almost thirty miles away. We shall manage!" I turned to my wife and touched the back of her hand. "When you have travelled leagues through the land of the Turk, this does not seem such a bad journey to have to make!"

"And we leave tomorrow?"

I shook my head. "No, Richard, for I have to go to Wigmore and tell Baron Mortimer what we intend."

Richard had been happy, but his face fell at my words. "You cannot, Captain, for he will forbid you to go!"

I watched Mags squeeze his hand. "Dick, the captain knows his business and he commands. Bend your stiff neck, for it has brought us to this place!"

I nodded. "Listen to Mags, for I know my mind on this. I will not risk this manor, for it is not just me who will be affected. Think of the others. The king has not returned yet and I believe that I can persuade Sir Roger. You may come with me if you wish but it will be my decision!"

Defeated, he nodded.

That night, as my wife lay in my arms, we discussed all the events of the afternoon and evening. I was happy we did so, for we were of one mind and that pleased me.

I was lucky, for the baron was at home when we reached Wigmore the next day. He could have been hunting or visiting one of his many homes. Lady Maud and her ladies were sewing a tapestry of Evesham. I knew without looking at it that it would be graphically gruesome!

The baron took us to his solar. "How is your wife? I heard she is with child!"

"She is, my lord, and she is well."

"Good. You are lucky to find us here. We had a letter from Sir Robert Burnell. The king will be back in England by August and he will be crowned at Westminster. Lady Maud and I are invited to the coronation."

"Finally, he is back!"

"I would not use such words when you meet him, Warbow, for they sound critical to me!"

"I meant no offence, my lord; it is just that before he heard the news of the death of his father, he was keen to return home."

Mollified, he nodded. "You may be right, and certainly we need a strong King of England once more. Prince Llywelyn has grown bolder in the absence of a king. Earl Gilbert de Clare did not sail with Lord Edward on crusade, because Llywelyn had destroyed his new castle. Although de Clare has recovered his lost lands and almost completed Caerphilly castle, it shows what Llywelyn is capable of."

I suddenly spied hope. "And have you heard of Lord Jasper of Alberbury's fate, my lord?"

He nodded. "A foolish man. His widow has left for the south and that castle is now deserted!"

"Llywelyn took captives, my lord, and one of them is Richard of Culcheth's son."

It was as though the baron saw Richard for the first time. "I am sorry, Richard! The king will put things right."

"My lord, by the time the king returns, then my son might be dead!"

"Richard! Curb your tongue! I am sorry, Baron. However, Richard is right in his urgency, and I intend to go to Wales and rescue my man."

"You risk the king's displeasure."

"From what you have told me, Gilbert de Clare did just as I intend and took back what was his."

"He is an earl!"

"King Edward and Queen Eleanor are both fond of Robin. If they were here, then I believe they would allow me to do this. I will not be taking an army. There will be but eight of us and we will wear no livery." I paused. "No one will know that you are our lord. We will just be eight archers rescuing a friend and a son."

"It is tempting, and I do hate the Welsh so." He smiled. "Thank you for telling me that you will visit with Robin, son of Richard. When I return from London and the king is crowned, you may speak to me about seeking reparation for his abduction."

As we rode back to Yarpole, Richard asked, "I am confused; does that mean we have his permission or not?"

"He is pretending not to have understood our intention. That way he can deny all, should the king be angry, and I alone will be punished. The baron is a friend of the king, but he will not risk his anger."

As I lay in my bed, the night before we left, Mary squeezed me tightly. "I know that you have to go and do this, for Richard cannot let his son stay a slave, but remember, husband, that you have a wife and child. Do not be reckless and throw your life away."

I could not see her face, but I smiled and kissed her. "I am never reckless. You should know that I am good at what I do. We have time to assess the situation and to plan for a successful rescue. Do not fret if we are away longer than you expect. It just means that we are being careful."

She sighed, kissed me and then nestled into me to sleep. I had meant what I said. Life was too precious to throw away. I had changed once I found Mary, and my life had a different purpose now. There was a family, and I would do all that I could to make my home safe. But I was still Gerald Warbow, and there was a bond with my men. I would go to Wales; the Welsh would learn to fear me!

Chapter 3

For some of my men, this was their first action in a long time. The last time I had seen Richard of Culcheth draw a bow in anger had been in the Holy Land, and for Robin of Barnsley, before I went on crusade. It was another reason why I had not brought John or Jack; an archer's reactions had to be swift, for hesitation could cost us dearly.

At the fore, I had William of Matlac and Will Yew Tree. They were both experienced and, having survived the Holy Land, were as sharp as any. Robin of Barnsley and Richard led the two horses. They objected but I cared not. I would do this my way. Tom and Martin brought up the rear and I rode with David the Welshman.

As we rode David said quietly, "I am pleased that you have taken me, Captain, for I felt I had fallen out of favour with you."

I turned, surprised, for I valued none higher than David. "Of course not. What makes you say that?"

"You did not take me on crusade with you and this will be the first time I have gone to war... for a long time."

I shook my head. "I left you behind along with John and Jack, for I wanted my home and my people protected. You did that, and I wanted my young men to have the opportunity to gain experience."

He looked relieved. "Then I am happy."

"Do you know this place to which we travel?"

He shook his head. "I have heard of it, but my service was further south. I know the Conwy Valley and I have served in Aberystwyth, but the silver mine? No. What I do know is that, along with the gold mines close to Dolgellau, it is where the Welsh rulers find their money. Anglesey gives them wheat and that feeds the people, but Wales is a poor country. Their towns are like large villages and they cannot be taxed like the English. A ruler has to dig for his money. The guards will be good, Captain, and this will need skill and cunning as well as courage."

"It is why we go in at night. This will be knife work and the ones who fought in the Holy Land are now more skilled."

"I am an archer."

"And you will be the one to slay those who patrol the slave hall. Who else would you take with you?"

"Will and Richard are the ones who will be the steadiest, and Richard will be keen to get to his son. That will leave you just four men to take the other guards; will that be enough?"

I patted my metal-studded brigandine. "I have the most experience with a sword and Martin and Tom fought on the walls of Acre. They will do. I plan on eliminating their three best warriors first. We will have to wait until we get to the horses before we use our hammer and chisel to rid Robin of his fetters."

The headwaters of the Severn are close to Crewgreen and the river narrow enough to swim on a steady horse. We saw many people on the road as we headed north, but they were the usual travellers; merchants heading to Ludlow or Shrewsbury, others heading north to Chester or south to Worcester. What we did not see were soldiers. The imminent arrival of the king meant that every lord would have been summoned to swear allegiance to the new king. Not to do so might result in the loss of lands. In Prince Llywelyn's case, failure to pay homage to Edward was tantamount to a declaration of war. That alone made me more hopeful that he would be nowhere near his mine!

Where we planned to cross, we also had the advantage of thick undergrowth and trees to hide us so that we could make a camp that was safe from spying eyes. We left the road at Coedway. The road to Wales went west and we headed for the River Severn, just before its junction with the River Vyrnwy. We ensured that there were no prying eyes to watch us cross, and we found somewhere with rocks on the southern bank to disguise our tracks. Of course, a good tracker would find where we had crossed, but by the time they had backtracked us, I hoped to be back at Yarpole.

The river was just fifteen paces wide and although it was lively, the water was not deep enough to necessitate swimming. Our breeks, however, were soaked. Once on the other side, David and Will went up and downstream to ensure that we were alone and to find a good campsite. David found one upstream, to the west of us. Here the river was young, and it twisted and turned in narrow loops. He found a wooded area between a loop of the river. The trees hid us, and it meant we had just the north side of the camp to guard.

We tethered the horses and took off our breeks to let them dry. We would not risk a fire but there was enough warmth in the air to begin to dry them. When we donned them again, they would still be damp but that was all.

Having ascertained that we were alone, I gathered my men around me. "According to Peter, the mines are just ten miles from where the Vyrnwy meets the Severn. If we rise early, before dawn, and follow the river, we will add three or four miles to our journey, but we have to avoid the village. Peter passed through it on his way home and said that there was a hall there, and that suggests some sort of lord of the manor. I would not risk a confrontation. When we find somewhere to camp, we will leave the horses and scout out the mine. If Peter's numbers are accurate then we may well attempt a rescue tomorrow night." I saw Richard nod enthusiastically. "But, Richard, if I deem it to be too dangerous, then we will spend another day scouting it out."

"But Captain, each day we delay makes my son weaker!"

"Better a little weaker and rescued than us dead and no hope of rescue. We are Robin's only hope!"

I waited for that to sink in and then, having arranged for one man to be on watch each hour, we wrapped ourselves in our cloaks and slept.

I was woken by Will Yew Tree when it was my watch. "Quiet as the grave, Captain, although there is a fox hunting."

I nodded and, after making water, I tested my breeks. They were dry enough to don. I ate some of the ham and stale bread we had brought and then sat with my back against the bole of a tree. I went over my plan and while I could find no fault in it, I knew the risks involved. We had to kill every guard who was awake. If we left one alive then there would be pursuit. I was keenly aware that if we succeeded then we might have twenty men. While I would not leave any behind, such a number

36

merely increased our chances of capture. I could do nothing about that. Robin was our priority!

When I had completed my watch, I had a mere hour of sleep before Tom woke me. I had barely got back to sleep.

We left before dawn and headed into the darkness of the west, guided by the sound of the river from our left. We followed the man-made path which followed its loops. At one point the path headed due west and we cut out one large loop.

As the sun rose, we saw tendrils of smoke to the north of us. That was the village of Llanymynech, and we became warier. We strung our bows. I had not brought the Mongol bow. It was more powerful than mine and I could use it from the back of a horse, after a fashion, but here I would be on foot, and the familiarity of my warbow more than compensated. As soon as we spied the smoke, I had us dismount and we led our horses; in that way, we would make a smaller target.

A short while later, as the river wound around, yet again, I spied the mine and its workings above us. There were buildings and there was smoke. I guessed that they would do some smelting there too, to save weight when they transported the finished silver.

That set me to thinking. We had forgotten the men who would operate the mine. The miners would be supervised by a senior miner and there would surely be others; experts in giving commands and extracting the ore. Peter had not mentioned them but there was no reason why he should. He had not been in the mine itself. The ambush had been at the other side of the village, and he had only been taken to the mine workings to have his hand and lower arm amputated. The fire there facilitated that.

He had said that he saw the workshop, for he had been tethered by his good arm to the anvil in there, while the other captives had been dragged inside to have their fetters fitted. When they had come out, they were taken inside a building with but one door and a bar on the outside, before all of the slaves were returned to their quarters as the afternoon wore on. Peter had been sent on his way with his message the next day. That alone had saved his life.

From Peter's account I had no idea how many men worked at the mine, only the number of slaves. The number of men we might have to deal with could be double our predictions. I wondered if I had taken too much on.

We found a sheltered and hidden spit of land close to the river and Will established that we could easily ford the water. There was no shelter on the southern bank; it was grazing and scrubland. We could keep any pursuers from it with our bows. I left Richard in charge of the camp while I went with David the Welshman to scout out the mine.

"Do not leave me here, Captain!"

"Can you speak Welsh?"

"No, but…"

"And that is why David is coming with me."

Taking our bows and swords, we headed for the River Vyrnwy. I hoped that there was a bridge or a ford. It made sense to me that there had to be one or the other. There would be people in the fields and travelling the small roads and tracks which crisscrossed the increasingly uneven land.

When we reached the river, it did not bode well, and I wondered if we would have to bring our horses. But the closer we came to the steep slopes on the other side of the river, the more likely it became. Eventually, we found a place where many people had stepped into the mud. It was a ford, but not an obvious one, made from rocks which had been dropped into the river. In the afternoon sun we could see them, but I knew that, at night, we would not. We would have to lead our horses here.

I could now see, above me, the shape of the mine, elevated amongst rocks, and its buildings. Peter had given me an idea of what to expect, but he had been no scout, and his account was not as accurate as I might have liked.

We took a wooded trail which seemed to loop around the side of the rocky hill. It was risky but we needed to find a way to get close to the workings. I soon realised that the path would take us above the mine. Perhaps it went around the hill to one of the other villages and hamlets which were dotted about this land.

Suddenly the trees ended and, halting, we slithered on our bellies to peer down, for we could see the mine, the buildings and the workings. The smell told us that they had many fires going. They were smelting. There was also the sound of banging. I knew that there were iron and lead workings to the west and north of us. I wondered if the workshop used material from those mines. They would need a source of metal for the fetters and the tools.

As I had expected there were few people there. Disappointingly I saw no sign of a stable or horses, but I did see a pigsty with four enormous pigs.

I saw just four large buildings; they would not keep the silver here. They would take it to the village and the hall that was there, although horses and wagons would be a temptation for the slaves.

I saw the halls used by the senior miners, other workers and guards. Each hall had at least two doors, and there was smoke rising from the fires they burned within.

I spotted the slave hall which was the smallest and meanest building. I heard the caw of a crow and saw the sudden movement of a couple of the birds. They were pecking at two heads which were atop two spears close to the slave hall. I could not detect any features. Was one of them Robin? I was happy now that I had left Richard behind. He might have reacted badly. This way I could warn him.

David tapped my leg and pointed. "I see one of the guards."

We were far enough away to be able to talk quietly.

I saw the man and realised that Peter had been right. He was a warrior, for he had on a leather studded brigandine and a mail coif around his neck. His sword was a good one. He was off duty, for he was drinking, and he was doing so alone. That was useful intelligence, for it showed a structure. The three senior guards did not associate with their men. Kill the three and the others might just decide that they would not take us on.

"Have you seen enough?"

"Aye, we can use this path. I see a way down to the buildings, and any guards would be looking towards the village."

After we had crawled back to the trees and risen, he said, "Do you think one of the heads was Robin?"

I shrugged. "We will gain nothing by speculating. I will tell the others what we have seen. We will have to bring the horses, for we are too far away from our camp to be certain of escaping to them."

We managed to return to the camp unseen before the sun started to dip to the west. My men gathered around, and it was a mixture of both eagerness and, in Richard's case, dread.

"We will have to go now and leave the horses closer to the mines, for we have another river to ford, and we need to cross it while there is some light. Coming back may be harder than we hoped. You should know that we saw two heads on spears close to the mine, but we could not identify them. It does not change what we do." I saw the grim determination on their faces. They were good men and knew that what we did was not without risk, but they were brothers in arms and Robin was one of ours. "Let us go. David will lead."

We barely made it across the river before the sun set in the west. If we were successful, then we would have to cross it in the dark.

Once on the other side, David led us, as we walked our horses, towards the small patch of scrubby bushes we had identified closer to the mine. We would have to leave someone with the horses to keep them quiet and that took away one more man. I had decided to leave Tom with the animals, for he was good with horses.

When we had tethered them, we strung bows and prepared ourselves. I pointed to Tom and the horses. His face fell but he nodded. I pointed to Will and Richard and then David the Welshman. The two of them nodded. I circled my hand to the others, and they showed me they understood. They would follow. These were my men and words were unnecessary.

As David led us up the path, I held two arrows next to the strung bow. My men all did the same. We could and would use swords if we had to, but we were archers, and even in the dark we preferred bows. There would be enough light, even on a dark night, to make out not only the body of an enemy but also the lightness of a face, and if we were within twenty or thirty paces, then we would not miss!

We all followed in the footsteps of the man in front and David was like a surefooted goat as he led us to our vantage point. We stopped at the top to calm our breathing and to allow everyone to see what lay below us. There was a fire and it burned in the centre of the four larger buildings which lay five hundred paces down the slope. The four guards Peter had described could be seen. The firelight reflected from the metal studs on the brigandine of the man at arms. There were occasional bursts of laughter or noise, which came from one of the two halls we had identified as the sleeping quarters of the guards and the senior miners and workers.

David looked at me and I nodded. He began the descent and I followed him. I let him get two paces away before I did so. I knew, without even turning, that Richard was behind me.

It was a tortuous journey, for we had to watch our footing as well as keeping an eye on the guards. If we were seen prematurely, then we would have to move quicker than we wished. Luckily for us, the path was not covered in loose material nor was it slippery, and we moved down. I knew that the four guards would not see as far as we could, for they were all looking at the fire. Even when they took a turn around the buildings and came back, the fire would soon destroy their night vision. So long as we moved slowly and silently, then we should escape observation.

Suddenly there was a flash of light from one of the other buildings. I saw that it was the guard hall, and a figure stepped out. We were two hundred paces away but still above the man's eyeline. We all froze. David had nocked an arrow when he had begun his descent. If he had to release, then there was a risk the bow might creak or that one of the other guards would hear the thrum of the arrow. David would only do so if he had to. I heard the hiss and splash of liquid. The guard was making water. When he had finished, he opened the door and returned. It had been handy, for that showed the door the guards would be likely to use and I would be watching that one.

When we made the flat, we stopped and listened. The noises were louder now, and we could hear the four guards talking. They were speaking Welsh, which was why I had placed David at the fore. He could understand them. He mimed pulling back on the bowstring and Will and Richard nodded. They nocked an arrow and when David moved, they followed him, one on each side of him.

I nocked an arrow and then mimed for Martin and William to go to the other door, the one on the fireside. Robin of Barnsley waited with me. I suddenly realised that if anyone came to make water, then the sound of their body hitting the ground might alert those within. I laid my bow on the ground and drew my dagger.

As I did so, from the corner of my eye, I saw my three men pull back with their bows and Richard fire off a second arrow as soon as his first had landed. There was a slight noise as one of the guards murmured as he died, and the four bodies fell to the ground, but those in the halls would have heard nothing. The four falling bodies made virtually no sound, for they were seated and had not far to fall.

I moved to the side of the door. The first part of the plan had succeeded. Now David had to get the door open and the slaves freed, but as they were fettered that would not be easy. I gestured for Robin of Barnsley to place himself where he could see the slave hall and he nodded and moved. The movement took him to the side of the hall.

It was then that I heard laughter within the guard hall and the door began to open. I pressed myself against the wall as a man stepped out. As he turned to close the door, he saw me. His mouth opened but my hand was swiftly upon it, and my dagger's edge slashed across his throat. Warm blood flowed over my hand and he choked, but there was no sound, and when I saw the life go from his eyes, then I knew he was dead. I am a strong man and I held him there. After sheathing my dagger, I took his body and slung it over my shoulder. As I did so I noticed that he wore a brigandine. The second man at arms was slain.

I carried the body towards the undergrowth. Perhaps they would think he needed to empty his bowels. At the very least, when he did not return, then they would have to search for him, so I laid him down, satisfied that he was hidden from casual view, and hurried back to pick up my bow. In my hand, I held his sword.

Robin of Barnsley waved to me and I joined him. I saw that the slaves were now moving from the slave hall. They held their metal fetters so that they would not make a sound. I saw Richard embracing one and knew that Robin was alive. There were not twenty slaves. I counted a bare ten who were following David to pass the other sleeping hall and head down the path to our horses. Even so, how would we escape with all these slaves? I forced myself to leave that problem until later. I saw that four dead guards had been disarmed and that meant four of the slaves had been armed with their weapons. We now had more men if we had to fight our way out.

44

David, Richard and Will shepherded the slaves while the rest of us faced the guard hall with nocked arrows. Amazingly none emerged, and we backed our way to the path. I could hear the noise of metal as the fetters inevitably clinked, but then it came to me that the guards and workers would be used to such noises, and I began to think we might have escaped.

We were halfway to the horses when I heard a commotion from the camp. The escape had been discovered. David was hurrying the slaves as fast as he could, and so I waited with the other three to watch the top of the slope. I heard a horse neigh and cursed. Tom was not to blame. The smell of strange men would make our horses do that, but the noise would attract attention. Sure enough, one hundred and ten paces above us, two faces appeared. It was dark but the white skin stood out like the centre of a target, and four arrows flew to smack into them. The faces disappeared.

"Move!"

We turned and hurried down the path. David had seen what had happened and I heard the sound of a hammer hitting a chisel as they began to rid the slaves of their fetters. Each bang sounded like the crack of doom, but it could not be helped and besides, they now knew where we were. We had rid ourselves of at least eight of them and we now had another few allies, but we were in the land of the Welsh and there would be pursuit!

We each nocked another arrow and, as it only took one man to remove the fetters, that left seven of us with bows. Burning brands appeared on the slope above us and I heard their shouts as they spied us. They sent arrows in our direction, but they were wasted, for we were more than four hundred paces from them and hidden in the dark. Even so, some hit the ground fifty paces from us. I turned and saw Robin. He was helping his father remove the fetters. Already some of those who had been freed were racing towards the river which bubbled not far from where Tom and the horses had waited.

One of the freed prisoners had tried to cross and had missed the rocks. Martin urged his horse into the water and leaned to grab the flailing arm.

I shouted to the others, "Hold on to our stirrups as we cross. Will, lead the way!"

I turned and nocked an arrow. It could be a wasted arrow, but better a nocked arrow than nothing. However, I could now see that our pursuers had realised the futility of chasing horsemen afoot. Instead, they were racing down the road to the village. They would seek help from the lord of the manor, and we would be pursued by horsemen.

I was the last to cross. The man who had fallen in grasped Martin's hand. "Thank you, friend."

"I couldn't let you drown."

All the faces looked to me as I was patently the leader. I sighed. "I am heading back to England, but we will be pursued."

One of them, a man with a large frame but who looked as though he had been starved, said, as he pointed northeast, "I come from Alberbury and it is just a few miles yonder. If you can escort us to the Severn, then it is but four miles."

The man on the horse next to Robin spoke. "There is no garrison at Alberbury. Robin, son of Richard, and I are the last two surviving soldiers."

The wasted giant nodded. "That may be, but it is my home and I know where to hide when they come."

I looked at the others. "And the rest of you?"

"You have freed us and that is enough. Get us across the Severn and we shall be in your debt…"

"Captain Gerald Warbow of Yarpole. Now let us move, for we waste time, and I would be across the river before daylight." I was aware that we would be slowed by stopping at Alberbury, but I could see no way around it. I was just grateful that only this handful had chosen to follow us.

David led us unerringly to the ford we had used. It was one thing to cross it on horses but quite another to risk it in the dark on foot. I was keenly aware that these men had been ill-treated and not in the best condition. The wasted giant had shown me that. I should have brought more food and ale, but hindsight is always perfect!

Richard was riding next to his son and the other man who had mounted a horse, the man who said he had fought with Robin. I did not know his name. I could also work out by their haircuts that the two heads on the spears were the other two captured in the ambush, the crossbowmen. I had planned well but fate, as ever, had intervened.

We would need to find somewhere on the other side of the river to hide. Technically, the land was England, but that would not stop the Welsh from seeking us. We had attacked Prince Llywelyn's men and they would try to take us sooner rather than later.

It was as we neared the ford that I heard, to the north, the sound of dogs. Every face turned to look at me. I could offer no words of hope. The river might disguise the smell but if they were good hounds, they would find us. We were forced to cross, and it was a hard crossing. One man clung to each horse as we laboured across the water. I had the wasted giant with me, and

I kept my right arm under his arm. As my horse struggled out of the water, I breathed a sigh of relief.

"Break out the food and the ale; let these poor fellows eat and drink."

"Thank you, Captain; you are a Christian. If I survive, then I will light a candle for you in our church."

"Just live and I will sleep easier."

We had brought little enough food, and more than half was taken by the captives, who would now make their way home. Four went with the wasted giant while the others took off in different directions. One man in each group had a weapon and I knew that they would not be taken without a fight.

The man with Robin said, "Captain, I served around here for six months. There is a rocky hill covered with trees a mile or so from here. If we were to ride our horses up the river, the hounds might not find us, and we could shelter there."

I nodded. "I bow to your local knowledge. Your name, friend?"

"Stephen de Frankton. I am, or was, a man at arms, but now I am just a freed slave who is glad to be alive."

"Then lead on, Stephen de Frankton. I will fetch up the rear with David the Welshman."

We left space before us so that the others could ride in single file. David was my most experienced man, and this was his country.

"Well?"

He turned and grinned; even in the dark, I saw his teeth as the first hint of dawn appeared in the east. "As I see it, Captain, we have done more than we might have hoped but it has put us in peril. On balance I am a happy man. We lost not a man and, if this man at arms knows what he is talking about, we can rest up until after noon and then try to get closer to Pontesbury and the Shrewsbury Road."

"You would not rest until darkness?"

He pointed to the south-east, where we could see the looming lump of rock and earth that was the hill Stephen de Frankston sought. "I know not this rock, Captain, and it looks a good place to hide, but I would not fancy descending in the dark. We need just a little rest, but the horses need more than we do. The fording of the river took it out of them."

It would be my decision, but everything he had said made sense. I had the best horse, Eleanor, and yet she was struggling. I would not kill a horse with exhaustion unless there was no other choice. As we had the hill, mountain, whatever one chose to call it, between us and the rising sun, it was still dark when we left the river and began to seek a path up its sides. Stephen de Frankton might have seen the rock, but I doubted that he had ridden up from this side.

"David, ride to the fore and find us a way up this slope. I trust your judgement and this de Frankton is unknown. I am grateful that he has found us this hideaway, but I will not gamble all upon his word!"

By the time the sun had risen and bathed the upper Severn Valley in daylight, we were in the trees and seeking somewhere to shelter. The horses had drunk well in the river, so we sought grazing. We had a bag of oats with us, but they would not go far. David had dismounted when I rode into the clearing, and that told me we had found a place to rest!

Chapter 4

I let the others eat first and, after setting a watch, I joined Robin and Richard. I knew that I was intruding but I needed to know as much as I could, and I was still the captain. "Speak, Robin, about your life since you were taken, and leave nothing out."

"You should know, Captain, that Stephen and I are shield brothers. If he had not been with me, then neither of us would be alive. I slew the Welshman who was about to kill him, and his shield saved me when another Welshman tried to take my head!"

I nodded. "I thought that there was a bond."

"The two heads you saw were the two crossbowmen, Jacques and Henry. They tried to escape the first night we arrived. I would have done so but I had drunk some bad water and I was vomiting. Stephen cared for me. They took their heads as a warning to the rest of us. Their bodies, and the others who died, were fed to the pigs. Rhodri ap Rhodri is a cruel man. He taunted us with the pigs."

I remembered the pigsty. "Was he one of the men at arms? He wore a brigandine?" Robin nodded. "Then know that we slew two of the three men at arms. Mayhap this Rhodri died."

Robin shook his head. "He is the spawn of the devil and we know that the devil looks after his own. He will be alive, and he will seek us out. We were told that he had once been a lord but had murdered his own brother. He lost his title, but Prince Llywelyn recognised his skills. Each day we worked from dawn to dusk in the mines." Robin pointed to the sun. "This is the first sunlight I have seen in a week. Two men died in that week. As they were not replaced, we had to work even harder. Rescuing all of us was a most Christian act, Captain, and I swear that I will not leave your service again."

Richard said, "And I will try to be a better father. Mags has told me that I turned my back on you and—"

Robin waved his hand. "I came back from the Crusades arrogant. I had been close to Lord Edward and his lady. I thought I was better than I am. I have learned humility."

I nodded. "Rest. We leave in the middle of the afternoon."

As if to emphasise our danger, I heard the hounds to the north of us. I wandered around the camp and spoke to Will Yew Tree. "Is everything quiet and secure?"

"Yes, Captain, but get some rest yourself."

"I will, but first I make sure that we are safe. We did not plan to come here, and so I need to check it thoroughly."

He looked over to Stephen who was making himself a bed using a pair of horse blankets. "You think he might be a spy or something?"

I shrugged. "Perhaps. Acre made me suspicious, and I look at every stranger with jaundiced eyes. It is easier and safer to say you are sorry for a misjudgement than to pull a knife from between your shoulder blades!"

He laughed. "I reckon he is all right, but it does no harm to be wary. I will keep an eye on him."

When all was checked, and I had seen that Eleanor was comfortable, I took my cloak, wrapped it around myself and fell straight to sleep.

It was Will Yew Tree who woke me. "Captain, the hounds are getting closer. David the Welshman and William of Matlac have slipped down the other side of the hill to investigate."

I was awake in an instant. "Get the horses saddled." I ran around the camp, waking the others who were asleep. "To arms, there is trouble!"

I strung my bow and, selecting two good arrows, headed along the path which David and William had taken. We had a place on the other side where we could observe the road and where I saw my two men peering around the boles of a pair of trees.

I sidled up behind David who whispered, "They have dogs and men on horses. It looks like a lord is leading them, for he is wearing spurs. There are four men at arms, and we have counted twenty men on foot. They have bows."

"Do the dogs have our scent?"

"No, for the wind is from the east, but they know where they are searching. They left the road and followed the path which crosses here. They will come up this path."

An idea began to form in my mind. I looked at the path which I saw twisted and turned along the natural contours of the hill. It rounded rocks and large trees. There was, however, a straight section just one hundred paces below us, where the path ran along from north to south. When they reached it, almost all of them would be in sight at the same time. "We will ambush them. We have no bodkins with us so we will have to aim at the knight and hope to hit his horse. Wait here and I will fetch the others."

I hurried back in a crouch, confident that I would not be seen. The Welsh had almost nine hundred paces to climb. "Robin, Stephen, hold the horses. The rest of you, fetch your bows, we have company."

The man at arms said, "I am a warrior! I can fight!"

"At the moment you are not. You do not even have buskins! I need two men to hold the horses and you two are the least use to us at the moment!"

The man did not look happy, but Robin said, "The Captain is right. We have barely eaten, and we are both tired. If I had a bow… but I do not. We will hold the horses, Captain, and await your command!"

When time allowed, I would have to explain the facts of life to the man at arms!

I caught up with the others, who were making their way to the other side of the hill, and as I passed, I said, "Wait for my command. I want as many men hitting with the first two flights as possible. Kill the dogs!" We could not allow any sentiment. These were large hounds and could easily maim or even kill a man. It was not worth the risk.

When we reached David, the others naturally spread themselves out to cover the path. I saw them each choose the best two arrows that they had. No archer worth his salt had a poor arrow, but there were always some that were as close to perfection as a fletcher could manage. I did the same. I had one bodkin in my arrow bag, but I was loath to change it. I would use a war arrow first.

The Welsh hunting party appeared and disappeared as they wound their way up the slope. My men would know the place

I had chosen for it gave us the clearest view of our prey. Rocks had tumbled from the summit and cleared away the vegetation, affording a clear view. But if the enemy looked up, they would have the problem of looking directly into the afternoon sun. They would be relying on the dogs, but the wind was against them.

As soon as the dog handlers emerged below us, I began to draw back on my bow. The path was flatter, and I heard the Welsh knight urge the men on. The dog handlers began to run. Tom and Martin were on the extreme right of our line, and they would first kill the dogs and then try to hit the handlers.

William was to my right and he, along with David on my left, would aim at the knight and the first two men at arms. Richard, Will and Robin of Barnsley would deal with the other two horsemen and the more dangerous of the men on foot.

David aimed at the knight, who was preceded by two men at arms. I let out my breath as I released my arrow at the second man at arms. All the power of my pull was transferred to the bow and it hurtled towards him. I heard two yelps as the hounds were slain by my men. My arrow struck the man's leather brigandine at the shoulder. Some men wear a piece of metal there. He did not, and the arrow drove down and through his body. The power was such that it knocked him from his horse. Still holding on to the reins as he fell, he was sent with his mount down the slope. I nocked a second, and in the drawing of my bow, saw that William had sent an arrow into the side of the head of his target, and David the Welshman's arrow had driven through the knight's thigh, his saddle and into the horse. The animal took off down the slope.

I switched to my left and saw that all the horsemen were down, but the Welsh archers were nocking arrows. My arrow slammed into the chest of one a heartbeat before Will Yew Tree's hit the same man in the arm. My third arrow was sent towards a Welshman who was trying to take shelter behind a rock. My arrow hit his right arm. A swordsman can fight one-handed, but not an archer.

I saw that all the Welsh had gone to ground. I heard moans from the wounded and the dying. Two of the horses stood inertly on the path.

I said, "David, tell them that we can kill them any time we like. I want them to leave and take their wounded with them. If we see them near us, they will die."

"Better to just kill them, Captain."

"True, but do you think we can do so without losing anyone?"

"No, Captain. They will be good!" I heard him shout and a voice answered. David spoke again and two Welshmen stood. They unstrung their bows and began to head down the slope. One went to take one of the horses, but David sent an arrow into the ground close to the man and shouted something. He chuckled, "Cheeky! They said how did they know they could trust us, and I said they had my word. Then they attempted to take the two horses. They won't try that again! I said I would have his jewels if he did!"

I turned. Arrows had been sent at us, but I had heard no cries. "Is anyone hurt?"

"No, Captain."

"Then go back and fetch the horses. David and I will see what we have."

With nocked arrows, we made our way along the path. It descended quite sharply before flattening out after the bend, and we saw the two dead hounds, a dead handler along with the other dead men. In all, there were six Welshmen who were slain. I saw, at the bottom of the hill, the knight having his wound tended to by one of the men at arms who had survived. In theory, they could still attack us, but I thought they knew that they would lose.

We searched the men at arms and took their weapons and their treasures.

I heard the horses and, looking around, saw my men coming towards us. "Robin, there are buskins here for you as well as daggers and swords. Stephen de Frankton, if you wish to be a man at arms again, then there are three dead ones to rob. Take what you will, but hurry. The lord is wounded and fled but he may raise the county against us. We will ride now until we reach Yarpole."

I saw the man at arms look at the dead and when he spoke there was less arrogance in his voice. "Thank you, Captain. This is good war gear." He spied the shield that had been dropped by the knight and he went to retrieve it. After he had hung it from his saddle, he continued to take the better pieces from the dead. He said, "From the shield, the lord is Maredudd ap Iago. It was he who led the ambush with his cousin Davy ap Cynfyn. Some of our dead are now avenged."

I looked at Robin. "This is the only raid we do for vengeance, Robin. I would not have a blood feud with the Welsh. We live too close to the border and my family is more important than some misplaced sense of honour."

I saw Robin nod towards his father. "Captain, I may be bull-headed, but even I can learn a lesson. My Welsh madness is gone."

I saw that Stephen had put his gear on his horse and mounted.

Will and Martin were leading the captured horses which were laden with the weapons and equipment we had taken, and I said, "Let us ride. David, lead us home!"

As we descended the twisting path, we saw the survivors of our ambush heading back towards Wales. Our divergent paths meant that even if they reached home and returned with more men directly, we would still have a good lead and they would not be able to catch us. Nonetheless, I kept a steady pace, and we reached my hall, walking our horses, but whole, after dark. We had saved our comrade and suffered little. I said a silent prayer of thanks to God as the door to my hall opened and I saw John of Nottingham with drawn sword. My family had been safe and well protected in my absence!

My men saw to the horses and John left my home. I embraced Mary. It had been only days since we had left but it felt longer. I was aware that I smelled of sweat and blood, but I hugged her anyway. She said quietly, in my ear, "Robin is returned to us and none were hurt. My prayers were answered."

I kissed the top of her head and pulled apart a little. "Aye, and we rescued other slaves. I feel that we were meant to go there. I was anxious when we left, but now, I am content. If King Edward chooses to censure me, then so be it."

"I do not think that Queen Eleanor would allow it. You know that she is very fond of you."

"She barely knew me."

"She comes from Castile, you know, and there they have a hero, Rodrigo de Vivar, who was known as El Cid. Although he was a knight, she said that you had much in common with him. You never baulked when the odds were too great and although you fought like a lion, there was honour in your fighting. So long as she is queen, then you have an ally and King Edward will not punish you, no matter what you do."

I had not known that the queen's feelings for me were so great. I knew that I had saved the lives of both of them but that was my duty. What I did know was that I would not abuse my position. I had risked what I had for Robin, but I hoped I would not need to do so again.

I bathed the next day, and that in itself took half a morning as water had to be heated and the bath we had bought in London filled. When we had returned, Mary had asked for little, but she had been brought up in Constantinopolis and was used to baths and cleanliness. Even the Mongol princess she had served had enjoyed clean water and baths. As it was the only request she had made, I acceded, and as I washed myself clean of the detritus of battle, I was glad.

The result was that it was the afternoon when I was able to walk out of my door and speak with my people. Men had been waiting for me and I saw Richard, his son, Robin, Peter and the man at arms, Stephen de Frankton, detach themselves from the others and head towards me. It looked ominous!

It was Robin who spoke, and I saw in his eyes and heard in his voice that he had changed. Incarceration will do that to a man. "Captain, I thanked you once for my rescue, but I would do so again, here at Yarpole, and reiterate that my father and I, along with Mags, are reconciled and my misbehaviour will cease."

"Good." I waited, for I saw in the looks he exchanged with the others that there was more.

"Captain, I have a boon to beg. I know you have done much and if you refuse, then I would understand. Peter and Stephen fought alongside me and while I have known them for a little time, they are now shield brothers. You know what that means, Captain. Both would like to serve you."

I had thought that this was what they wished, and I nodded. "Peter, my wife said we would not throw you out and you know that you have a home here."

He nodded. "I know, Captain, but I do not wish charity and I am no farmer. I know that I cannot fight as a man at arms, for I am one-handed, but I can still fight. My right hand is still what it was, and I can fashion a buckler to strap on to my arm. I would stay here but Robin is right; we are shield brothers and I would fight for you. If nothing else I can train your archers to use the sword better."

I smiled, for I liked his attitude. "You had a place already, but I am pleased that you still wish to fight. Of course, you may serve me as a warrior. We brought some war gear back. Choose what you will. The rate I will pay will be the rate for an archer: three pence a day." That was less than a man at arms. He nodded and I added, "Go get your gear and I will speak to Stephen de Frankton alone." Peter nodded and turned. Robin looked as though he would stay, and I said, "Alone!"

Richard said, "Come, son, let us help Peter choose the better pieces."

I looked at the man at arms in the eye. "Peter was promised a place by my wife and I would not throw out a wounded man. You, however, are without wounds and you could ply your trade elsewhere." He made to speak, and I held up my hand. "Let me finish. You did us great service with your knowledge on the way home, but I will have no man argue with me. I am a captain of archers, I am Lord Edward's archer, and if I offer you a position then you must understand this. The pay is that of an archer and all of my commands will be obeyed." He nodded. I shook my head. "I cannot see why you agree to this, so explain."

"Captain, I hate Prince Llywelyn and the Welsh. They took all from me. You are right; I could seek service with a lord, de Clare or de Bohun, and I could be paid more, but you are Lord Edward's archer and you will be there when King Edward finally realises that he must destroy this snake. I know from Robin that you are not wasteful of men's lives. Lord Jasper was, and I know of other lords who are, reckless with the ones who fight for them. If I serve you then I have more chance of survival and of fulfilling the promise I made to myself to rid this world of Llywelyn."

I liked his answer and it made sense to me.

He smiled. "And I think that I can give your company something you do not have at the moment, protection, for even with one arm, Peter is a good warrior and with the two of us before your archers, we could buy you the time to loose another ten arrows each. I have seen the skills of your men and know that your company is the equal of any Welsh band. We will make Captain Warbow's Men the finest company of archers in England."

I held out my arm. "Then, Stephen de Frankton, welcome to my company!"

I had my doubts, even as I accepted his offer, but he was right. As archers, we were vulnerable, and having two swordsmen, even a one-armed one, gave more protection to my family.

It was August and that meant there were no idle hands. Crops were harvested and animals tended. Food was preserved and game was culled before winter. It was also when Lord Edward was crowned and became King Edward I! I was a mere gentleman, and I was not invited to the coronation, but I knew, from messengers who travelled along the road from Shrewsbury, that Prince Llywelyn had not travelled to London. I became a little uneasy. Had I been responsible for his non-attendance? If so, then I could expect an angry response.

I had sent David and Will Yew Tree to Alberbury to see if retribution had been meted out. They found four of the men we had freed, including the wasted giant who we learned was called Ralph of Alberbury. The others had also escaped but they had fled the borderlands. Lady Alberbury had closed up and emptied the hall. There was no longer a lord of the manor and King Edward would need to address that particular issue. The Welsh, it seemed, had been hurt by our rescue and escape. That did not mean that they would forget us, but Llywelyn was busy fermenting dissension in the lands to the south. We were safe.

We began to improve our defences. It was simple enough to do. Without the permission of the king, we could not crenulate, but there was nothing to stop us from building walls and gates.

The road through Yarpole headed west to Wales and then northeast to join the main road which went south from Wigmore to Leominster. The houses which lined the road belonged to those like the smith, Sarah and others who had lived in the village before we had come. My hall lay behind them and I had built the warrior hall parallel to mine. Behind the halls were the barn and the stables. It occurred to me that we could use the barn as a sanctuary for other villages in case of an attack by the Welsh. By building a wall with a gate from the warrior hall to my hall, and then a wall from the warrior hall to the barn and another from my hall to the stable, both of which lay to the south of us, we had a defensive structure. We put a second gate in the stable-barn wall. To the south of that lay the cottages and smallholdings belonging to my men – Richard, John, Jack and the others.

We did not build the walls all at once. We built the foundations first and then added a wall at a time. The first was the north wall and gate, and we put two small towers on either side of the gate. With a fighting platform, the eight-foot wall was surmountable, but defended by the villagers and my men, an enemy would pay a high price for entry.

The two easy walls were next, and one benefit of them was that we were able to build a larger bread oven against the barn wall. It increased our capacity to bake and we allowed the villagers to use it.

By October we had the last wall and gate in place. We had all laboured on the defences and that brought us all closer together. Even one-armed Peter showed hidden talents. He had skills in bricklaying. He could not lift the stones, but he knew how to mortar.

It was while we were building the last wall that Sir Roger Mortimer and his men arrived. I had heard that he had returned from London, but I had not had the chance to visit with him. He reined in and dismounted. While his horses were watered and his men fed, I took him along my defences. I wondered why the old knight had come to see me.

"These are good walls, Gerald. I hope that they will offend the king." He shook his head and smiled. "You were lucky, you know? I heard about your rescue, for it was the talk of the court. Those who arrived late for the coronation could not wait to tell the king. Not everyone is your friend."

I knew that but it did not bother me. "Baron, they had fed the bodies of dead Englishmen to the pigs!"

He waved a hand. "I realise, but you know King Edward. As it happens, Prince Llywelyn chose not to attend the coronation and that displeased the king mightily. He is due to come to Shrewsbury in November when King Edward will accept his homage." He paused. "You are ordered to attend too!" I nodded. Then the baron smiled. "Know that I am happy with all that you have done," he gestured towards my new walls, "and all of this pleases me." He put an arm around my shoulder. "And now I need you to do something for me. Have you heard of Gruffydd ap Gwenwynwyn, a lord from Powys?"

I shook my head. "I have not heard the name."

"It seems he was involved in some sort of plot against Prince Llywelyn, and his son was taken as hostage. He also lost some of his lands. His family were powerful and ruled Powys in times past. He and his wife live in Rhayader. It is thirty miles to the west of us. King Edward asks that you find this man and offer him sanctuary."

"Here?"

He shook his head. "No, either my castle or Shrewsbury. King Edward sees him as a pawn to be used."

"Will not this make the prince think that King Edward was behind this plot?"

"The king was on crusade with you when it occurred but, in any event, the king cares not. I fear that the snub from Prince Llywelyn will not easily be forgotten."

I did not like this, for I would be travelling through the heartland of those who supported Prince Llywelyn. Was it a trap? I hoped that King Edward would never deliberately seek to put my life in danger, but this seemed reckless. "I am not happy about this, so let me clarify what I must do. I do not have to bring back this plotter?" The baron shook his head. "I just deliver a message and return home?"

"That is all. The king trusts you and he knows that if you say something is done, then it is true."

"And if Gruffydd ap Gwenwynwyn does not believe me? He may suspect a trap. Do I have any written assurances to give to him?"

The baron shook his head. "You have a certain reputation, Warbow. It is another reason you were chosen."

"That and the fact that I am expendable. I am not a lord, and if I fail then no blame can be attached to you or the king."

The smile the baron gave me was sad. "I see that you know how to play this game, Warbow."

"That does not mean I have to like it. Can I refuse?"

"Had you not raided the mine and killed his people then perhaps, but now…"

I was defeated. Robin and the men I led were more important to me than any king. I dared not lose that which I had, and I would do as I was ordered. This was not a request. It was an order. "And when do I leave?"

"The sooner the better. At the moment, Prince Llywelyn just has Owain ap Gruffydd as a hostage. His mother, Hawise, is with Gruffydd ap Gwenwynwyn. The king needs his potential ally safe." I was silent, and I think the baron took that to be an attempt by me to negotiate. It was not, but he said, "And you need pay no taxes for a year."

"I will do this, my lord, but I hope that King Edward does not need me to be his emissary again. I have a family now and I do not wish to jeopardise their future."

The baron's eyes became hooded. "Then you will continue to do as the king commands!"

The Village After the Work on the Defences

Chapter 5

As I had expected, Mary was less than happy with my news, and it took all that I could to persuade her not to write to the queen. Mary was, despite her time at the Mongol court, naïve. The queen had influence, but she would not interfere in such matters. She might only make things worse by annoying her husband.

"I will do this, for we will have one more year without paying tax and that will make us more comfortable. There should be no need to fight and if I go with a small band of men, four or five, then we can remain hidden. The journey there should take just one day. I will be returned within five days."

She hugged me and tears coursed down her cheeks. "I thought it would be different in this realm. The Mongol lords and ladies were happy to use slaves like me to their own ends, but I thought that your service to Lord Edward, and that you were a free man, meant it was different for you."

"I fear not, my love."

I sought David the Welshman's advice. He knew the land. Like me, he was resigned to obeying the king. "Who else do we take, Captain?"

"Tom and Martin have shown themselves to be handy."

He nodded. "And how about the new man, de Frankton?"

I wondered at that. He hated Llywelyn, and so should have been a perfect choice, but he was not an archer. Then I realised that his presence might help. He seemed to have intimate knowledge of the world of Welsh politics and the lords who held the power. I nodded. "Then let us tell them what we plan."

David had not heard of the Welsh lord Gruffydd ap Gwenwynwyn, but Stephen had. "Captain, he is not a clever man; if anything, he is a fool. What had he to gain from plotting against Prince Llywelyn? He wants a piece of land which the prince refuses to give him, but is that worth having your son taken hostage? I do not like the prince, but I know that he is popular. This reeks to me of his brother Dafydd. He is a treacherous man and has already sided with King Henry. Why Llywelyn forgave him I know not."

I nodded. "Thank you, for all information is useful, but it does not change what I need to do, does it? I do not have to get into bed with him. I just deliver my message and come home. It does not even matter to me if he refuses the king's offer."

"I just thought that you should know the kind of man you are dealing with."

"Stephen, I have a low opinion of all men until they redeem themselves in my eyes. It has enabled me to live longer!" That made them all smile. I addressed David. "And is there any danger twixt here and there?"

"There are no castles if that is what you mean, but the people have no love for the English."

"It is thirty-odd miles and we will do it in one journey. If we rise early then the first part, to Leominster, can be travelled in the dark, for the road is familiar to us. We will leave the day after tomorrow. That will allow each of us to prepare."

We travelled as though to war and each of my men wore a leather brigandine and a cloak. They all had a good sword and knew how to use it. Their war bows were in a leather case and each had a warbag of arrows; this time I had them take five arrows each which were tipped with a bodkin.

We made good progress along the road to Leominster. Despite the hour, there were still travellers on the road, but they were heading in the opposite direction. There was a market in Ludlow, and some were heading there to sell while others to buy. The fact that they might have a three-hour journey in each direction meant that they only took the road when it was necessary. We waved and spoke to all of them. It was not mere politeness. We were each listening for a Welsh accent. Not all Welsh travellers were a threat, but a Welsh voice would make us wary.

"Stephen, forgive my interest but you seem to know a great deal about Welsh politics. How is that?"

"I was in Gascony, fighting for King Henry, when I heard of the deaths of my family. The news took four months to reach me, and so I knew that even if I left directly, I could not do anything for them. I resolved to discover as much as I could about the Welsh, and I began by asking questions of the Welsh who were on campaign with us. None were Llywelyn's men, but there were men at arms and archers who had served in the Welsh Marches. I began to gather nuggets of information. I left the service of my lord during a truce and headed home. I went to London. It might be a cesspit of the worst of England but, if you know where to look, you can find men who know what is going on all over this realm. I had their names and I sought them. By the time I reached Alberbury, I knew as much as any about who was who in Wales."

"You chose Sir Jasper?" I was beginning to see inside this enigmatic man.

"Sir Jasper was not a subtle man. He made no secret of the fact that he intended to raid the Welsh. It is why we were ambushed."

"And yet you still went?"

He nodded. "I am good at what I do, Captain, and I always believe that I will survive. No man, neither knight nor man at arms, has ever bested me. I assumed that I would survive, but the chance to steal the silver from Prince Llywelyn was simply too great an opportunity for Sir Jasper."

"Sir Jasper sought the silver?"

"Sir Jasper had ambitions, but to further those ambitions he needed coins. He sought to build a land inside Wales that was English. He looked to Gilbert de Clare as his hero." I was silent and Stephen said, "So, you see, Captain, you can trust me, for I am a driven man, and my motives are purely vengeful."

I turned sharply. He was a clever man and had read my mind. I would still be wary of him, but his answers were plausible, and I was content.

I was an emissary and Mary had insisted that I rode in my second-best clothes, for I was acting for the king. They were hidden beneath the good riding cloak and my brigandine. I had no livery as such, but my men and I all liked to wear green. It was practical and gave us some protection from observation in our normal environment, the woods. The difference between my clothes and my men's was that theirs were crude; I had better quality garments. I even owned one set that had been made in

Acre. It was manufactured from the finest and most delicate of material. I confess that I had only worn it twice. Once when we had dined with King Edward and Queen Eleanor on the night before we parted in Sicily and then on my wedding day. I was even wearing a hat. The time of year dictated that it was a beaver skin hat to keep my head warm. A hat was a sign of my status.

By the time dawn broke, we were well inside Wales. The travellers on the road had stopped appearing when we neared the border. The Welsh used their closer markets.

We knew we were in Wales when the surface of the road deteriorated. Even the lesser roads in England were well made with cobbles and ditches. The ones in Wales were serviceable, but carts and wagons would suffer damage when they used them. The exceptions were the roads in the north of Wales, for they had been built by the Romans.

Rhayader was the largest place we had seen on our journey thus far and had been well built where the road rose towards the mountains. There was a castle, but it was more like a fortified manor house and, as we approached, I saw archers keeping watch from the top. We had been seen and, whilst we had no weapons in our hands, we were strangers, and they would be wary.

We were still four hundred paces from them when I turned to Stephen and said, "No matter what your feelings towards the Welsh, I command here."

He smiled. "Do not worry, Captain; if these plot against Llywelyn, then their lives are as safe as any man in Wales!"

We reined in and a man, a steward by his livery and his dress, emerged. "How can we help you, stranger? We are off the beaten track here. Do you seek refreshment?"

He spoke in English and that told me much.

"I am Captain Gerald Warbow, Lord Edward's archer, and I come here at the behest of the new King of England."

A voice from within said something and David said, quietly, "We are to be admitted."

The steward said, "If you would leave your men and horses here, I will admit you."

I shook my head. "David the Welshman will come with me." My tone suggested that I would brook no argument and he nodded. "Stephen, keep watch!" He would not only keep an eye on the horses but ascertain any risk or danger.

"Yes, Captain!"

The entrance was not wide and reflected the fact that the house was fortified. Only one man at a time could enter, and I saw that there was a second door inside what looked to be an entrance chamber. The interior was gloomy, and our passage was illuminated by a lighted brand through a windowless corridor to a larger, better-lit room. An attacker could be held up in the corridor by one to two men. I noted the arrangement and wondered how I might incorporate the same into my own home.

Inside the room, there were a dozen people. Two of them were women and one was patently a servant. The two best-dressed men were seated at a table while the rest stood. All bore swords.

"I am Lord Gruffydd ap Gwenwynwyn and that is my wife, Lady Hawise."

My first impressions were later confirmed. Lady Hawise was a lovely lady and a devoted mother. Her eyes, when she spoke of her son, showed care and distress at his abduction.

Lord Gruffydd ap Gwenwynwyn appeared to me to be slow-witted. I had learned that was not unusual amongst the nobility, but perhaps my view was jaundiced by normally associating with quick thinking archers! His speech implied his dullness of wits, but it was his movements which confirmed it. He was a big man, and I guessed that in combat that would give him a physical advantage but, as we spoke, I realised that he could not have devised a plot to take the prince's crown.

"I am Captain Gerald Warbow and King Edward has sent me here to offer you and your family sanctuary in England. He knows of the abduction of your son."

He said nothing but Lady Hawise said, bitterly, "He was not abducted, Captain Warbow, but taken as hostage by Prince Llywelyn." She threw a hateful glare at the two men seated at the other end of the table.

Lord Gruffydd ap Gwenwynwyn looked at the man next to him. He was a little younger than Gruffydd ap Gwenwynwyn and I did not like him from the first glance. His eyes reminded me of Sir Henry, who had killed my father and I had subsequently slain.

When he spoke it only added to the antipathy I immediately felt. "Out of deference to you, we will speak your language. I am Lord Dafydd ap Gruffydd, the brother of Llywelyn. I too, it seems, have incurred the wrath of my brother, who persists in the belief that others plot to take his pathetic little crown! Nothing could be further from the truth. My brother is deluded, and I fear for his sanity."

In that single sentence, I saw who the real plotter was. Gruffydd ap Gwenwynwyn was merely a figurehead. I now had a dilemma. Fortunately, I had served Lord Edward and knew his mind. He would happily offer sanctuary to the brother of the prince, for that way he could use him as a puppet.

"And I am sure that King Edward would offer another so persecuted sanctuary, my lord."

The two men smiled but I saw the hand of Lady Hawise go to her mouth. If they came to England, then Prince Llywelyn might execute her son. She said nothing.

"You have the authority to make such an offer?" Dafydd's silkily smooth voice made me want to say no, but I nodded.

"Then we will accept." There was no discussion and that confirmed who the leader was. His eyes narrowed. "This sanctuary, it is not to be the Tower of London, is it?"

I shook my head. "Wigmore or Shrewsbury are both close to the Welsh border and it is your choice. I will escort you to Wigmore Castle and you can tell my lord, Baron Mortimer, your decision."

"Good, we—"

"I will not leave without my son!" Lady Hawise's voice contrasted with the Welshman's. It was firm and assertive. She would brook no argument.

"My love, be reasonable!" The ponderous voice of Gruffydd ap Gwenwynwyn would have made me do the opposite of whatever he said.

"Do not '*my love*' me! You have been led by the nose by this man and our son paid the price, and now you would leave him to suffer the vengeance of the man his brother tried to kill."

Dafydd ap Gruffydd coloured and held up a hand. "Lady Hawise, there are strangers!"

Her eyes flashed. "I care not. I have just met this Englishman and already I would trust him more than either of you." She turned to me. "Captain Warbow, do you have children?"

"My wife is due to give birth in December."

She smiled. "And would you desert your child and leave him to be murdered?"

"No, my lady."

She turned to her husband and his master. Her words were icy. "You two may slink off to England but I shall stay here, and I will go to plead for the life of my son. I have knowledge I can trade!"

There was a real threat to her words, and I saw the panic in the eyes and face of Dafydd ap Gruffydd. "You would not do that!" He turned to Lord Gruffydd. "She is your wife, Gruffydd, command her!"

He shook his head sadly. "She will not listen. We must try to rescue Owain."

Lady Hawise beamed. "You have a backbone after all!"

Dafydd ap Gruffydd snarled, "Not from where I am sitting!"

It was my time to speak. "My lords, I have to be back home in five days. Either you come with me in the next two days or seek your own way to England."

"Do not be hasty, Captain. Your king would wish you to escort us. Lord Gruffydd's son is held just twenty miles from here. If an attempt to rescue the youth was made tomorrow morning, then we could leave here the day after. I will send Caradog, the captain of my guards, to lead the rescue attempt." I saw a huge, black-bearded warrior, with a leather brigandine and a hand-and-a-half sword, nod. Then Dafydd turned to me. "Surely you can wait a day or two?"

I nodded. I had resigned myself to two days sitting around in the hall when Lady Hawise, her voice cold and commanding, said, "You think me a fool, Dafydd ap Gruffydd? Do you think that I do not know what you plan is? My husband may be a dullard, but I am not. Your man will slay my son and put the blame on your brother. You will garner support from the people of Wales and the cost will be my son's life."

I was watching the face of the would-be Welsh prince and I saw the truth of her words. King Edward was getting into bed with a bag of vipers.

Lord Gruffydd was slower on the uptake or perhaps he genuinely believed Dafydd's words. "My love, Captain Caradog is a good warrior, and he shall bring home our son."

It was as though her husband had not spoken and she turned to me. "Captain Gerald, I have just met you, but your words and eyes bespeak a man who has truth and honour." She suddenly turned to David the Welshman and spoke a torrent of Welsh, none of which I understood. He nodded and answered her. She smiled and addressed me once more. "Your Welshman here confirms my thoughts. You are well respected. I beg you to go with these men and rescue my son. If you and your men are with the party, then I believe that there is a chance he may be rescued. Without you, he is a dead man."

I was aware that all eyes were on me. I did not want this attention. I had been ordered to come to Wales, and what had seemed a slightly dangerous but minor excursion now threatened not only my life as well as Owain ap Gruffydd's, but also the lives of my men. I glanced briefly at David who smiled and nodded. I thought of Mary, not as my wife but as a mother. If my unborn child was ever in danger then she, too, would beg another for help. I nodded. "Reluctantly, I will agree, but know that I am less than happy about this." I also knew that King Edward would like another ally.

The scowl which passed across the face of Dafydd, brother of Llywelyn, told me that I had upset his plans. However, he quickly mastered his emotions and smiled. "Thank you, Captain Gerald; your assistance is unnecessary but shows that King Edward chose a good man."

As we went to tell our men, David said quietly, "I would not trust that Caradog."

I nodded. "And I do not. Find out all that you can about this place we go to rescue the boy. Do you not think it strange that his father does not go with us?"

"I did wonder, Captain, but I can see that he follows his leader blindly. I believe that Lady Hawise is right. If we were not there, then the boy's life might be forfeit."

We told my men, and none appeared to be upset at the prospect of rescuing a Welsh prisoner. Stephen nodded after he had heard the frank explanation of what had been said and what we had to do. "What you have told me confirms all that I had heard on my travels. The brothers do not get on and each seeks to undermine the other. King Edward has chosen a wise course of action. He can win Wales without losing too many men."

There was more to my new man at arms than met the eye. He was highly perceptive.

We discovered that the youth was held at Caersws, a small town eighteen miles to the north of us at a crossing of the Severn. There had been a Roman fort there, but the stone had been robbed to make the small stone hall where Owain was being held.

I spoke with Captain Caradog to discover what sort of opposition we might meet. I did so while Lady Hawise stood to listen. The cunning captain was forced to speak the truth, for Lady Hawise knew the place well.

"They have a garrison of no more than twenty men, Captain Gerald."

"Will there be a knight or lord in command?"

He nodded. "Cynfyn ap Meurig is the lord there. He is a young knight and seeks to win favour with Prince Llywelyn."

"This garrison of twenty men; how are they made up?"

"There are six men at arms and the rest are archers." His precise knowledge and answers told me that they could have attempted to rescue Owain any time they chose, and it begged the question of why they had not.

"What was your plan, Captain, before I was invited to join you?"

He gave me a wry smile. "I have just ten men and my plan was to try to rescue him at night. It would have been tricky, for if they have any sense, they will bar their doors at night and, in the dark, it might have been easy for us to be trapped. Now that you are coming with us, what do you suggest?"

I would not risk the night, for in the darkness it would be too easy for a knife to end the youth's life, and I agreed with Lady Hawise that the opponents of Prince Llywelyn would use that to raise a rebellion. Ironically, if we succeeded then King Edward might disapprove of my actions, for he wished to ferment rebellion.

"You may be right, Captain Caradog; daylight might be better. My men and I are unknown to this Cynfyn, and if it is daylight, then the guards may well be more relaxed. I would suggest that we ride in to offer our services to this Cynfyn and, while we fix their attention, then you and your men can attack them unawares."

Lady Hawise put her hand on my arm. "My son, Captain!"

I smiled. "Do not worry, Lady Hawise; if I see your son outside of the building, then we will protect him and, if he is within, then when the attack begins I will enter to ensure that he is safe." I held her eyes. "I have done this before, and you should know that in the Holy Land I was charged with protecting Lord Edward and Lady Eleanor. If I say that your son will be protected," I looked to Captain Caradog, "then he will be. You have my word."

She smiled. "And I believe you!"

We left before dawn and there were eighteen of us. We had a spare horse for Owain. My men and I had been given accommodation in the stables and that suited us, for it was warm and we could speak.

My plan was based on the fact that we would have to rescue Owain ourselves and we would have minimal help from Captain Caradog. That was where our preparations in Yarpole came to the fore. My men were good with a bow and a sword. Also, we were well protected by our brigandines. Perhaps our most important asset was that apart from Stephen de Frankton, we had all fought together many times. We each knew how the others would react. With our plans in place, we slept as best we could before we rode together the next day.

The road we took twisted and turned over rough and rocky ground. The nature of the land meant that it was hard to see too far ahead. When we were just three miles from Caersws, Captain Caradog and his men left us.

Before they parted, I said quietly, "Captain Caradog, you do not know me and so I shall give you a warning. If we are betrayed, then there is nowhere you can hide from me. I am a hard man to kill and the men I lead are all better warriors than you. If you do not attack, then expect me to come for you."

His eyes flickered and he gave me a false smile. "You misjudge me, Captain. Lady Hawise is wrong; I would do nothing to harm her son and we will attack."

David the Welshman said something in Welsh and Captain Caradog flushed and then jerked his reins to lead his men away.

"What did you say, David?"

"I just told him the truth, Captain. I said that I would not wish Captain Warbow on my trail, for I would be a dead man walking."

I nodded and we headed down the road. It dipped and fell closer to Caersws and the river. I saw the bridge and the stone hall. None of us had weapons in our hands but we could reach our swords quickly. The fact that our bows were in their cases would allay their fears, for I knew that few archers knew how to use a sword well. My men were the exception. Our paucity of numbers would also make them relax their vigilance.

As we drew closer to the hall, I saw men appear on the crenulated roof and I was aware of others lurking, with nocked bows, at the sides of the hall. It was what I had expected, and I smiled. A smile often disarmed an opponent.

There were two men at arms lounging by the door. There was a gate and a low wall around the property, but neither were guarded. I knew that at night-time they would be locked, manned and patrolled.

I reined in just inside the gates and dismounted. My men did the same. I had counted ten men already. According to our information, there were twenty men. Some must be the night guards and they would be indoors, resting.

I approached the two men and deliberately spoke in English. "I understand that there is a Lord Cynfyn who lives here, and he might be interested in hiring warriors."

The man who spoke was surly, but he spoke English. "We have all the men we want and do not need some poxy Englishman who does not know one end of his bow from the other."

"Begone!" the other man said.

I nodded. "Then you are Lord Cynfyn?"

"No!"

"Should you not at least ask him? After all, he may well want to know what information is in our heads. We served with King Edward on his crusades." All the time I was talking, buying time, I was just waiting for Captain Caradog to begin his attack. We needed the guards and sentries to be looking at us and not their unknown assailants. Stephen and I would rush the men at the door when the attack happened.

Just then the door opened and a mailed warrior stepped out. He wore spurs and I knew that he had to be Lord Cynfyn. He looked suspiciously at me. "From the colour of your skin, you have been on a crusade, but you are a fool, Englishman, for I serve Prince Llywelyn and—"

He got no further, for there were cries from above and two of the sentries pitched to the ground at our feet. It is a natural reaction to look upwards. My men and I did not. Martin knew to wait with the horses. I knew that he would be drawing his bow from its case and stringing it. I was drawing my own sword and had stepped so close to Lord Cynfyn that we were almost nose to nose, and I punched him hard in the face with my sword.

Stephen and David, backed by Tom, had eliminated the two sentries and I stepped into the gloom of the hall. It was fortunate that I had been in a similar hall or I might have been skewered. One of the guards from within ran at me with a spear. Flattening myself against the wall, I grabbed the spear behind

80

the head and then rammed my sword up under his chin and into his skull. I pushed his body from me and ran towards the doorway illuminated by the glow from the fire within. Behind me, David the Welshman began to shout in Welsh. I knew that he was telling Owain that help was to hand.

A voice shouted from the glowing room but was curtailed and ended with a cry. I leapt into the room and saw a young man, who looked to be about seventeen summers and I presumed was Owain, lying on the floor, nursing a bloody coxcomb.

There were four men in the room; three of them were drawing weapons while the fourth held the sword whose pommel had just felled the captive. He lunged at me, and I blocked it with my own sword while drawing my dagger with my left hand. I had no compunction in doing what I did. I had another three opponents, and I knew not if my men had managed to follow me. I rammed the dagger up between his ribs. He was a strong man, but his grip on the hilt of his sword weakened and I was able to smash it into the side of his head.

Even as the other three drew their weapons, Stephen de Frankton lunged with his sword and slew one with a strike to the throat and, as he withdrew it, he hacked across the side of the head of a second. The third man dropped his sword and fell to his knees. He jabbered in Welsh.

David said, "He surrenders."

"Disarm them. Tom and Stephen, protect our fore. David, watch our backs." I held my hand out. "Owain, your mother, Lady Hawise, has sent us. You are safe."

He nodded. I could see he was still dazed. I reached down and took the sword from the man I had stabbed. I handed it to the youth. I knew that we were not out of danger, for I still did not trust Captain Caradog. When we emerged there could be a flurry of arrows and our sad deaths would be reported to Lady Hawise. I knew that I was risking the lives of Stephen, Tom and Martin. They wore good brigandines beneath their cloaks and that would have to protect them.

Lord Cynfyn was attempting to rise as we emerged, and Stephen kicked him in the head to knock him to the ground. Until we were safely back in the hall of Lady Hawise, there could be no honour.

It all seemed quiet. I had expected some opposition from the villagers, but they were behind doors which were firmly shut.

Stephen and Tom mounted while Martin scanned the hall with a nocked bow. David cupped his hands to help the young Welshman on to the horse and, when that was done, we mounted and, whipping the heads of our horses around, galloped away from the hall. There was no sign of Captain Caradog but then I would have been surprised if there was. The fact that none of his men had loosed an arrow at us told me that Prince Llywelyn's brother had decided to cut his losses and allow Owain to live. I knew that I had made another enemy, a pair in fact, but that appeared to be my lot in life!

Chapter 6

We reached Wigmore a few days later. Once Lady Hawise had her son safe in her charge, she emptied her hall, and we rode as fast as four wagons can manage. She pointedly rode next to her son and insisted that my men and I ride around the two of them. She still did not trust Dafydd!

I did not mind, for we were not simply ignored by almost all of the others but shunned. It was clear to me that I had spoiled their plans. A dead Owain was of more value than a released prisoner. The only one from the conspirators who appeared to show any remorse over their plan was Lord Gruffydd ap Gwenwynwyn. He was not a clever man and he had been duped. I think the bruises and the wound his son bore told him that he had been used by Dafydd and Captain Caradog.

Baron Mortimer was delighted that I had managed the rescue, and he and Lady Maud wished me to stay. I shook my head. "I have been away long enough. I have served my king, again, but I have a family that deserves as much attention." I gestured for Sir Roger to come closer and when he did, I spoke quietly. "I would not trust this Lord Gruffydd ap

Gwenwynwyn, lord. Speak with Lady Hawise and see if my suspicions are correct."

He stepped back and his eyes examined me. "You are a clever man, Gerald. Go back to your family, but remember that in spring you should be at Shrewsbury, for King Edward comes to accept the homage of Prince Llywelyn and he will not be happy if you are absent." I nodded, for I knew my place. "And I dare say that the king will reward his loyal subjects for the service they have done."

"Thank you, my lord."

I would rather have been left alone than be paid a reward that would tie me even closer to the king. Yarpole was a gift but it did just that. I knew then that Sir John had been lucky to have been given Malton. That was as far from the king's enemies as anywhere in the land. He could get on with his life!

As we rode back to Yarpole, I reflected that the rescue had not only been successful but had also shown me that Stephen de Frankton was a loyal man and a good warrior. He had dispatched two men in a blur of blows.

We arrived back to find my wife still healthy and my manor burgeoned with the fruits of our work. We had no time for reflection as every man was put to work harvesting the crops and beginning the cull of those animals we could not keep over winter. This was a time of collection and preservation. The windfalls and the damaged fruits were cooked and added to meat which would not last the winter. Soaked in cheap sack, they would provide a feast at Christmas. We were luckier than most, for Sarah had many spices to use and the hall was filled with the smell that Sarah and James called Christmas. Other meats were preserved in salt, brine and vinegar. The animals from the cull were butchered and every part used. Even their bones were burned with the fallen leaves and the remains of the bone fire collected to be used as fertiliser. I had learned, since becoming a farmer, that you wasted nothing in the countryside.

I went with Father Paul to see which villagers needed help. I knew that winter was hard, especially on the old and the poor. We were lucky in Yarpole; we had few who were poor, but we had many who were old. It was not coins that they needed but kindling and food. When the harvest was gathered, we took around the wood and excess food collected by my men for them to use. Sarah had ensured that we had plenty of vinegar and salt, and that was taken too so that they could preserve the food we had given to them. Father Paul and I visited the same people each week. I did it because I felt responsible. I knew that not every landowner did the same, but I remembered my childhood and people who starved to death over winter. That would not happen to my people. King Edward and Sir Roger might not be concerned about the poor and the old, but I was.

As Mary's time drew close, so I kept close to the hall. My men still hunted and collected wood for winter, they still practised, but I rarely strayed more than a few paces from the hall. The exceptions were my weekly visits with Father Paul, and Sundays, when Mary and I went to church. It was at the service on Christmas Eve, when the first really hard frost and cold spell descended, that her waters broke. I did not know the term but Sarah, who was with us in the church, did.

"Captain, let us hurry home, for your child is come!"

All thoughts of the Christmas feast disappeared as we hurried back to my hall. My men were sent ahead to begin to put on pots of water to boil. Sarah seemed to think that was important. James and I carried Mary, who kept apologising. I know that it was fear, for she had confided to me that she was unsure if she could bear the pain of childbirth.

As a man, I was ushered from the birthing chamber, our bedroom, and Anne of Yarpole – the village midwife, Mags and Sarah, aided by John and Jack's wives, saw to my wife's needs. I sat with my men in the hall we used for dining. After my men had built up the fire, Jack fetched the ale, which had been intended for Christmas Day, and he used a poker to heat it. I was reluctant to drink, for I feared I might be needed.

Jack had many children and he laughed. "Captain, you have done your part! The women would not thank you for interference and they know their business. It is Mistress Mary's first and this could take some time."

Robin, now fully recovered, nodded. "Aye, Captain, and what a propitious day! The bairn will be born on Christmas Day, Jesus's birth date!"

I took the ale and drank it without even tasting it. The date of the birth had escaped me but there was something significant about it. Mary and I first knew that we would be wed when we were in the Holy Land and within a few miles of Bethlehem. The date was momentous.

My men began to talk about what the date might mean. Most of us had no idea when we were born. Dates of birth were for nobles and those who were important. We just knew that we were so many summers old. My child would be different, for although we were not noble, all would remember the date.

As warriors do, it was a small jump from talking about birth to speaking of death and those who had fallen in battle. I had lost many comrades and I was silent as I remembered them and my father. I wondered what he might have thought of my rise from outlaw and murderer to gentleman and confidante of lords. I hoped he would have been proud, but we had never spoken a great deal and there was much about him that was a mystery. When my child was born, I would ensure that we were close. I would make sure that words were spoken so that my child could know a little about me, for I knew that when I was dead there would be tales and rumours which were untrue.

I drifted in and out of the conversation until, after he had returned from making water, David the Welshman returned. "It is morning; it is Christmas Day!"

As was the custom, we each clasped arms with the others who were in the hall. This time it seemed more significant.

James, Sarah's son, said, "Perhaps we should begin to cook the food. I have heard little from upstairs and, in my experience, birth is normally preceded by shouts and even screams. The women will be busy. What say we men set to and make the feast ourselves?"

It seemed a good idea and we went into the kitchen to prepare the Christmas feast. The vegetables were all ready and all that was needed was for us to prepare them. The wild pig we had hunted three weeks since had been skinned, gutted and hung. Alan had been tracking the old boar for a month before we killed him. He had told us that there was a younger boar and the old one had served his purpose. The animal had fought to the end and that was good.

Richard of Culcheth and his son, Robin, now brought it into the kitchen. It should have been started the night before when we had returned from church but there was still time. Jack and Martin put the metal spike through it and hung it above the fire. It would be constantly turned by one of the sons of my men. We then set to plucking the fowl we had to accompany the pig. We would cook far more than we needed, for whatever was left would feed us all for the next ten days or so.

The work distracted us so that when we heard the scream, we all started. John came over to me. "Do not worry, Captain, that is part of the birthing, but in my experience the babe will be here soon. Tom, take the captain and help him to clean himself up. We will finish here, Captain."

I nodded dully and went obediently with Tom. He chattered to me, but I heard not a word. There were more shouts and then the sound of feet running along the floor above us.

Tom smiled when I started. "I reckon they will call for you soon, Captain. I am the oldest of eight my mother bore, and such a rush normally precipitated an announcement."

Why did everyone else seem to know more about birth than I did?

As I passed through the kitchen, I heard Mags's strident voice from the top of the stairs. "Captain! You are a father!"

My men all cheered but my heart sank. What about Mary? I took the narrow stairs two at a time to get there quickly.

Mags laughed. "The bairn and Mistress Mary are going nowhere, Captain. You do not want to hurt yourself, eh?"

"How is she?" I needed to know before I entered the chamber.

"Tired, but that is normal. You have a stronger wife than you know, Captain."

I entered the chamber and saw bloody sheets and towels being gathered by other women while Sarah brushed my wife's hair. Mary looked pale but happy and, in her arms, swaddled in white, lay my child.

Mary said, "Husband, you have your wish; you have a son!"

I smiled broadly. "And has he…?"

Sarah laughed. "You see, Mistress, it is as I said; the first thing men want to know is if the child has the required number of limbs and organs." She turned to me. "He is whole, Captain; a good weight and has a set of lungs on him. We will leave you two alone, but not for long, Captain. Your wife is tired and needs rest. Alice will come back and sit with her." Alice was the wife of Jack of Lincoln. She had lost a child a month since and if it was needed then she could wet nurse my son.

The door closed and I went to kiss my wife on the top of her head. She smiled and held the boy. "Take him and hold him."

"But I might drop him!"

"No, you will not, and the Mongol warriors do this as soon as the babe is born, for they wish them to be warriors. You wish the same for our son, do you not?"

I nodded and took him. He seemed so fragile that I was almost afraid that my rough touch and archer's arms would crush him. His eyes were closed, and he was red of colour, but he looked content.

"Have you a name in mind?"

I looked up, startled. "A name?"

She laughed. "We cannot call him boy, can we? It makes him sound like a dog."

I nodded. "I did not give it much thought, for I did not know if we were going to have a boy or a girl. I do not want him to have my name, for that way men might think I was vain."

She smiled. "I have had time to think and I knew it would be a boy. Only one name came to mind. Hamo. I would name him after the man who helped you and Sir John to rescue me. He was a kind man and a good warrior." She smiled. "And I know of no other who has his name."

I looked at the babe and said, "Hamo, son of Gerald, aye; I like that name." At that moment he opened his eyes and stared at me. He did not cry, and I took that as a sign that he approved of the name.

If the night before had been celebratory then that Christmas Day was like no other. Of course, Sarah and the women complained about the way we had prepared the food, but we expected that. We had entered the domain of women. But as their carping was gentle, we guessed we had done something right.

The men who had their own families of children only stayed with us for Grace before they departed to their own homes with their portion of food. Even so, the table was full. Sarah liked to do everything correctly and so we all sat with a napkin over our right shoulder to wipe our hands. We took the proffered food with our left hands and none took too much. Sarah's vigilant eye saw to that.

When Tom, who had a very healthy appetite, took a whole turkey guinea fowl, she said, "Tom, I think your eyes are bigger than your belly! If there is any of that fowl left, then there shall be no pudding for you!"

That was a dire threat as the highlight of the feast, for many, was the spiced pudding made of fruit and meat. Sarah's was especially tasty, and Tom made sure that all that was left on his bread platter were the fowl's bones. To be truthful, the turkey guinea fowl were not particularly large. I smiled, for after the bones were taken away, Tom still had appetite enough to eat the bread platter which had been soaked with all the gravies and tastes from the savoury foods.

We all drank well, for there was plenty of ale, and I broached a barrel of the sweet wine they made in western Spain. It was sweeter than sack and I liked its deep red colour.

When the rich pudding was brought in, steaming and aromatic, silence fell upon the table. It was so rich that we were all offered a small portion. As head of the house, I could have demanded more but, in truth, I was satiated and wished to see my wife. I had seen her before the feast, and she had said she wished to sleep.

When I entered the chamber, Hamo was nursing.

"Alice, go down, for they serve the pudding and Sarah has saved a portion for you."

"If you do not mind, Captain?" I shook my head. She grinned. "I am fond of Mistress Sarah's pudding. I hope that one day she will share the recipe with me."

She left and I put my arm around Mary and the nursing baby, who was sucking greedily.

"The feast went well?"

"It was perfect, my love, save that you could not be present."

She gave me a wan smile. "I was a little busy."

I nodded. "All went well, and they were all happy."

"We have good people, my husband, and I am happy here." I knew that Mary had been worried about coming to a community as a stranger, but I had reassured her of the spirit of the people of Yarpole. The previous landowner had almost sucked that spirit from them but, thanks to Sarah, James and Father Paul, it had recovered, and we were now strong enough to withstand any calamity.

We had Hamo christened on Saint Stephen's Day and gave him Stephen as a middle name. Father Paul thought it was a propitious naming and we went along with it.

I rode, when the weather improved a month later, to tell Baron Mortimer and Lady Maud of the birth. Their Welsh guests had decamped to Shrewsbury and, from Lady Maud's face, it was not a day too soon! She gave me a gift of ten marks for Hamo to be kept for him until he was old enough to need a sword. It was a thoughtful gesture and suggested that she expected me to rise above being a gentleman. I returned home knowing that I had until the spring to myself, and then I would need to ride to Shrewsbury, where Prince Llywelyn would pay homage.

I put those thoughts from my mind as I played, for the first time, a dutiful husband and father. I stayed close to home and ensured that my wife and child were cared for and protected.

It was something of an anti-climax when the date arrived and the messenger came from Sir Roger to tell me that the king was unwell and would not be attending the meeting he had ordered. Ominously, Prince Llywelyn did not attempt to attend, yet he would escape censure as the king was unwell and would not know of the snub. However, what followed was worse.

As summer began, Dafydd ap Gruffydd and his allies began to raid across the border. They raided the mines we rescued the prisoners from, for the silver and to butcher the locals. War came to the northern Welsh Marches, and our home was in striking distance of any warband that chose to raid an easy target.

I knew from men I had served with when on crusade that border warfare was the same on the Scottish borders as the Welsh borders and, indeed, the border between Outremer and the Seljuk Turks. It was rarely the war of armies but more a tit for tat battle with sides choosing easy targets. As soon as we heard, in June, that Alberbury had been burned by Welshmen, I organised our defences.

Following our return from Rhayader, I had built a stone entrance to my hall. It was narrow and had a good door. We could easily defend it. If, however, the enemy, whoever they were, managed to attack the door, then our main line of defence, our wall, had failed.

I went around all the villagers and told them that when they heard the church bell toll constantly, they were to get to my hall with their families. These were not the same people who had hidden behind their doors when I had first come, after Evesham. These were my folk, and they would defend my walls, knowing that any mischief which damaged their homes would be repaired by my men and me.

I had Peter organise my defences. He was the unofficial Captain of the Guard. Even Stephen deferred to him. He made a rota so that we had men on the gate twenty-four hours a day. Of course, if an enemy came at night, then our people would suffer, for they would not have enough warning to get within my walls.

The walls themselves, and the gatehouse we had spent so long on before my son was born, would now come into their own. We had added a wooden palisade which was crenulated so that archers could shelter and loose obliquely at an attacking enemy. The ditch, which ran around the wooden outer wall, was well maintained, and we set to placing stakes in the bottom to injure any who tried to cross. There was one wooden bridge across the ditch. We began to raise it at night, hoping that would probably deter a night-time attack. We left it down during the day to allow people to enter.

Our last defence was vigilance, and I rode out each day with two of my men to look for any signs of intruders. This was where

I had the most experience. I had learned to scout and look for signs of an enemy when I had been barely a youth. While I always set out along the Welsh road, I rarely came back the same way. Instead, we would follow the waterways and the paths which crossed fields. I looked for footprints muddying the crossing of streams. I searched for horse dung where it should not be, and I looked for places where a warband might camp. For three weeks we saw nothing, but we heard of raids to the north and south of us. Dafydd ap Gruffydd still sent Captain Caradog into Wales to raid his brother and I knew that someday, and soon, the war would come to Yarpole.

It was a strange time, for while we worked in the fields, picking the summer crops and tending to animals, we all watched over our shoulders. Men worked in the fields with whatever weapon they could find. Many simply used their billhooks. Those who had them strapped on a sword or a dagger. As every man old enough had a bow that he could use, they were encumbered by those too. I knew that this would wear down my men and their families but there was no other choice. The whole of the county was doing the same. We were watching and waiting for violence to strike. I cursed Dafydd ap Gruffydd for his ambition. This would cost lives. King Edward had thought that Welsh treachery might win Wales for him. Now it appeared it might lose him the borders!

Chapter 7

Inside my home, we tried to keep life as normal as we could. In the months since Christmas, I could not believe the change in my son. For the first month or more he had either been attached to my wife or asleep. If he was doing neither then his wails would tell the world that he needed attention. Then, seemingly suddenly, he began to take notice and to make sounds. He started to smile when I walked in and spoke. I had learned to use a different voice when speaking to him. I was softer and gentler. Mary smiled when I did so. I was always rewarded by smiles at first and then giggles. Despite the threat from beyond our walls, those smiles and giggles warmed my heart and made me feel that we would prevail. God had sent us a son and he had given me something as important as Mary to defend.

John and Jack both had sons who, whilst not old enough to be either archers or men at arms, could, like every boy their age, use a slingshot. Pebbles from the streams had been gathered and the four boys would be part of the defence of the hall. John, son of John, was an agile ten-year-old and he had managed to scale the roof of my hall before. He had been in trouble with his father and wished to avoid a beating by escaping up there. We now used that skill, and he would clamber out of the door we used in the roof to lift heavy objects, and then he would sit astride the roof, watching the roads into Yarpole.

On one particular day, I had been down the Welsh Road with John's father and we had seen nothing.

"Perhaps they have better targets, Captain. Yarpole has little to offer to a raider."

I shook my head. "Alberbury had less and that was chosen. This is about vengeance. They cannot get at Dafydd, for he squats inside Shrewsbury's strong walls. Wigmore, Leominster, Hereford – all of those places have castles. Wigmore is the strongest in this part of the Marches. The Welsh have not forgotten Llanymynech. They will wish to punish us but, perhaps, our new defences have made them think again."

Just then we spied my hall and I saw John's son, John, waving from the roof. John waved back at his son, but I knew that it was not a greeting. That was confirmed when he pointed to the south-east.

"They have come – ride!"

I dug my heels in Eleanor's flanks. John's son must have only just spied the danger, for there was no tolling of the bell. That would come. As we passed houses and people, their waves of greeting were stopped when I shouted, "Get into the walls! The Welsh are coming!"

Whatever happened, my village owed a debt of gratitude to John, son of John of Nottingham. I heard the bell tolling and knew that we would have men to defend the walls. More importantly, the families would also be safe. We would lose animals and the Welsh would try to destroy our crops, but seeds could be replanted and animals bought. People were harder to replace.

We were not the first to ride through my gates. Those whose houses were the closest were already pouring through. James was in charge of them and he was already directing them to the barns and outbuildings. We would be packed inside but, thanks to my new walls, we would be safer than in the village.

I shouted up to John, son of John, "Where away?"

He cupped one hand and pointed with the other. "They have fired Luston!"

Luston was a small hamlet a mile and a half to the south-west. There was little there, and the people used our church and our mill. Without a lord to protect them, they were helpless. I hoped that they had had warning and been able to escape but, even as the thought entered my head, I knew that there would be English captives heading back to Wales unless we defeated the Welsh and reclaimed them.

"Can you see any?" I meant, of course, the Welsh, but if there were survivors they would be coming across the fields.

"The woods hide them, but I can see flashes of metal as the sun catches them!"

I pointed to the south-east corner of our walls. "Peter of Beverley, they have fired Luston. Man the tower and keep a watch for survivors."

He waved his acknowledgement and rattled out his orders.

I ran inside my hall. Mary was feeding Hamo and I gave her a wan smile. "Danger comes."

"But the people are safe?"

"Aye, the Welsh will find us a little large to swallow. I must arm. Fear not, my love; we have good people."

She smiled. "Aye, and a leader who knows how to fight! Hurt them so that they never return!"

My wife had lived amongst Mongols and knew the way that they fight. Mongols do not take prisoners!

I already wore my brigandine and had my sword, but I grabbed my helmet and not only my war bow but my Mongol bow. This might be the time to give the Welsh archers a taste of its power! I hurried to the centre of my walls and saw that all the walls were manned. My own retinue; archers and men at arms, were on the south and western walls, facing Luston. The others were spread around.

Alan was the last to arrive. We now called him Alan of the Woods as his home was so close to the wood to the south of us. His wife, Anna, and his two sons rode his horse.

As he helped his family down, I said, "Alan, ride to the church and fetch Father Paul. All else are within the walls."

"Aye, Captain. We saw men heading through your wood."

I nodded. "The south wall is manned too. Hurry!"

He sprang onto the back of his horse and galloped off to ride the short way to the church.

I took my bows and ran to the barn tower. The barn was at the junction of the south and west walls. We had built the walls so that we had the protection of the barn behind us and there was a small wooden tower at the corner. Tom and Martin were there already.

When I reached them Tom shouted, "I see them, Captain; they are heading up the Luston Beck, and I also see some of the villagers – there are just six of them."

I strung my Mongol bow and took an arrow.

I stood next to the tower and John of Nottingham shouted,

"I see them. It is Harold of Luston and his family!"

"Cupping my hands, I cried, "Harold, run to the main gate and we will cover you!"

They were three hundred paces from us, but he waved acknowledgement and urged his wife, sons and daughters on. In his hand, he carried his scythe.

"Do not waste arrows. Loose only when you are sure that you can hit one."

I saw the Welsh as they emerged from the shallow stream. As I had expected, the ones who were chasing were the archers. My dilemma was that they were closer to Harold of Luston than they were to us. They would be able to slay them before my men were in range. Had it just been Harold then he might have had a chance, but his wife was struggling.

I saw the Welsh archer stand and draw. I had an arrow nocked. The range was extreme, even for me, but I was elevated and that would give me more range. The Mongol arrow was long, and it was a barbed arrow. It was one I had brought back from the crusade. I loosed but was aware that there was a breeze from my left. I had not allowed for it. Despite that, I saw the Welshman draw fully back and then watched as my arching arrow plunged from on high to smash into his skull. His bow and nocked arrow fell from his dying hands. It was not just the fact that I had saved Harold that was important, it was the fact that I shocked the Welsh archers. They knew their range and ours. My single arrow made them not only stop but rush back to the protection of the stream. Harold and his family would be safe, and they would try to find another way in.

John of Nottingham was my most experienced archer. He had not been on a crusade and had not seen the bow used in anger. He shook his head. "Captain, if we only knew how to make such bows… None could defeat us."

"But we do not. This one will have to suffice, and we have set them a problem."

Stephen de Frankton joined us. He pointed to the sun which, whilst still in the sky, was beginning to drop to the west. "If they have any sense they will wait until dark."

"And get closer to our walls?"

He nodded. "They cannot have brought ladders, but they may try to cross the ditches and scale our walls. Of course, if they do then they will be hurt!"

The Welsh would not know that the bottom of the ditch was covered in sharpened spikes. There was an ankle breaker to stop them leaping. With luck, they would try to cross, and we might be able to discourage them.

"The danger is if they have fire arrows, Stephen. They are my only fear."

David the Welshman was studying the ground. "We know how to make them, Captain, but I doubt if these raiders do. I will ask Harold of Luston how they were attacked." He disappeared down the ladder.

We could no longer see the Welsh and had no idea of numbers. They had gone to ground. The fields around my hall gave us a good line of sight but there were four small dwellings, behind which they could hide, and there were fences too. But Stephen was right. We had put good defences in place and we had to trust them. What we did know was that there would be no help coming to us, for none would know of our plight. I smiled and shook my head.

Stephen de Frankton said, "Something amuses you, Captain?"

"No, Stephen, it is just that it is not long since I was last besieged with no sign of help, but that was in Acre! Somehow this seems more precious."

Just then John, son of John of Nottingham, who still had his precarious perch, yelled, "They come!"

My men had arrows nocked and there were darts and stones for those without a bow. None of my people needed encouragement from me, and any words might make them think I lacked faith in them.

Stephen said, "It seems they have no sense, Captain!"

For all that it was foolish, the Welsh showed great skill and courage. They rose from the ditch and, with two dozen men protected by shields, they ran towards the abandoned houses. They were followed by more than thirty archers.

I spied a half dozen men at arms and what looked to be a knight, well out of range. I say looked like, for he had mail and a good helmet. The livery seemed familiar. The men at arms wore brigandines.

The men with shields left the houses and advanced together with the archers close behind. They were now within range of us.

John of Nottingham said, "They have fewer men than I would have expected."

I had thought the same. "Then there may be others ready to attack while our attention is here. John, go to the village gatehouse. Your presence might stiffen the resolve of our people. And get your son down from the roof. He has done all that we might have hoped."

Stephen was staring at the advancing men. The ones with shields were fewer than two hundred paces from the walls – we had stone markers to give us the range – and we could have risked arrows, but with the relatively small number of archers I had to hand, the men with shields would be able to see the arrows and block them. Had we a hundred or more then we could have loosed a shower and guaranteed some hits.

"Captain, I recognise the man at arms who is with the knight," said Stephen. "It is Rhodri ap Rhodri, who was our gaoler. Put him within reach of my sword and he will die."

"And the knight?"

"From his livery, he is Maredudd ap Iago."

I nodded. "The one who ambushed Sir Jasper and chased us from Wales." He nodded. "Then we have scores to settle here."

The men with shields were advancing confidently as no arrows had headed their way. My single arrow had warned them of our power, and this was their solution. I saw that ten more men with shields had moved to protect the men at arms and the knight and his squire. I saw, however, that the squire was a little overconfident or perhaps he was tired. Whatever the reason, his own shield dropped a little and he had allowed a gap to the man with the large kite shield, who protected him.

Looking around I saw that the sun was lower in the sky. It would still be hours until sunset but there was a chance for a cheap victory. I nocked an arrow and, in a swift and practised motion, drew and released. The squire was a little blinded by the sun and his hand was slow to rise. My arrow smacked into his shoulder.

My other archers seized their opportunity and, as men looked around to see who had been hit, arrows were sent towards them. None were wasted. Every arrow hit. More than half hit shields and three struck helmets. The arrows would have made the head ache and ears ring, but the men were unharmed. Six men, however, were hit by arrows that found flesh. That was six wounded men.

The Welsh archers responded but we had wooden walls, behind which we could shelter. More importantly, it exposed the archers and, when we rose and sent our arrows towards them, we were rewarded with hits, two of them mortal.

The knight shouted something, and the shield men and archers began to pull back. It cost them two more men who were struck. One did not move and had an arrow in his head. The green and white flights told me that it was Richard of Culcheth who had killed the Welsh bowman.

David the Welshman had returned in time to send his arrows at the enemy and now, as the Welsh withdrew, he spoke to me. "Captain, Harold of Luston told me that the Welsh surprised them by surrounding the hamlet. He and his family only escaped as their farm is at this end of the hamlet and they were in the fields picking beans. When he heard the shouts and screams, he ran with his family."

"Did he know numbers?"

"He said he saw the Welsh ponies in the distance, and they had riders upon their backs."

It was not the answer I needed, but it told me that they were mobile and suggested that there were more men available to this Welsh knight than we could see.

When the sun set, I knew that they would now wait for dark of night to draw closer. I had two men in three go for food and then to rest. Sarah and the women had baked bread and cooked pottage. We would not starve, and I guessed that the Welsh would retire to Luston to eat whatever they could find.

I spoke with David, Stephen and Peter of Beverley.

"We lost no-one, and we hurt them, Captain."

"Aye, David, but night will give them a cloak to allow them to come closer and, perhaps, even scale the walls. It is why I have sent two-thirds of the men to rest and to eat. We four may well have to forego such luxuries. I cannot see these Welshmen tarrying long and I can go one night without sleep. I want one of us on each wall tonight. We will know the signs."

Stephen de Frankton said, "There is another way, Captain. We could send a few men out tonight and kill their sentries."

I shook my head. "That had occurred to me, but we do not have enough numbers to guarantee success and I cannot afford to lose a single archer or man at arms. Peter, have all the spare weapons from the armoury spread out along the walls."

"Aye, Captain!"

I walked the walls and told each of my men what we had planned. I went to the barn and sent a third of the men back to the walls so that another third could eat and have an hour of rest. I ate but I did not taste the food. I put on a smile and exuded confidence for my wife and Sarah.

Sarah shook her head. "My son, James, has told me the numbers you face, Captain. This will be a hard fight. You make sure you eat properly and do not fear for your lady. She will be protected by us!" She took, from beneath her voluminous dress, the carving knife she used to butcher meat. A Welshman who took her on would be lucky not to lose a limb or worse!

The food, the smiles from Hamo and Mary, forced in the case of my wife, refreshed me as much as a night in a goose feather bed, and I returned to the walls. I went to the barn wall, for it was the closest to the Welsh and the one I thought they would use.

The fighting platform seemed empty with only a third of the men remaining. Alan and Robin were the nearest to me and Tom was in the wooden tower. We did not speak, for that would give away our position. With our hoods over our heads, our faces were shielded, and so long as we did not move, we would be invisible. We stood protected by the wooden crenulations and looked out at an angle. There were enough of us so that we could see the whole of the ground before us.

I think I was the first to spot the moving shadows but Alan, with his hunter's eyes and senses, was not far behind. We each tapped the men close to us and I sent Jack's son Wilfred to fetch more men to our wall. I was desperate to visit the other walls and see how they fared, but I had to trust Peter, Stephen and David.

There was little point in wasting an arrow, and so I picked up a couple of the darts the blacksmith had made. With a lead-weighted end and thrown at close range, they could be deadly.

Tom nocked an arrow. The shadows skittered across the ground. The Welsh would have to negotiate the corpses which lay where they had fallen. If they had been my men, I would have made some attempt to recover them for the sake of the morale of the remaining men, but Lord Maredudd seemed not to care.

Tom must have had good eyesight, for he released an arrow that brought forth a cry as it struck a man. Realising that they had been seen, the shadows stopped the slow, creeping motion and ran towards the ditch.

My archers close by me sent their arrows into the white faces. I saw a face on the other side of the ditch. He had an arrow nocked but I hurled my dart. He was not expecting it. A bow would make a thrumming noise when released. The dart was silent, and it struck his right hand before being deflected, by his reactive jerk, into his eye.

Men were still joining us and some of the Welshmen jumped into the ditch. Their screams told me that they had found the sharpened stakes. I threw a second dart into the back of a wounded man who was trying to climb out. There could be no mercy for these men. It struck his back and he fell backwards to be impaled upon our stakes. Seeing the body deterred the others, who turned and ran.

I could hear fighting on the other walls and now that we had beaten off this attack, I said, "Alan, take charge here while I see how the others fare." I grabbed my bow and ran.

Our fighting platform was not continuous. We had deliberately ended it at each building so that if one section of the wall was lost, we could defend the others. I descended the ladder and ran to the main gate. I climbed up and saw that we had lost men. Ned, the miller's son, lay with an arrow in his head. They had not had time to clear away the bodies from this part of the wall.

I looked out and saw that there were more men here, for the houses were a little closer to our walls and had allowed the Welsh to get a little nearer before our bows could be used. The battle was in the balance, but more of those who had been resting were now joining Peter and his men.

I nocked an arrow and sent it into the shoulder of an archer who was aiming at one of my men in the two wooden towers. Our extra numbers swung the battle in our favour and, as with the south wall, the Welsh fell back.

I checked the other two walls and discovered that they had beaten off their attackers too, but we had injuries. All of my archers survived unhurt, but the village had wounded men. Father Paul tended to them.

Dawn brought the grisly sight of the Welsh dead in the ditches and beyond. In all, we had slain eighteen men, and with more of them wounded, I wondered if that might discourage them.

We ate on the fighting platform. The little rest my people had enjoyed was all that they would get.

I saw no movement towards Luston, and I wondered if they had departed. A cry from the main gate told me that they had not.

I ran and climbed the ladder. Rhodri ap Rhodri and Lord Maredudd were approaching. They were bareheaded and had their hands open. They wished to speak.

I did not let them speak first; I simply said, "If you have come to surrender, then know that there must be reparations for those whose property you took."

That made both men colour, and Lord Maredudd said, "We have come to demand your surrender."

I pointed to the bodies. Some had fouled themselves in death and begun to stink. "That is the price you will pay for attack!"

Rhodri turned and whistled. Two hundred paces away, four bound men were dragged out by Welshmen and forced to kneel.

Lord Maredudd said, "Unless you surrender, we will execute these men."

I heard Harold of Luston shout, "You bastard!"

I shook my head. "If you do that, I will see you hanged, but I will not accede to your demands, for you would do the same to us."

Lord Maredudd raised his arm and I wondered if he would really do it.

Then Father Paul said, "I am a witness to this crime, Lord Maredudd. It is murder, plain and simple!"

I saw hesitation and then Rhodri said, "I have a solution, Captain Gerald Warbow. Come out of your walls and fight me for them. If you win, they will be handed over to you, and if I win, they will die! We have more captives. Luston was not the first place we raided. Perhaps you would like to see your women despoiled?"

Stephen de Frankton shouted, "Fight me, you butcher!"

The Welshman laughed. "I will get to you in time. First I kill Warbow and send a message to Longshanks that he does not rule here!"

Stephen turned to me. "You cannot do this, Captain. He is a trained man at arms and—"

"And I am just an archer. I know, but know that I have done this before, and it is my Christian duty to try to save them."

Will Yew Tree was close by and he said, "I will have an arrow nocked, Captain, in case of treachery!"

I shouted down, "Pull your men back to the houses, and that includes you, Maredudd, for I trust you least of all! Have the rest of your captives brought out where we can see them!"

"I am Lord Maredudd – show me respect!"

"I will show respect when you have earned it, but know that I have an arrow with your name upon it, and when your snake here lies dead, then I will hunt you down. Wales is not big enough for you to hide!"

I descended. At the foot of the ladder, I handed my bow to Robin.

Stephen said, "Do you wish a shield, Captain?"

I shook my head. "Fetch me a hand axe that is sharp." I had a dagger in each buskin and my sword was a good one. Beneath my brigandine, I wore a padded gambeson. I would try to use speed. I took off my helmet. I wanted to have good vision. "Have they cleared the area?"

Will shouted, "Aye, Captain, and I think you have their lord worried. He is mounted on his horse. The captives are there. He has twelve of them. The others are women and children. They are closely guarded."

Stephen handed me an axe and I said, "If I fall then you command."

"And if you fall then not a Welshman shall live."

"Open the gates."

As I stepped out of the gates, I realised that I had not said goodbye to Mary nor offered an explanation. I hoped that she understood. I was not sure that I did. The villagers were not even mine, but if I did not try to protect them then who would?

I had to put such thoughts from my head as I saw the Welshman facing me. He wore a helmet and, like me, he had a brigandine, but he also had a shield. I had chosen an axe and though I was unfamiliar with its use, I could use either hand, and two weapons might be better than one.

He strode towards me eagerly and I deliberately slowed so that he might think I feared him. I did not. I would also let him have the first blow, for I wanted him tired. He might have more skill, but I was an archer and could use my arms for longer periods than he.

"Englishman, I will hack your flesh from your body, piece by piece. You slew my brother at the mine, and I will have vengeance."

I said nothing, for I was weighing him up and seeing where I could gain an advantage. The sun was behind me and it had yet to rise above the hall. When it did, then he would have light in his eyes. I could not allow him to turn me.

He took my silence and slow approach for fear, and he moved quickly for a big man. He was using his shield and his sword together so that he punched with his shield while he slashed with his sword. It might have mesmerised another but not me.

I spun on my right leg so that his shield and his sword struck fresh air and as I spun around his back, I hacked the axe into the rear of his brigandine. The metal studs prevented it from cutting too deeply but I hurt him. I kept spinning until I was back in my first position. From the walls came a cheer. I had not wounded him, but I had injured his pride, for I had struck the first blow and he was angry. Angry men do not fight well. Archers always fight cold because we are fighting at a distance. I used that coldness to keep me calm.

"Trickster! Stand still!"

He would not try that again, and he came more steadily and this time measured his approach, keeping his shield up for protection. He now knew that I could use my left hand. I wanted him to think that I did not know how to use my sword and when he swung his own at my head, I did not block it with my sword but my axe. I did not want to blunt my weapon. He was strong but an archer has a left hand as strong as his right. Sparks flew as the sword struck the axe head and the edge of the blade came perilously close to my head.

As he pulled back his sword, I punched the head of my axe up under his chin. The crack on his mail coif sounded loud to me and when he reeled, I knew that I had hurt him. I went on the offensive and I hacked at his shield with my axe. It was a short axe, but it had a head that was very heavy in proportion to its size, and I cracked his shield.

I still had the east behind me, and I used it to my advantage. I raised the sword as though I was going to strike down and, when he raised his sword to block the blow, the sun caught the two blades and blinded him. I swung the axe, and he must have sensed it, for he brought his shield around to block it, however, I was not aiming at his shield but his thighs. The mail skirt he wore protected only his groin and the axe head drew blood.

His reactions were fast, and he almost caught me out. His sword came down towards my shoulder, but I managed to block it, not with the edge of my sword but the crosspiece of the hilt. He tried to use raw strength to force the sword towards my unprotected neck, but he was bleeding, and I was an archer. As I pulled back my left arm, he lifted his shield to block the blow and I rammed my right knee between his legs. I hurt him and I saw him struggling for breath.

I had to end this before my luck ran out, and I pulled back my right arm and rammed my sword through his screaming mouth. The blade came out of the back of his skull and when I ripped it to the right, I tore out half of his face. He dropped to his knees and then rolled over. He was dead.

I saw Lord Maredudd raise his sword, but from behind me I heard David the Welshman shout, "Loose!" and arrows flew towards the Welshmen whose spears and swords were ready to end the lives of the captives.

I lifted my sword and ran towards them. From behind me, I heard a roar as Yarpole manor emptied and every man and boy who could hold a weapon raced out. Lord Maredudd's men still outnumbered us, but our arrows had hurt the men with the spears, and the sight of our charge made Lord Maredudd turn and flee.

The Welsh had seen their champion die and now they were threatened too. They ran. Those who could mounted ponies and headed west. My men and the villagers were not in a merciful mood and any they caught, they butchered.

The fight had taken it out of me, and I waited with the captives as Stephen de Frankton led my men on a day-long chase. They returned at dark with four ponies laden with weapons. The Battle of Yarpole was over, but not its repercussions.

Chapter 8

Of course, Baron Mortimer, when we told him, was outraged. It was a pity his outrage had not stretched to sending men to check on our safety. My gain was the hamlet of Luston. The village became part of my land. It was a double-edged sword, for while I received some of their taxes and could levy their men, I was responsible for their protection. My wife pointed out that I was the kind of man who would protect them in any case and the small reward was the least I could expect.

As I led my men back to Yarpole, I learned about the flights of arrows that had turned the tide in our favour.

David the Welshman nodded towards Stephen de Frankton. "It was Stephen's idea, Captain. He asked if we could send arrows accurately over the captives' heads, and I said we could but not the farmers. Instead, I ordered the farmers to send their arrows to hit behind the houses, for I knew that men would shelter there, and then we hit the men with the spears. It was Harold of Luston who opened the gate and led the folk out to kill the last of the Welsh. One of the captives was his sister. We could not stop them."

It had been a mixture of luck and anger that had won the battle for us. If the Welsh had been led by a braver warrior then it might have gone differently. I had killed the real leader and I knew that the combat could also have gone in a different direction, but I had angered him and that had swung the fight in my favour.

What the baron did do was to have his men at arms patrol the roads of the county, and he wrote to King Edward to inform him of the depredations of the Welsh, both of which helped us.

It was that letter that yielded results, although they were not the results that I wished for. I was summoned to London to speak with King Edward. I had not seen him since the day he had learned he was king. I thought, perhaps, that he had forgotten me, and that did not displease me.

It was good weather when I left but I only took Tom and Martin with me. I left the rest to guard my home. We had learned from the attacks, and the men I left would continue to improve the defences. We would add more of the wooden towers. Some of the houses had been badly damaged, and they would be rebuilt, but in a different place to make our defence stronger.

I resented being summoned to London and I wondered why I had been. Baron Mortimer would have been able to deliver the same news as I! I determined to get there as soon as I could and return quickly.

The journey to Windsor was one hundred and twenty miles. We took spare horses and made the castle in three days. One of the reasons for taking just a couple of men was that I knew the castle would be filled. King Edward and his court required many servants. While I was found a small chamber in the castle, Tom and Martin had to make do with the stable.

Despite the urgency of the letter, I was kept waiting while King Edward dealt with affairs of state.

It was Queen Eleanor who saw me first. "Gerald Warbow! What a delightful surprise. What drags you here from your home?"

I bowed and kissed the back of her proffered hand. The fact that she had offered it showed my status to the waiting guards. None of them knew me and I had noticed their sneering and haughty glances. The proffered hand changed all of that.

"The king, Queen Eleanor, has sent for me."

She frowned and then nodded. "And he is within, speaking with his counsellors. It was ever thus, Gerald. How is Mary?"

I was on more comfortable ground, for I would not have to criticise the king and, with waiting guards who would report every word to him, domestic matters were a better choice. "We are wed, and we have a son, Hamo. He was born on Christmas Day!"

Her joy was genuine, and she clapped her hands. "How propitious! I am pleased, for I know how much she wished to be married to you. They are both well?"

"They are." I hesitated and then decided to tell her. "My hall was attacked by the Welsh, but we survived intact."

She became serious. "We had heard that there was trouble in the Marches but did not know that there was bloodshed."

"The next hamlet to mine was burned to the ground. We have rebuilt it."

She nodded. "I will find time to speak with you before you leave. I expect you will wish to return to the bosom of your family as soon as possible."

I smiled. "I would need a horse with wings to return as swiftly as I wish!"

"Just so." She shook her head and looked about to say something and then thought better. This was not the royal apartments in Acre, where she knew and trusted all those around her. This was England and the very walls had ears. Where she might have spoken in confidence to me now, she could not.

I was left alone again to wait without the doors. The difference was that the sentries spoke to me and did so deferentially. I might have been dressed as some common archer but the queen herself had spoken with me. I found it strange, for I was still the same man who had entered!

Eventually, the doors opened, and a servant dressed in the king's livery emerged. "Yes?"

"I am Captain Gerald Warbow of Yarpole, and I was sent for by King Edward."

He scanned the document he had before him and said arrogantly, "You were due here two days since."

I might hold my tongue before one of my betters, but this was a clerk and a weasel-faced one at that. "And I am here now and, having waited without for longer than I ought, perhaps you should announce me so that the king can tell me why he has summoned me!"

The smirk from the two sentries told me that the pompous little man was not liked. He coloured and, turning, said, "Captain Gerald Warbow of Yarpole!"

I stepped into a court filled with nobles as well as clerks and clerics. The king rose from his throne and his long legs strode over to me.

There was genuine joy on his face. "You came!" He put his arm around me and spoke loudly so that the whole court could

116

hear his words. "This is the man who helped me slay the assassin sent by my enemies! He is a friend!"

I nodded. "You are too kind, King Edward; it was little enough that I did. How is the arm?"

"The flesh regrew." He shook his head. "God works miracles, does he not? When that doctor cut away the poisoned flesh, I thought I would have lost the use of my arm. When I was in Rome, I thanked God for all that he did for me, and now it is completely healed. Come, I would speak with you." He strode to his throne and gestured for me to stand at his side. He waved an imperious arm. "You all have duties to perform – give my archer and me space to speak!"

It was as though a wind had come to disperse them, and the two of us were alone with just two bodyguards, who were ten paces from us.

"How stands the border?" That was King Edward, straight to business. His wife had asked after my family but that was not his way.

"The man we rescued on your behalf, Dafydd ap Gruffydd, is causing much mischief on the borders. He raids Wales and they retaliate!"

"Watch yourself, Warbow. You have a special place here, but I am the king. If he does annoy Llywelyn, then perhaps that will stir the miscreant to pay homage to the crown of England! The nobles in the Marches enjoy special privileges. This is the price they pay."

"But it is not the nobles who pay, King Edward! They have castles and walls. It is the ordinary people who bleed."

He was silent for a moment. I do not think he cared over-much about the ordinary men and women of England, but

I could see he worried about unrest. "You know that Llywelyn is still speaking of fulfilling the contract to marry Eleanor de Montfort?" That confirmed my suspicions, for there were still many in England who admired the philosophy of the de Montfort family. The Battle of Evesham had crushed their military might but not the spirit. "I need you and your special skills."

My heart sank, for that normally meant I would be placed in danger. Hitherto that had not been a problem but now I had a wife and child. I nodded. "I am ever your servant!"

He beamed. "That is more like it, Warbow. I thought for a moment you had been softened by a year or more away from war." He lowered his voice. "Soon, we ride to Chester. There I will receive the homage of Prince Llywelyn and tell him that I forbid the marriage to the de Montfort girl."

"And will he agree, do you think?"

"If he does not agree then I will take his land by force. I no longer need Llywelyn; I have his brother as an ally and he will agree to anything I demand."

"He is not a trustworthy man, King Edward."

"That is for me to judge, and besides, it will only be temporary. My father had his new castles at Dyserth and Deganwy destroyed. Chester and the rich lands of Cheshire are at risk. I must build castles, but that will take time."

I nodded. "And what is it you wish me to do, my lord?"

"I have sent messengers to Prince Llywelyn but received no reply. Perhaps the messengers were less than truthful, or they wish me to be deceived. You, I can trust. If you say that you have spoken to him then I know that it will be true. Once I know that for certain, I can act accordingly."

"You wish me, an archer, to speak to the Prince of Wales?"

"I wish you, Gerald Warbow, gentleman of Yarpole and known confidante of the king, to deliver a message. That is simple enough."

I decided to be blunt. "And if he has me killed?"

"Then I will have my answer!" He smiled. "But you are a cunning and wily fellow. You will not let him kill you. This way my honour remains intact. Only you and I will know of this quest. Your return or non-return gives me the answer I seek. You will return to Chester when you have the answer."

"Then I had better leave early in the morning, my lord, for you have given me little time to find this elusive prince."

He nodded. "I have a courser for you to make the journey swifter and I will have one of my clerks draft a document to give you authority for shelter and sustenance." That was the least he could do. It meant I could use the monasteries and religious orders who offered accommodation for travellers, at a fee, of course. "I hold a small feast here this night and you are invited. I am sure that the queen would like to see you. She is very fond of you and that girl you saved." He stood, a sure sign that I was dismissed.

I went to the tiny chamber I had been accorded. It was in a remote tower with neither heating nor a proper bed. It just contained a jug and bowl of water, a pot in which to piss and a straw-filled mattress. The straw smelled fresh and I had slept on worse.

Of course, when I was summoned by a lowly servant, I knew that I would be the worst dressed at the feast. It could not be helped. I had my napkin, wooden spoon and eating knife. I assumed that there would be goblets provided. As I had expected,

I was at the low end of the table with the poorer knights, most of whom looked down their noses at me.

The exception was Sir Payn de Chaworth, who had been at the Crusades with us, and he gave me a fulsome welcome. "Gentleman, we are honoured, for here we have a real hero. Do you not recognise Lord Edward's archer? He was the who one saved King Edward from an assassin's dagger and rode through the Turkish army to fetch Mongol warriors to our aid!" That made the younger knights view me differently. "I expected you to have been knighted for your deeds, Captain Gerald."

I smiled. "I am content. How goes your life then, Sir Payn?"

He lowered his voice. "The king has entrusted me with a force of men, and I am to lead them from my castle at Kidwelly. I am charged with the prevention of encroachments from Prince Llywelyn. And you?"

"I am now a farmer, although I may be needed if war does come to the borders."

One of the other knights laughed. "There is no if, Master Archer! It is here now, and we just await the king's command to take back those parts of Wales which his father gave away!"

Just then horns sounded and we all stood as the king and queen entered. We waited until they were seated and then we sat. I saw the queen look around and her eye fixed on me. She turned and spoke to the old priest who was seated next to her. He stood and came down to our end of the table.

He gave me a sad smile. "The queen wishes you to sit next to her. I am afraid these young knights will not enjoy your tales of the Crusades and will have to listen to the crusty old confessor of Queen Eleanor."

"You should stay at the other table, Father."

"No, Captain Gerald, the queen wishes it, and I am sure that your conversation will be more entertaining than mine."

"Thank you." I headed towards the king's table. All eyes were upon me. I had not asked for this honour and I was not sure that the king would even have thought of it.

Queen Eleanor patted the cushioned chair next to her. "I know not what the king's steward was thinking. You are an honoured guest!"

The king smiled and nodded. "Welcome, Warbow." He then turned to speak to another crusader, John de Vesci, whom I knew from Acre.

To be seated at the king's table and next to the queen meant that I had almost the first choice of the food that was offered. Thanks to Mary and her time as one of Lady Eleanor's ladies, I knew the etiquette. I only picked the food from the platter that was proffered with my left hand, and I did not return any to the platter once I had selected. It all looked delicious, but I saw some lords whose fingers hovered like fruit flies, seeking the most succulent cuts. I was less fussy.

I was then interrogated by the queen. It meant I did not get to enjoy the food as I might have wished as I was thinking of the correct phrases and words to use in such company. She wanted to know of the birth and how my son had looked when he had been born. She herself was the mother of five children. The youngest was Henry, who was almost twelve. Then she began to delve into the lives of the men who served me, for she had met then in Acre. It meant I blurted out about Robin's abduction. She was a clever woman, and she wheedled the other information from me.

"You know, the Welsh border seems much like my home in Castile. We have disputes with Aragon and Navarre as well as with Portugal. Living here in the south, where there are no wars, makes it seem as though we live in a peaceful realm. The reality is that nothing could be further from the truth." She leaned into me and whispered in my ear, "I asked the king to knight you, for I believed you deserved it, but he said that the time was not yet right. You know the king; he has plans and ideas which must be adhered to."

I then asked about their journey through Italy and France. I had not yet travelled in Italy, but it sounded much like Spain and with the same intrigues.

One problem with a royal feast is that no guest may leave until the king has retired. I had had an early start and the queen tried to encourage the king to leave by leaving the feast early herself, but he was too engrossed in speaking with his senior knights. It was far later than I might have wished before he retired, and I was able to scurry up the stairs to my chamber.

In the chamber, I found a present on the bed. There was a note from the queen. It was a gift for my son. I was asleep almost as soon as I had made water.

I had trained myself to wake at a particular time and I heard the bell tolling for the priests in the castle to attend Matins. It was still dark. I made my way out of the castle to the stables.

As I was about to leave the main gate, a clerk rushed up to me. "Captain Warbow, here is your pass from the king!" He handed me the parchment bearing the king's seal. I knew without looking that the careful king would have assigned it to me alone so that no other could use it. "I will take you to the stable, for he also has a horse for you there."

Eleanor, my horse, was at the end of the stable that was closest to the stable door. The clerk woke the horse master, who was about to complain until he saw that it was the king's clerk who woke him.

"We have come for Captain Warbow's horse, the gift from the king."

I heard Tom and Martin wake at the noise. The horse master's eyes widened. "I thought it was meant for a knight at the very least! This is a kingly gift, Captain, and is worth thirty marks! It comes from the king's stud just down the road. Lion is a warhorse. I hope that you know how to ride!"

The clerk shook his head and said, "Do you not know who this is? He rode with the Mongols and they are master horsemen!"

That stopped the man in his tracks. "You are that man! I would dearly love to have a conversation with you, Captain, for—"

"We have little time for gossip, horse master. The captain is on the king's business!"

I was intrigued at the gift. I recognised the quality of the horse immediately.

I expected to have to lead him on a tether, but the horse master shook his head. "Lion does not like to be led. When you have ridden him and he knows you are his master, then he will accept a tether, but you must master him first. We have a saddle for you. He will lead your mare."

He was a magnificent horse and he stamped and nodded his head to show me what a fine beast he was. I had learned much when riding amongst the Mongols and I kept him on a short rein for the first five miles or so. Each time he threatened to question me, I stopped him and waited until he was compliant. Tom and Martin were in awe of the horse, for they had seen him in the stable and knew him to be a king of horses. I told them how he had come into my possession, but I did not tell them of my mission. That would wait until we reached home.

I rode him all day and did not make as many miles as I might have hoped. My pass gained the three of us entry to an Augustan monastery, as well as a room and food. Tom and Martin were happy, for they were used to a barn.

The next day I rode Lion hard and stopped briefly at a tavern in Oxford. I let the other two alternate their horses with Eleanor so that we made good time. By the afternoon, he seemed happy to be led, and we made it to Cheltenham by dark, where we were welcomed by Sir Roger of Bourton. The pass gained us entry once again, and my horse and name guaranteed the three of us a warm welcome, although Tom and Martin ate with the servants and not the lord and lady of the manor. Everyone who discovered my name wished to hear the story of the assassin's attack!

We reached Yarpole before dark the next day. Both of my horses were tired, and I was weary of the saddle, but I had made the journey half a day faster than with just one horse.

Tom and Martin saw to the horses and I went into my hall and gave the queen's package to my wife, who opened it. It was a gown of fine English lace. I guessed it was for a christening, but as he had already been christened, it would do for my next child. If there was to be one.

While I ate, I told Mary all that had been said and my orders. I had no secrets from my wife. Like me, she was not happy, but she, above all others, knew the power of a khan or a king.

"You will be careful, my love?" I nodded. "Sarah and Mags think I am with child once more."

I squeezed her. "And you?" She nodded. "Then I am content."

That night, tired though I was, it took me longer to sleep, for I had a storm in my head. All that I wished to do was to be a father and a landowner. I wanted to care for those who were close to me, but it seemed I had a king to serve and that would always come first.

The next day, the joy of the prospect of a new child meant that I had almost forgotten Lion, but my men had discovered him in the stable and were gathered within. I saw Tom and Martin telling them the tale of the gift.

James came from the hall with me. He knew horses and he said, "Magnificent, Captain, but how could you afford him? He must be worth at least ten or fifteen marks!"

I smiled. "He is from the king's stable, and the king's horse master told me thirty marks!" Their eyes widened and I saw Tom and Martin nodding, for they knew his worth too. "He is a warhorse and should be treated accordingly. James, I would have a separate stall built for him. You have time, for I shall be away for, perhaps, a couple of weeks."

The attention of my men switched from the animal to me. "War, Captain?"

"No, Robin, but the king's business. I will need David the Welshman and I will take Tom and Martin."

Stephen said, "Captain, why no men at arms?"

"Because, Stephen, I have but two. Peter has one arm and as the man I seek is Prince Llywelyn, I thought it prudent to keep him further than the length of a sword from you!"

"He would be safe, Captain."

I shook my head. "This is a mission of peace and I dare not risk it. The four of us will be enough. When we have found him, we head for Chester to meet with the king."

David nodded. "And when do we leave, Captain?"

"Tomorrow, but I need to know where to find him!"

David smiled. "That is easy, Captain. There are still raids across the border and the prince will be close enough to react if one escalates. I would put good money on the Clwyd Valley or the Conwy Valley. We can try one first and then the other. You say the king will be at Chester?" I nodded. "Then we try the Conwy valley first. By the time we reach Bala, we will know if we have guessed aright."

"And how far is that?"

"Sixty miles to Bala and then either sixty miles to Conwy or sixty miles to the Clwyd. Either way, we have four days of hard riding."

"Then I will take my new horse and we will need two sumpters. See to all, David. Stephen, I leave you and Peter to command my men."

I could see that none were happy about the few men I was taking, and Robin voiced their worries. "And if you are taken? Do we rescue you?"

My voice was resigned as I answered him. "If I am taken, then Prince Llywelyn is tearing up the Treaty of Monmouth and declaring war on King Edward. I will either be dead or about to die!" The finality of my words hit them. I saw the determination on their faces. If I was murdered, then their vengeance would be terrible!

Chapter 9

We were heading into a part of Wales I did not know and so I listened to the advice of David the Welshman. "Bala has a lake and it is a large town. We Welsh do not use many castles but there is a small one there. There is a risk, Captain, that we may be stopped by those who do not wish you to speak with Llywelyn."

"Then let us avoid people until we are close to this town."

"It means camping."

"We have supplies and it will only be for a night or two. Is there a bishop at Bala?"

"There may be, Captain. Why do you ask?"

"In my experience, they are more likely to listen than knights or nobles. We try the church first."

The hardest part was getting across the border. In this part of the borders, the River Lugg was still the line that separated England from Wales, and so we found a ford to slip across. We were still relatively close to home when we did so, and we headed through the small back roads, which were used by local farmers, both Welsh and English, until we found the uplands close to Dutlas. This was bleak and rocky sheep country and we saw no-one, not even a shepherd. We camped when the light went and had a fireless camp.

As we sat around, Martin said, "Why on earth does King Edward want this country? The people are poor, they have little that we want, and they have more rocks than land to plough.

David growled, "This is my land, boy! Be careful what you say!"

"You are partly right, Martin, but further south is rich farm-land. I spoke to the Lord of Kidwelly, Sir Payn de Chaworth, and he told me that his town is as prosperous as any in England. King Henry did his son great harm by signing away so much. The Welsh now seek to take the land which has been English since the time of the second King Henry. They are prosperous because of the English. Who knows, if we put English farmers here, then this land might become as prosperous." I was aware that David had been silent and that suggested that he disagreed with me. "If I am wrong, David, then tell me so. I do not mind. I confess that the politics of all this are a little beyond me."

"You may be right, Captain, but a man can never truly leave the land of his birth and while I do not like Prince Llywelyn, nor his brother, I do not think it should be ruled by King Edward."

"That, I fear, is what will happen, but we will not fall out because of it, will we?"

"Never, Captain."

It was important to leave no doubt about such matters.

The next day saw us riding through equally empty land. Lion seemed to enjoy the chance to open his legs and to gallop along roads that had little sign of horses upon them. I had to restrain him or risk losing the others.

When we neared Bala, I stayed with Tom and Martin in the wood we found less than a mile from the town.

David walked into the small town. He left his sword with us and took just his bow, arrows and dagger. He would try to find out what he could. As a Welsh archer, he could walk through the town with impunity. It was dark and so late when he returned that I had begun to fear for his safety. It struck me that travelling through the land of the Seljuk Turks had been easier but, perhaps, that was because the land was so empty and we had the services of Ahmed, the Mongol archer we had travelled with.

"Well?"

"He is not here in Bala, Captain, but in Rhuthun, the Clwyd Valley. I am sorry, Captain, we could have found him already."

I nodded. "No matter. How did you discover this?"

He hesitated. "One reason I brought us here was that my sister's son lives here. He is a priest. He was always a good boy and I knew we could trust him. He knows that Prince Llywelyn is at Rhuthun because Iago, Lord of Bala, left to join him there a week since."

"And that explains why it took you so long. I feared for you, David. You should have told me of your family ties. I would have understood."

"I am sorry, Captain, but the good news is that Rhuthun is but twenty-odd miles from here. We can visit with the prince tomorrow if that is still your plan?"

"It is, and hopefully tonight will be the last night of cold fare, eh?"

Despite David's apologies, the diversion to Bala helped us, for we were approaching the Welsh prince from the south-west and doing so meant that we aroused less suspicion. Many people took me for a knight as I rode such a fine horse and many armed men were heading for the town.

We fell in with a group of Welsh spearmen and David spoke to them. He made out that I was an arrogant warrior who looked down on others. Tom and Martin had enough Welsh to be able to nod or shake their heads at appropriate moments. We only rode with them for a mile and when David gave me a subtle nod, I knew that we had all the information we were likely to get and I dug my heels into Lion's flanks, and we galloped away.

When we were a mile from them, David laughed, "They cursed you, Captain, for an arrogant man whom they wished to cut down to size."

I smiled. "Then I could be a mummer, eh? What did you learn?"

"That Prince Llywelyn fears that King Edward will use his brother Dafydd to rule Wales in his stead. He is gathering an army in case he has to fight."

I knew that was not the case – yet. King Edward merely wanted homage. Perhaps my quest might not be so hopeless after all. I just needed to persuade Prince Llywelyn to travel to Chester.

The town was an armed camp, and I could see as we rode in that work had begun on a castle. The Welsh had simply destroyed the work begun on Dyserth and Deganwy, although they were close to the coast. This new castle was being built as a bastion against the English.

It was my horse that was our undoing. He drew eyes to admire him and then they saw that the man who rode him wore neither surcoat nor mail. Even more telling was the lack of spurs.

We almost managed to reach the hall, which was patently being used by the prince, before we were stopped. Two knights whom I did not recognise approached us. They spoke in Welsh, which merely confirmed their suspicions. When David the Welshman answered, weapons were drawn and there were shouts.

David turned to me. "Captain, they think that you have stolen the animal and we are ordered to surrender our weapons."

One of the knights shouted, "English spy!" in English.

I spread my arms with palms uppermost to show that I was unarmed. "I am an emissary for King Edward of England, and I am here to speak with Prince Llywelyn."

By now we had drawn a large crowd. Even worse, I recognised a knight who angrily stormed towards me. It was Lord Maredudd and he shouted something in Welsh and then said, in English, "You will hang, Gerald Warbow! I shall do it myself!"

Men dragged us from our saddles, and I saw others fetching ropes. This was a mob and they cared not for the rights or wrongs. They behaved as a mob always does. They changed from men who, alone, might be quite reasonable, to men among others, transformed into a single beast that had neither mind nor reason.

"I am an emissary of King Edward and this can only end badly for Prince Llywelyn!"

Maredudd backhanded me across the mouth and the metal strips on the back of his gloves tore into my cheek. "Silence! Dog! You killed good men and you will pay!"

There was a huge oak in the centre of the small town and the first of the ropes was hurled over it. I had always thought I would die in battle and not hanged like a common thief.

A Welsh voice commanded, and everyone stopped. Lord Maredudd answered in Welsh, but as I was pinioned, I could not see to whom he spoke. There was another voice and then I was released.

"You say you are from King Edward?"

I turned and saw, for the first time, Prince Llywelyn. I would have known him, for he bore a striking similarity to his brother,

131

except that he was older and greyer. I nodded and reached into my tunic for the pass the king had given to me. As I handed it to him, I said, "I am Captain Gerald Warbow of Yarpole."

He looked up from his reading. "The man who attacked my silver mine!"

I said firmly, looking him in the eyes, "The man who rescued his men from captivity and did not take a single piece of silver."

I saw the glimmer of a thin smile upon his lips. "Aye, they say that you speak the truth and care not whom you offend." He seemed to see my bleeding face for the first time. He looked to the side and snapped something in Welsh. Lord Maredudd answered and when Prince Llywelyn spoke there was ice in his voice. Lord Maredudd stormed off.

The mob, their fun spoiled, also began to disperse. I saw that my men had not been touched. I was the only one with a wound.

"Captain Warbow, I am sorry for your treatment. Lord Maredudd is a bitter man. Give them back their weapons." His men handed us back our swords. They had not discovered the daggers in my boots.

I nodded. "And a coward! He behaves thus with a mob behind him but when he faces warriors, he runs! The next time my bow has an arrow nocked and he is before me, he will die."

The prince laughed. "And I believe you, but you are here to talk of peace." He nodded towards my horse, which was being tended by men wearing the prince's livery. "A fine horse. How did you acquire him? War?"

I shook my head. "A gift from the king."

"He will be cared for and you and your men will be my guests, but you will understand that you will have a guard on your chamber." He smiled. "For your own protection, of course."

I smiled back. "Of course."

The hall he was using must have belonged to a rich Welshman, for it was furnished well with fine tapestries and wall hangings. There was no sign of a woman in the place and I remembered that the prince, although more than fifty years of age, had yet to marry. Eleanor de Montfort would be his bride if King Edward allowed the marriage.

The prince seated himself on a large chair before the fire and gestured towards another that was close by. "If you would surrender your sword and your men leave us, we can speak privately, for I think that what you have to say to me will be delicate."

I nodded and unstrapped my sword. "Of course." I did not hand the sword to the captain of the guard, who held out his arms for the weapon, but to David the Welshman.

The prince smiled and said something in Welsh. My men were taken away and a servant brought in some wine and two goblets. We were left alone, and the prince poured the wine. He handed me a goblet and the pass. "You are a brave man, Captain Gerald, for you have annoyed many of my men."

"I have never attacked your people wilfully. When I rescued Robin, son of Richard, it was because he had been taken. When Lord Maredudd destroyed Luston and attacked Yarpole, we merely defended ourselves."

He held up his hands. "And that is why I am speaking with you. I know my own people." He wagged a finger. "You did attack my men and rescue Owain ap Gruffydd."

"I did so at the request of his mother, Lady Hawise. I am sorry if your men were hurt in the process."

His face darkened. "My brother's hand was in that! Do you have brothers?"

"I am the only son my father had."

"Then you are lucky! Blood binds us but my brother is ambitious and would kill me if he could. I have never threatened him and yet he would kill me." He drank some of the wine. "So, what is it that King Edward proposes?"

"It is simple enough, Prince Llywelyn; King Edward awaits you in Chester. When you go there and pay homage, as is his right, then the matter is ended. He just requires what you promised to his late father."

He nodded. "And I will be safe in Chester?"

"Safe?"

"There will be no knife in the night to end the threat of a free Wales?"

"That is not King Edward's way. I have served him for many years, and he is not dishonourable."

The prince laughed. "He may not be, but so long as my brother and the snakes with whom he surrounds himself are abroad, then my life is not safe outside of my borders. You know that he plotted to have me killed?"

"You have my word that he will not get close to you."

The prince was shrewd. "You do not like him!"

"My personal opinion is immaterial, Prince Llywelyn; the fact is that if I give my word, then I will keep it."

He nodded, almost absentmindedly. "That is what I have heard of you." He drank some more. "Tell King Edward that if he comes across the border to Mold, which is halfway twixt Chester and here, then I will bend the knee."

It was my turn to drink and to choose my words carefully. "Prince Llywelyn, I am just the emissary from the king. I will return and give him your request, but I know the king and he will not stir from Chester. If you do not go to him, then he will take it that you refuse to pay homage."

"And that will mean war?"

I shook my head. "I am an emissary and I do not know what is inside the king's head, but he will be displeased. You must know, Prince Llywelyn, that despite the strength of the Welsh mountains, you cannot defeat King Edward. He is a warrior, and his father was not!"

"You have a Welsh name, Warbow; are you from a Welsh father?"

"I grew up not far from here, but my father served the English. I am English."

He smiled. "You know, despite your reputation I wondered if you came here to kill me. It is why I had your sword taken away."

I smiled and in one motion drew one of the daggers from my boot. "If I had wanted to, Prince Llywelyn, then you would be dead." I replaced my dagger. "I made that demonstration to let you know that you can trust me and my word. If I say you will be safe at Chester, then you will be."

He nodded. "I will consider your words. It is too late to leave this night and besides, there may be danger on the road. I will have my men escort you to Mold on the morrow and you may tell King Edward that I will consider his words."

"Do not be tardy in your response, Prince Llywelyn. The king has waited more than a year and his patience is wearing thin."

"I do not trust my brother, but you seem an honest fellow and I will give your words and the request due attention."

The meal was endured rather than enjoyed. The prince was distracted and whilst he was friendly enough, the barbed comments and hateful glances from the other lords who attended made it a trial I could have done without. The prince had forbidden Lord Maredudd from attending but that was a double-edged sword. Where was he if not at the feast?

When we departed the next morning, we were escorted by two knights and ten men at arms. They said nothing. Mold was neither Welsh nor English, and so when we reached the outskirts, the knights and our escort simply turned and left.

We had just twelve miles to go and so we watered our horses and I spoke with my men. It was the first opportunity I had had to do so. "Well?"

David the Welshman rubbed his chin. "I like this not, Captain. They could have escorted us to the Dee. That is the real border; why did they not do so?"

I nodded. "String your bows. It is important that we reach the king. He is a patient man, but if he has no word from either us or the prince, he will assume the worst and there may be war."

Our horses refreshed and with strung bows, we left and headed for the Dee. I had no bow with me, and I felt naked. We passed Buckley, but the doors were closed as we rode through. This was the border, and any armed men were dangerous.

Ahead of us was the remnant of a huge ancient forest. I knew it, for when I had fled the wrath of the men of the lord I had killed, I had fled through part of it. Some outlaws lived within it, but they did not worry me. I had managed to deal with them when I had been alone, but I knew it to be the most dangerous place we would have to pass. Broughton, the next village, was nothing.

As we approached the tree-lined road, I said, "Be wary."

My two words were enough, and they each nocked an arrow. I drew my sword and led them in single file along the tree-covered road. There was fresh horse dung on the road. It was not steaming but it had yet to set. Under normal circumstances that would mean nothing, for this was a major road which led from Wales to England, but these were not normal times.

I peered into the gloom of the trees. I had yet to ride Lion into danger. Had this been Eleanor, then I would have known the signs that told me that there was trouble ahead. I would have to rely on those instincts that had kept me alive thus far.

None of us spoke and the only sound we heard was the hooves of our horses on the road. It was the bird, some fifty feet from us, which suddenly took flight, that alerted us to the danger. To many men, it might have just been a shock, which made them look, but I had well-trained men and their bows came up.

The ambushers made another mistake; their first had been that one of them had moved too soon and alerted the bird. The second was to spring their ambush prematurely. My men had practised loosing bows from the back of horses and, whilst not as accurate at a range of fifty feet, they were well within range.

The ambushers had no archers with them and Lord Maredudd and his ten men at arms simply galloped from within the eaves of the trees. Had we fled, there was a chance they might have caught us, but they struggled to leave the safety of the trees as there was a ditch alongside the road, and three arrows stuck the leading three men.

I dug my heels into Lion. This was what he had been bred for, and his turn of speed took not only me by surprise but also Lord Maredudd and the two closest men. Swinging my sword, I slammed it across the shoulder of a man at arms, and Lion snapped at Lord Maredudd's mount, making the animal veer off to the side, the knight barely managing to hold on.

The other man at arms was a little way behind Lord Maredudd and the first man at arms. I lifted my bloodied sword above my head as Lion, the bit between his teeth, began to open his legs. My courser was larger than the sumpter ridden by the man at arms and his horse baulked. It saved the life of the rider, for my blow just struck the man on his brigandine. It sliced through to the flesh, but the cut was not deep.

I risked turning in my saddle and saw that my three men had drawn their swords and the Welsh were fleeing. Once again Lord Maredudd's actions had weakened his men, but I took no chances and when the three of them joined me, we galloped hard for Broughton.

It soon became clear that they had given up on their attempt on my life. I shook my head as we neared the village. We had been lucky. I should have brought more men. My three companions, however, were elated. We had driven men at arms away and that was to be celebrated. None were sure if they had seriously hurt the men they had hit, but one thing was certain, they would remember Captain Warbow's archers and be even more cautious the next time.

We reached the bridge over the Dee in the late afternoon. As we rode across the river, the city seemed almost empty compared with what I had expected. The king and his entourage had yet to arrive. For us that was good.

My pass gained us chambers in the castle, albeit a small one, and better stabling for our horses. It also gained us food, but we did not eat in the Great Hall, which was reserved for the great and the good. Instead, we ate with the garrison. The food was good, and we did not have to worry about etiquette. While my men regaled those on our table with the tale of our journey, I was silent. I had done all that was asked, and yet I did not know if King Edward would be pleased or angry.

We ate with what I called real soldiers. These were the men who did not ride to war on horses and did not own the finest of weapons. For all that, they had a great skill, for they had learned to survive on a battlefield where the odds were all in favour of the men in mail who rode warhorses. We learned that the Dee was the real border. Some lords lived on the other side, but they had no real security and what was needed was a castle.

Old Geraint of Abergele knew what he was talking about. "I know, Gerald Warbow, that you lived in that land, but when you lived there, we had men who fought against the Welsh along the Clwyd. I know it does not do to speak ill of the dead, but old King Henry did not know one end of a sword from the other. He only did well when he brought down some of the warlords from the north to fight for him. Then we held back the tide, but the Scots saw how weak King Henry was, and when his son went to crusade, then the barbarians were banging at the door."

Ralph was another long-serving soldier. "Hold hard there Geraint. They are not barbarians, but you are right, they need a strong hand. Captain Warbow, you fought with King Edward – is he a warrior?"

"Through and through! We would not have won at Evesham but for him, and he scoured the land of rebels. You are both right. We need castles here. With stout walls, then King Edward could control the valleys, but he needs a castle with access to the sea. That is why Dyserth failed and, from what I have been told, Deganwy was seen as the stronghold to keep them in check."

"Aye, well." Geraint rubbed his stubbly beard. "First we have to beat Llywelyn, and that cannot be done from London. We need buskins on the ground and to meet them beard to beard. This is not the country for knights." He nodded to me. "This archer knows that, and I take heart that King Edward listens to an archer!"

I realised then the responsibility that I bore.

Chapter 10

The king arrived two days later. His journey had taken much longer as there were over two hundred following him who were not soldiers. Cooks, weaponsmiths, armourers, minstrels, servants, priests, clerks and clerics were some of those who followed the colourfully mailed snake that made up the household knights of King Edward.

If he needed an army to fight, he would have to raise the levy. Men like me would bring our spearmen and archers to fight on foot. Of course, I had a special position, but the reality was that when King Edward went to war, then the ordinary men would be arrayed before the knights and be the first to die. They were far cheaper than a horse that a lord might ride.

The king, Otto de Grandson and John de Vesci, along with the Earl of Warwick: William de Beauchamp, almost dragged me into the Great Hall to hear my news. Two of them had been with us on crusade but I knew Sir John better than Lord Otto. Sir John de Vesci and I had exchanged words when the assassin had struck in Acre, but when his life had been saved, his attitude change. He now trusted me. I wondered why Sir

John Malton was not here. He had been Lord Edward's squire in Gascony and while we were not as close as we once had been, I still held him in high esteem.

"Well?"

There was no way to honey my words. "He wishes to pay homage, King Edward, but he does not trust his brother and the Welshmen at your court." I paused and as I said the words, I mentally prepared myself for the storm. "He asks for you to meet him at Mold, just over the border."

He was silent for a while and I wondered if he had heard me. When he spoke it was in a quiet voice. "Does he take me for a fool? Is he making a woman of me? I am Edward, King of England – he is the one who will pay homage to me! He will come to Chester and I will see him on his knees."

That was the moment when the last chance for peace vanished. War did not come immediately but Llywelyn must have known what his words meant, just as King Edward must have realised that harbouring those who had tried to kill Prince Llywelyn would make him fear for his life.

"Tell me, Warbow, has he a large army with him? Could we launch a sudden attack and take him by surprise? If we put him in the tower, then I could appoint his brother as prince and rule Wales through him."

I shook my head, remembering how Prince Llywelyn had been so well supported by both men and his people. "His army outnumbers yours, King Edward, because he has his archers, spearmen and the levy there. I have no doubt that man for man our knights are better, but this is the land of my birth, and I can tell you that it is the graveyard of fine horses and knights." I hesitated, for I was about to offer the king advice.

"You could use your knights and not require the levy, but you would need castles."

He smiled. "You are right, and we have none." He slammed his hand on the table. "Then we shall build one!" He clapped me about the shoulder. "You are right; we need spears and bows. We will use the archers of Cheshire and see if they will serve me as well as they did de Montfort. I shall need your men too, Warbow, but not for a month. Then you can pay me the service you owe. I will need you and your men to act as scouts. I need all of your archers, mind! None of this leaving your outlaws behind. I shall need every one of your cutthroats if I am to succeed! And when my castle is built, then you and Baron Mortimer will claw back my lands in Powys. Be back here in a month, for by then we shall need men to protect my builders from Llywelyn's brigands!"

As we headed back to my home, I thought of the king's words and those of the garrison. I valued both equally. I could see why I had been chosen by the king. His strength still lay in his mailed and heavily armed men riding warhorses. The land of the Dee Valley and the Clwyd Valley would be disastrous for fine horses such as Lion. I patted his neck. "I fear you will just be exercised, and you will have to wait for war until we find a better land for you."

David shook his head as he heard my words. "Then I fear that will not be for some time, Captain. I know my countrymen and they do not like the English. Even if they think they are going to lose they will fight on. They will hope that we give up as King Henry did."

"King Edward is not the same man as his father, David. I sensed determination, but you are right. This will not be a quick war."

Mary was just pleased that I would be back for slightly less than a month. "And if he demands forty days, then you shall be home for Christmas. From what Sarah and the others have told me, this is not the land to fight in during winter. I will take your company until the spring and Hamo can get to know you. He changes each day."

And so my life changed. I divided my time equally between my wife and child as well as running the manor and training with my men. Stephen spoke to me at length about Llywelyn. "I shall have the chance to fight the Welsh this time, Captain."

"War is not yet declared. I do not think that Llywelyn will pay homage, but King Edward is honour bound to wait for a month, which is why he has given us this time to prepare."

Peter of Beverley had been listening to the conversation and he added, "We do not have enough men, Captain. If you take away all the archers, as you say the king requested, then that leaves just me here. The border is still a parlous place. We could do with hiring men."

I shook my head. "I have gold from the Holy Land and I could pay them, but any warrior worth hiring will now be joining the great lords and King Edward himself. If any come, then hire them. The sons of John and Jack, as well as James's boys – are they ready to begin their training as archers?"

Peter rubbed his chin with his stump. "Aye, but it takes years to make an archer, Captain."

"What I have in mind is a mixture. Jack and John's will replace their fathers in the fullness of time, but until then we pay them to guard my home and you train them with the sword. In the armoury are the weapons we took from Lord Maredudd's men. They can use a sling until they are ready to use a bow, and you can have them use a sword. Train James and the other men of Yarpole and Luston to use a sword. Harold of Luston promised me that his men would fight for Yarpole. Use the time after services on Sunday. The men of Luston will be here then. I will seek warriors in the camps to serve us."

Peter looked a little happier. "Aye, Captain, that might do."

"One more thing – can you ride Lion with just the one hand? He will need exercise and I would have him ridden by a mailed warrior."

He grinned. "I might fall off the odd time, but to ride a warhorse, it is a price worth paying."

Stephen gave me a shrewd look. "Do you see yourself in mail, Captain?"

I smiled. "I have a mail hauberk that was made for a rider, and now that I have not only one son but the prospect of another, I would protect myself in battle so that I may live to train them. I shall not abandon them as my father did."

"An archer wearing mail cannot use a bow."

"Blunt words, Stephen, but you are right. I am still an archer and can still draw a bow, but I am no longer a young man and whilst I am in my prime, I know that the day will dawn when I shall no longer be Lord Edward's archer but King Edward's gentleman at arms. I will be ready for that day!"

Later that week, as I sat with James and his mother to go through the accounts of the manor, Mary joined us. Hamo was at the stage where he liked to crawl and to play. Other youngsters lived in the manor and Mags and the other mothers supervised their play. Mary was a good mother, but her upbringing and her mind made her aware that Hamo's need for her would lessen as he grew older and she wanted a position that was her own. We had spoken of this as we lay together.

James looked up, although as his mother was there, he should not have been surprised to see Mary.

"Mistress Mary wishes to know how the manor prospers, James. If I am to be away on the business of the king, then she will need to have her hands on the reins."

He smiled. "I can do that, Captain. Mistress Mary need not worry herself."

Mary was not cold but she was firm as she said, "James, I wish to know this, for if my husband is killed in one of the king's wars, then I will be the one who will run the manor." She smiled and it took any harshness from her words. "I do not seek to usurp you nor even to take over the day to day running, but I need to know whence comes our coin and how the villages prosper."

Sarah's voice was colder. "James, I am surprised at you! Captain Warbow does not question me and I am a woman. Mistress Mary is far cleverer than you and do not forget it!"

I smiled as James tried to make himself as small as possible. "Yes, Mother!"

Once that was out of the way, it proved to be a constructive meeting. The manor was, despite the wars, prosperous. That was mainly down to better management of the people and the land. Matthew of Yarpole had been a bad landowner who just took from the farms and did not care for them. Now that Luston was added to my lands, they too benefitted from our practices.

We rotated crops. I had introduced, at the request of James, more animals to my lands so that they were able to graze the fallow fields and fertilise them. A mixed farm was more economical.

We also used the markets to our advantage. We were welcoming to travellers, and we learned when there were shortages and surpluses so that we sold our produce at a time that made the greatest profit for us.

I was pleased that my wife had asked for the lesson in husbandry, for I realised that I could hire another four or five archers. We had the coin, and there was enough land to let them farm a hide or two and become connected to the manor.

When I left for the muster and the building of the first castle, I was a little worried about leaving the manor with so few experienced men, but not enough to make me lose sleep. Hamo was even able to stand, wave and shout goodbye as I left. He was growing!

The king had not left Chester, but things had moved on apace. Eleanor de Montfort had been arrested and placed in Windsor. She had made the mistake of trying to hide her father's banners when she landed in England. She was seen as a threat, for she was a symbol of the rebels. Her arrest was also a message to Prince Llywelyn. By declining to pay homage to the king, he had, in effect, declared war on England. As yet there was no formal declaration, but as autumn passed, the king intended to begin work on a castle at Flint. There was no room for my men and me in Chester castle and so we camped in the loop of the Dee amongst the Roman ruins. I did not mind.

There were still too few archers to be had. The men of Cheshire had provided but a hundred. Their leader, Matthew of Tarporley, was younger than I was and had not been at the battle of Evesham when the men of Cheshire had sided with Simon de Montfort. The captains from that time had either been killed or had lost their right hands when they refused to serve King Henry. The result was that the men who joined King Edward were all good archers but few, if any, had battle experience. A couple had been on the crusade with us and I knew them, but Matthew of Tarporley was more than happy to place his men under my leadership. That suited me, for I knew how to fight!

I had taken my Mongol bow. I had fewer arrows left from that time, but I found a fletcher who knew how to make good arrows and he was happy to produce new ones for this bow.

The other archers were all keen to see the bow in action. I mounted Eleanor to show them how it could be used while riding. Of course, I was nowhere near as fast as the Mongols, nor was I as accurate, but the lesson was useful. More than that, it enhanced my reputation. I had seen when serving with men like Hamo l'Estrange that such reputations were useful, for others fought better with a leader they respected and admired. When I had been a bow for hire, I had often had to use my fists to show other archers that I knew my business. Now my reputation did that, and if I could give a practical demonstration, then so much the better.

I was sent for, a few days after my arrival, and entered the mighty castle of Chester. I saw that the Earl of Warwick commanded and that pleased me for he was a warlord. De Vesci and de Grandson were also there, but so was Dafydd ap Gruffydd, looking smug. It spoiled the meeting for me but, thankfully, he was neither invited nor did he offer to speak.

"Warbow, I need you to take the archers and secure the land eleven miles from here on the Dee. Richard L'engenour will supervise the building, and you must protect him and his workers until there is a ditch and an armed camp. You will be needed until the end of November, by which time the construction should have protection and there will be men at arms who can defend the place. Your task is to ensure that there is no mischief to slow down the work. I have sent for the Savoyard master mason, James of Saint George, but he will not be here until next year. The stone will be arriving then too."

I nodded. "They will be digging ditches and building earth ramparts to protect the site."

King Edward smiled. "See, Warwick, I told you he knew his business. Aye, Warbow, we can supply the castle from the river and the sea, but Llywelyn may well try to slow down our progress, and labourers are expensive. You will ensure that he does not harm any of our workers."

"And how long is the contract and what is the pay, King Edward?"

He smiled. "You have become more astute of late. You are quite right, of course. Your men can give me their forty days of service which they owe me!"

"King Edward, we have already served some of that. Indeed, I have given you more than forty days."

"Hmm, I like not paying for men who owe me service."

"Yet you know that we will get the job done when those who give their time as service might not."

"Then I will hire your men for forty days and they shall be paid three pence a day."

"Crossbowmen will be paid fourpence a day and you know, my lord, that my men are better than any crossbowmen."

Shaking his head, he said, "There are not enough of you to quibble about. Fourpence, and there is an end to it!" I nodded. "I leave you to speak with the earl. I leave for Wigmore and then

149

South Wales to see how Payn de Chaworth fares." He nodded and left, followed by a gaggle of courtiers and senior lords.

The Earl of Warwick shook his head. "He can be like a whirlwind, can he not? I have every confidence in you, Warbow, but this work will not be easy. You know this land, for you lived here. Will we be able to continue working during the winter? King Edward is desirous that we do!"

"I believe the site is close to the river and you should be able to work, but the workers need to get the foundations as deep as possible before the onset of winter."

"I had planned on doing that, but first we need to get defences up. We will ride on the morrow. I have men to guard the camp, but it is your archers who will have to act as our guard dogs." He smiled. "No, offence, Warbow!"

"It is a good comparison, my lord, and my guard dogs keep my family safe whilst I am here." I looked at the sun, which was a thin one trying to peer through grey clouds. It was just a couple of hours past noon. "I will take half of my archers this afternoon, lord. You build the castle to the northeast of the town?"

"We do."

"Then that is where we shall camp, and I will take some men out in the morning while you and the wagons travel. That way we can aggressively scout."

"Aggressively scout?"

"Aye, my lord; question and disarm every man with a weapon. I would rather upset a man than risk a blade between my shoulders!"

Having travelled part of the Dee with just three men, I was not in the least fearful when I rode out with half of my archers.

We had sumpters with tents, tools, spare bows, and sheaths of arrows. We also had food, but I planned on raiding and eating from the Welsh supply. A starving enemy was more likely to hunt food than King Edward's archers!

I had an idea where the castle would be sited and, although we were the first of the men to reach the banks of the Dee, the rocky knoll above the river yet close to the waterline was an obvious choice. I could not believe that no one had placed a castle here before. I guessed that there might have been one, but it would have been of wooden construction. Despite the abundance of stone, the Welsh, if they built at all, used wood.

The first thing I did was to set my men to cutting down saplings and beginning a ditch. This would be to protect our camp.

Then I rode with David the Welshman and Stephen de Frankton to speak with those who lived in the village that bore the name Flint. They were largely fishermen who put nets in the river and took boats out to fish. They would not be a danger to us, for they already relied on the English who lived in Chester. Without English coins to buy their fish, then the village would not exist. When I told them that a castle would be built there, they did not seem surprised. If anything, they were pleased as they would have both protection and an income! They sold us some fish and I happily paid. You do not bite the hand that feeds you, and I wanted these hands on our side. I knew that the Earl of Warwick could also use them to help build the castle and it would be erected far more quickly.

Our camp would not stop an army but there was no Welsh army close by. Our men were watching the road from Chester, however, to ensure that we remained undisturbed. I would ride out early and find them.

Leaving Stephen in command of the camp the next day, I took my archers and ten of the men of Cheshire. I took my Mongol bow, for I now had more arrows and could afford to use them.

For once it was I who knew the land, and I took us not along the roads to reach Llywelyn's camp, for that was a journey of twenty-two miles. Instead, I took us over first the misnamed Halkyn Mountains and then over the much more desolate Clwydan Mountains. The Halkyn "Mountains" were a patch of lumps and bumps, which had more sheep than people, and there were few of either! The Clwydan Mountains were higher and, as I had recalled, empty. However, they afforded a good view of the Clwyd Valley. I led us confidently through the only two settlements on our route, the half a dozen mean homes of Rhosesmor and the tiny village of Rhydymwyn. Neither had a lord, and we were through both of them less than an hour after leaving the campsite.

David pointed up to the wooded slopes of the mountains that rose ahead of us. Compared with the mountains of Snowdon they were no more than a line of pimples, but they rose high enough to be an obstacle. "Captain, is there a way through there? Surely the road would be faster?"

I shook my head. "I spent my childhood exploring these hills. I hunted with my father here. It looks like a formidable obstacle, but it is not, and there are hunters' trails that cross it. We are heading for an old hill fort. There are many of them, but Moel Arthur gives a good view along the whole valley. There we will rest the horses after the climb and see if there are Welsh warriors in the valley."

It was strange to be riding in this land. My circumstances had changed. When I served as a young archer, I had, more often than not, travelled on foot. It was only when we had left the valley that I had ridden, and then either a pony or a poor sumpter. Eleanor afforded me a good view. I was still vigilant, but I doubted that any of Prince Llywelyn's men would think to guard these paths.

It was a steep climb but a short one, and when we emerged from the trees on the lower slopes, the air and the breeze cooled us and our horses. As we wound our way around to the hill fort, which had been there since before the Romans, I became warier. The fort had been designed to shelter those in the valley when invaders came. The side from which we approached must have been deemed the safer side, for it was sheltered from potential prying eyes in the valley.

I dismounted a hundred paces from one of the entrances and we walked our horses into the centre of the fort. It was a typical hill fort. There were ramparts and ditches and, over the years, they had softened. It was not the defensive stronghold it had once been.

I dropped Eleanor's reins to let her graze. There were puddles that she could drink from. I left my bow on the saddle and bellied up to the largest rampart, which faced south-west. There were higher peaks but this one hid me from view. I was not exposed on the skyline. I could see Rhuthun clearly and I scanned it to get my bearings. David joined me. I saw that in Rhuthun, they too had men digging on the slightly higher piece of ground to the south of the town and the river. There were few men, and it would take some time to build. Compared with the efforts the Earl of Warwick was making, it was more like a rabbit scrape than a place to defend.

"To me, David, it looks as though their camp is slightly smaller than ours."

He studied it. "Aye, Captain, and I cannot see the standard of Prince Llywelyn!"

"You have good eyes."

"I just remember the building from when we passed through, Captain, and it is without a standard."

We could have ridden into the small town to scout out closer but there was no point. If Llywelyn was not there, then who would order a war to begin? I scanned the roads around the town but could see no movement. The Welsh warriors were in their camps.

It begged the question where Prince Llywelyn was, but my task was to protect the work so that by the time the Welsh realised what we were doing, the Earl of Warwick would be able to defend his workers from the safety of partly built secure walls. We had lost Deganwy while it had been under construction because it could not be resupplied. Chester was close enough that even if Flint was cut off, then supplies could be sent by river. King Edward would not repeat the mistakes of his father who built a fort too far!

We reached the building site in the early afternoon. Already the Earl of Warwick had his labourers digging the line of the walls, keep and towers. Others were further away and digging the lines of the curtain wall. While this castle would not be a huge one like Windsor, it would have concentric lines of defence. King Edward had learned from his crusade. He had seen the crusader castles and knew how to build.

I saw not only the soldiers whom William de Beauchamp had brought to protect his workings but also the workers themselves, who trudged along the road from Chester. It was a trickle at the moment but soon there would be hundreds. There were mortar makers, mortar carriers, sand throwers, water carriers, hodmen, barrowmen, carpenters, diggers and watchmen, not to mention the elite: the stonemasons.

I reported directly to the earl. As I spoke with him, I got the impression that he would be spending little time at the works and would base himself in Chester. I did not blame him. On a fast horse, he could be at the site in just over an hour and so long as his subordinates got on with their work, then all would be well.

"Is there danger?"

"The Welsh are busy building a castle at Rhuthun, my lord, and many of their men have departed. As I do not think the prince is there, then I assume that his knights will be with him. My men and I are employed for another thirty-seven days. I assume that the archers of Cheshire have a similar contract." He nodded. "Then that gives us another thirty-odd days to secure the land around here and discourage the Welsh from interfering with your works."

"I would that you were here for the winter, Warbow."

"I know, my lord, but there will be little point. The Clwydan mountains and beyond become impassable with snow during the winter or if there is no snow, then they are slippery, icy death traps. No one will be heading here until spring." I smiled. "King Edward pointed out that my men owed him the service and we shall discharge that." I waved a hand. "The expense of this is exorbitant enough without the king's treasure wasting money on archers who will sit on their backsides. We will take the fourpence a day."

"Fourpence? I thought the rate for archers was three pence a day?"

"King Edward views my men as the equal of the crossbowmen, and as they are paid fourpence a day, then we earn that rate too."

He smiled. "You know your own worth then, Warbow?"

"I believe so, and I do not think much of crossbows. We shall see."

"You have your own camp. Make sure you report to me at least once a week while you are here. You and your men have a nose for trouble, and I would snuff it out before it becomes an inferno!"

Matthew of Tarporley came over when the earl went to ensure that the pegs for the foundations of the donjon were correctly positioned. The rest of the castle would be based upon their position.

"Well, Captain Warbow? Are we here for the winter?"

"I am contracted for forty days and we will leave at the end of that time, but I am sure that if your men wished for pay until spring, then the Earl of Warwick would compensate."

"But after forty days I may decide we head home. There are only so many fish my men can eat."

I gestured behind me with my thumb. "That is Wales, and now that war has been declared we can hunt and raid there at will. My men will eat game!"

Over his shoulder, I saw that the foundations for the curtain wall were being dug. It was a scratch at the moment but by the time I returned, next year, then there would be mortared stones which might be as high as a child's leg. Such would be the slow progress we would make. The castle might take two or three years to build.

"And what do we do apart from hunt?"

Some sand for the mortar had been delivered and I flattened a patch of it. "Here is the Dee." I drew a line. "Here is Chester and here are we." I drew another circle. "These are the Clwydan Mountains, and they are passable. My men and I will cover those. I need you and your archers to divide into two groups. One will head down to the coast at Dyserth and watch for incursions coming from that direction. The other half should invest Mold and watch the road from Rhuthun. I have fought the Welsh before, and they will send scouts down the road to test our strength. When they do that, we can prepare a welcome for them. It may be that they do nothing, in which case this will be the easiest money I have ever earned."

While I knew that our task was the harder of the three, I was happy for us to do it. We left before dawn and were at the hill fort as the sun rose. The Welsh workers were not as hard-working as ours and it was the third hour of the day before work began. Some riders left the workings, but they were on ponies and there were just four of them. They headed along the valley to Dyserth. There they would find archers.

"Do we follow them, Captain?"

"No, John. Even if they evade the Cheshire men and reach Flint, there are too few for mischief. However, we will wait here until they return."

It was not long after noon when four ponies returned. There were just three riders. Our sentries at Dyserth had done their job.

We headed back to Flint and the news was confirmed; the sentries had killed one of the Welsh scouts.

Matthew said, "Do we prepare to meet them at Dyserth, then, Captain?"

Shaking my head, I said, "I think not. First, they will send either more men or seek an unguarded route. Our vigilance will reward us."

The next day we saw no riders heading to Dyserth, but we did see six men on ponies heading towards the hill fort and the pass. They would be in for a shock. I was surprised that they had not tried the path first as I knew of it because I grew up in the area, and there must have been Welshmen who knew of its existence.

We did not have to move as the path passed beneath the ramparts and we nocked arrows and waited. Half of my men were behind the ramparts on the north. Tom and Martin were to the south of the path and I waited with Richard, Robin, son of Richard, and Jack on the path but beyond the eye line of any riders ascending. By the time they saw us, they would be surrounded.

We did not draw our bows but stood and waited. As the first of the Welshmen crested the rise just twenty paces from us, they saw us and reined in. I pulled back on my bowstring, as did the others. A pulled bow could not be held for long.

David the Welshman shouted something and the two men we could see turned to flee. I guessed that David had given them a command, and four arrows flew to slam into the two men. At that range, we could have almost picked our targets and I had chosen the right shoulder.

The four arrows knocked them to the ground, and I heard the thrum of another bow and then a voice shout, "We surrender!"

When we reached the top of the trail, we saw that three of the six were dead or dying but the other three had their arms in the air.

"What do we do with them, Captain?"

I could see by their fearful faces that the three men thought they were going to be executed, but that was not my way. "Take

158

their weapons and their ponies; send them back to whoever commands them."

"Should we not ask them questions, Captain?"

I turned to Robin, son of Richard. "And what do you think these three know? It matters not who is in command, save that it is not Llywelyn."

David spoke to them and they answered. He then turned to me. "They asked if we will bury the bodies of their dead?"

"Tell them that they can either bury the bodies or take them back to Rhuthun. It is their choice."

They spoke amongst themselves and then, hoisting the three bodies over their shoulders, headed back down the trail. Would they try the Mold road the next day?

I dismissed them from my thoughts immediately. My men took their weapons. None were particularly good, but we had young boys who might need them back at Yarpole. We waited until we saw the men on the road to Rhuthun at the bottom of the valley before we mounted up and headed for the workings.

Matthew of Tarporley had a wounded man with them. They had found trouble. The last Welsh patrol, from Dyserth, had arrived unharmed. "We saw nothing, Captain, except for what looked like a Welsh ship off the river. The men on patrol saw our horses and they turned back."

Matthew of Tarporley said, "We were caught out. I had my men watching the road, but a second party flanked us. We sent them packing but Egbert was wounded."

"The road has cover and the other two places they could use are bare and exposed. It was my fault."

It was not. Matthew should have realised the danger, but he was unused to such land as the road between Rhuthun and

159

Chester. There were no rolling fields and hedgerows. Here it was a twisting road, which rose and fell. You had to be more cunning than an enemy.

"Tomorrow we send just four men to each of the other two vantage points and we will take the rest of the archers and Stephen de Frankton and head for Mold, in case they try a reconnaissance in force," I said.

"A man at arms?"

"A very experienced man at arms. He may be able to tell us more about the Welsh formation. I will head, tomorrow afternoon, to Chester, to report to the Earl of Warwick."

That night I kept watch with Stephen. We had a comfortable camp, for we had hide tents made from cattle captured the previous year from the Welsh. It meant we were not only dry but, as the autumn nights became chillier, we were not as cold. We ate well as we all passed through woods and were able to take animals and birds, which were fed into the stews we made. We had been well supplied with beer and ale and I had endured worse campaigns.

"Well, Stephen, what do you think?"

"I think that I shall go mad if I have to stay in camp one more day and hear builders complain about everything!" I laughed. "But I think you have the reading of this right. They lost men at Moel Arthur and their ship saw that we had a sizeable force at Dyserth. If they are to find out what we are doing, then they have to try the Mold road. From what you told me, Captain, Mold is regarded as Welsh. If Prince Llywelyn felt comfortable meeting the king there, then they must consider it safe. If we hold the road then they have lost part of Wales."

"After we have seen them on the morrow, or not, as the case might be, then I will visit with the earl. If the Welsh are flexing

their muscles, then we may need knights and men at arms rather than just archers."

"From what you have told me, Captain, it is a local lord at Rhuthun. When Llywelyn returns, then they may try something."

We had more than a hundred archers when we left the next morning before the sun was up. We were able to take more than I had expected, for we had taken six ponies, and I took it upon myself to commandeer some of the draught animals from the wagons.

I sent Matthew and forty archers to the wood where he had been ambushed. I rode with the rest to Mold. I intended to ride along the Rhuthun road and also to let the villagers of Mold know our numbers. It was why I had taken more horses. They might have counted how many men we sent previously. While they had not seen the building at Flint, for we had a line of spearmen preventing any from travelling along the road, they must have known that we were doing something.

We reached Mold at dawn and clattered noisily through the cobbled road that ran between the houses. Heads appeared and then quickly vanished when they saw who we were. It took some time for us to pass and I knew we would be reported. After it was dark someone would hurry along to Rhuthun and speak of archers mounted on horses. It identified us as English.

One of Matthew's riders met us a mile north of the small town. "Captain, there are men on horses heading down the road."

"Horses or ponies?"

"Mainly ponies, Captain, but there are some horses with them.

I sighed, for this was always the problem when dealing with men you did not know. My men would have made a more accurate report. "How many?"

"We did not count them."

I snapped, "I shall have to ask Captain Matthew to send me a scout next time who was not dropped on his head as a baby!" I turned in the saddle. "David the Welshman, choose fifteen archers and head along the western side of the wood, which flanks the road. Captain Matthew should be to the east."

"Aye, Captain!"

I turned to the scout. "You ride back to Captain Matthew and tell him that we are heading for him. If he can engage the Welsh, then he should do so. Can you do that?"

I think I had terrified him. It was not his fault; the Cheshire man should have chosen a better messenger. "Yes, Captain!" He dug his heels in his horse and fled to the east to find his captain.

Stephen turned to me. "If there are horses and ponies, then they might have men at arms. These trees mean that your men do not have the range."

"I know." I slipped my bow from its case. "String your bows and have an arrow ready. Horse holders, be ready!"

Once again, I knew how my men would react but not the Cheshire men. It might well be that in the coming fight I could only rely on my men. It was not a satisfactory situation.

The sun was a weak one and although it lightened the road, I could see that the undergrowth and the trees, which had yet to shed their leaves, made shadows and provided places where men could wait. Before I could even order my men to dismount and prepare to advance on foot, I heard fighting from ahead. I had my Mongol bow in my hand and, nocking an arrow, I dug my heels into Eleanor's flanks and took off down the road. There were cries and shouts as well as the clash of metal.

The twisting road and the gloom meant that we came upon the fight suddenly. It was fewer than forty paces from us. I took in that there were mailed men on horses, but I saw no spurs on the leading men and that meant they were not knights. This was a strong force; even as I nocked and released an arrow into the head of the archer who was aiming into the woods to my left, I realised that we were evenly matched in terms of numbers.

My men dismounted and two of them held the horses. The others began to send arrows into the sides of men, and then David the Welshman had his archers send their arrows into the backs of them too.

I chose a Mongol bodkin arrow. I only had four of them. From the back of Eleanor, I sent it into the left shoulder of a man at arms. I must have hit something vital, for blood spurted and he fell from his horse.

Stephen de Frankton had not dismounted, and he charged towards the Welsh. I could not let him go alone and I dug my heels into Eleanor's side. I managed to send one arrow as I galloped. It would have disappointed Ahmed, but I was pleased, for it pinned a Welsh light horseman's leg to his saddle and his horse.

As Stephen sliced his sword through the shoulder of a Welsh horseman, a horn sounded, and the Welsh fled. The fight was over almost as soon as it had begun. The only two on our side who were mounted were Stephen and me. A pursuit was unnecessary and reckless. Now that I had seen the road at close hand, I could offer better advice to Matthew.

"If there are prisoners, then bring them to me. See to our wounded and any Welsh wounded who might live. Give those too badly hurt a warrior's death. Fetch the horses forward."

As I turned, I saw that I had not lost a single Yarpole man, but there were at least two dead men of Cheshire. Matthew looked embarrassed more than anything when he finally led his men to meet me. This was neither the time nor the place to dissect what might have been a disaster.

"Take the horses and weapons back to Flint. I will ride with the prisoners to Chester. Stephen, David, Tom and Martin, come with me!"

"Captain, I …"

"I blame myself, Matthew, for I am so used to fighting alongside my own men that often I do not realise that not all are trained the same way. I will return before dawn. Until then, you command!"

Chapter 11

We had the prisoners tethered to one another and, with Tom leading, Martin followed up with a spear taken from a dead man at arms to encourage them. It was just ten miles to our camp, where we would stop on the way to Chester, but we did not relent, and our horses kept such a steady speed that there was little likelihood of the prisoners being able to escape.

Stephen said, "Captain, do not be so hard on Matthew. His men are good, and he leads them well." I turned and stared at him as though he was a fool. "The trouble is, Captain, that your men all meet your high standards but not everyone has those standards. I have fought with other lords and captains. You have the drive and wish to be the best but, I confess, I know not why. We both know that lords will discard you when you are old, wounded or too expensive. You need not jump every time that King Edward snaps a command." I gave him one of my harsh stares. He smiled. "The trouble is, Captain, that I know your heart and you are a good man. I know I can say what I say for that reason. You might shout at me and censure me, but you will hear my words and you will reflect on them." He leaned over. "You do not have to try too hard; I listen at table and in the camp. All the lords, and that includes King Edward, value you, more than you can know. You could be paid more coin and receive more honours if you but asked for them!"

I heard his words and, I suppose, I knew that he was right. What was it deep within me that made me do what I did? "I need no more than I have, and I am content!"

He nodded. "Perhaps that is why men do what they do for you. They know your heart and cannot help but follow you." He laughed. "Listen to me! I came to you as the man who would slay Prince Llywelyn, and now, I am as much your man as John of Nottingham!"

We rode in silence. I found myself riding a little faster until I realised that I could hear the panting of the Welsh captives and I slowed. What had made me what I was? I knew I had changed but thought that was down to Mary and Hamo; they had nothing to do with my warrior life.

We crossed the bridge at Chester, and I was recognised by the sentries, who smiled at the eight panting prisoners. We headed into the city and the castle. We left the prisoners with the sergeant of the guard and while Stephen, Tom and Martin went to find an alehouse and food, I sought the earl. He was eating but it was just with his senior men. He waved the steward to fetch a seat and then food.

"How goes it?"

I told him of the Welsh patrols and how we had dealt with them.

He seemed pleased despite the losses that we had suffered. "I can see why King Edward has such faith in you. I confess that in the Holy Land I thought you had been lucky. Now I see that you are skilled. What do you need, Captain Warbow?"

"We can hold their scouts and archers, but if the Welsh bring a determined army and attack using spearmen and archers, then we might lose."

He laughed. "I doubt that, for you would find some way to win, but let us not try to use all of your skills up so quickly. I will send Sir Walter de Beauchamp and forty men at arms on the morrow. He is keen to impress King Edward and, between you and I, my nephew is a little too enthusiastic for my table!"

I knew the knight to whom he referred. He was a young knight who was using some of the items on the table to illustrate a point. "You will need to tell him, my lord, that we camp. There will be neither table nor fine food."

The Earl of Warwick laughed. "My nephew will not mind; he sees himself as the reincarnation of the Spanish knight El Cid!" I nodded, for I had heard of the legend from Mary. "He has seen just twenty summers, and yet he reads as though books are food, and he strives to be the best knight that he can be."

I heard the pride in his voice, and I knew that I would have to take care that no harm came to the young man, for the Earl of Warwick and his family were powerful. "Then I will find my men and leave."

"No, Captain, you will eat with me and you can tell my knights of how you saved Lord Edward from the assassin. They would know the true story."

I had no choice and, if the truth be told, I was hungry. I told them a version of the truth, but I gave more credit to Lord Edward for his actions. It seemed to satisfy them and when I had gorged myself, I sought my men.

It was dark as we headed back to Flint, but we had all eaten well and Stephen had even paid for a doxy. I would speak with

Matthew in the morning. There seemed little point in disturbing my good humour!

The next day, my captain of Cheshire archers was waiting to see me when I stepped from my tent. "Captain, I am sorry I have let you down. Your name is held in such high esteem that I would do nothing to jeopardise your good opinion of me."

I had thought about this on the way home. "Then do not try so hard."

"What?"

"If I were not here, then how would you have ambushed those Welshmen?"

"I would have hidden men on both sides with a few scouts ahead of us to warn us of danger and, when the first Welshman passed, had my last archer begin the attack!"

"And why did you not do that?"

"I thought to let you garner all the glory for the attack!"

I laughed. "By all that is holy! I care nothing for glory! I wish to win and leave the battlefield with as few dead friends left upon it as possible. Evesham was a harsh lesson! You are a good archer and a good leader, Matthew. Trust to your instincts!"

He looked at me and I saw the scales fall from his eyes. "Truly?"

"Truly! When my contract is up, I shall go home, and I am more than happy to recommend you lead the archers in my absence."

He stood a little straighter. "Then I will try to live up to your expectations."

"And today we have a knight with his men at arms come to help us, so let us not make any mistakes while he is here!"

Sir Walter de Beauchamp arrived not long after dawn. That showed me he was keen and he realised the dangers of travelling unknown roads in the dark. Unusually, he also spoke to me with greater respect than I was used to from young knights. Normally, they looked down on archers until they had learned their worth in battle. Sir Walter had yet to fight in a battle, and yet he asked me all the right questions.

"I realise that you have your own plans, Captain Gerald, but it would help me if you could show me the Clwyd Valley. If I am to do as my uncle wishes and defend the castle workings, then I ought to see the lie of the land."

"Very good, my lord. Stephen, would you ride with David the Welshman and patrol the fort today? I will ride with Sir Walter and show him the valley."

"Aye, Captain." Stephen grinned. "I have no doubt that your archers will try to test my skills!"

Sir Walter brought just his squire, John, with us, and that showed sense in one so young. He had brought his men to guard the camp and they would do that.

I took with us my Mongol bow and I saw the knight looking at it as we headed to Dyserth. I would end our ride at the site of the skirmish we had fought. As we rode towards the coast, he looked around and made comments about the land, which showed he was perceptive and was here to do what he had been tasked by his uncle.

When we reached the tiny hamlet of Dyserth and he saw the wrecked remains of the castle King Henry had been building, he dismounted and, while his squire held our horses, walked with me amongst the ruined fortifications. He nodded towards the sea. "I can see why this was abandoned. It was simply too far from the sea, Captain, but what a shame that it had to be so. Were you here?"

I shook my head. "No, my lord."

169

"I have little doubt that men died and it was unnecessary. The Welsh could be controlled by a castle, but not here."

We mounted our horses. "I think, my lord, that King Henry chose this as a site as the Welsh had already done work to make it defensible. We shall see, when we climb the Clwydan Mountains, many such sites, but the Welsh do not have castles as we do. They are learning but, in the past, they just built hill forts where they would shelter until an enemy left them. It worked for almost a thousand years, but I think that King Edward will end that."

As we began the climb, I saw him looking around. "Captain, where is the road?"

I pointed to the narrow track upon which we rode. "This is it. A road is needed when you use wagons. The Welsh rarely use anything bigger than a pony."

He laughed. "And if I attempted this alone, then my squire and I might well be lost."

"I grew up around here, my lord. There are few Englishmen who know the land as I do."

"Then you are Welsh?"

"No, lord. I was born in the land controlled by an English knight, and my father served him. I was born in Wales, but I am English."

He nodded towards my bow. "When I read of the exploits of Don Rodrigo de Vivar, I came across accounts of Muslim horse archers. Is that one of their bows?"

I shook my head. "The Seljuk Turks use a similar bow but this one is Mongol. Both nations use them from the backs of horses."

"Can you use it thus?"

I shook my head. "After a fashion, but the man who gave it to me would be embarrassed by my attempts. I am much more accurate with the earth beneath my feet and my war bow."

"After which you are named." I nodded. "It is a pity we cannot train our own archers to fight from the backs of horses, for then we would be unbeatable."

"It would be useful, lord, but it is an idle fancy, for we cannot make these bows and the men who use them are part horse. I rode with the Mongols and they do not need to use their hands to ride. But you are, with respect, my lord, wrong; no army is unbeatable. The Mongols did not defeat the Turk but then the Turk was beaten by King Richard. It is a combination of a good leader and the best of men that determines victory."

We had reached one of the highest points in the range, Moel Famau. We reined in. There was a hill fort at the summit, but it was smaller than Moel Arthur.

I swept my hand around me. "The Clwyd Valley, lord." I pointed to the fort of Moel Arthur. My men were hidden. "Stephen de Frankton and my archers are there."

"I cannot see them!"

I laughed. "And I would be most unhappy if you could, my lord." I looked up at the sky and saw it was approaching noon. "Come, my lord. We should be in time for some food!"

I watched the knight and his squire as they tried to pick out my men. They would not be able to, for the ramparts of the old hill fort afforded cover. We would see them but only when we were right on top of them.

I led us around to approach the fort from the Flint side. Will Yew Tree rose like a wraith from a rock and smiled when the squire jumped and made his horse rear.

"Any sign of the Welsh today, Will?"

He shook his head. "No, Captain; I think we burned their fingers the other day. There is food ready."

"I know, I can smell it cooking."

Sir Walter said, "I saw no smoke, nor did I smell the fire."

"My men used dry kindling and the wind is blowing the smell east, but I detected it. A word of advice, my lord – when you ride in unknown land, always take an archer or two with you as a scout. They have all grown up in woods and hunting."

"I have hunted!"

"With respect, my lord, you went into woods to hunt, but it was men like me who found the game and drove it towards your spears and arrows."

I saw him thinking about that and he nodded. "Aye, you are right. This is an education, archer."

My men had set snares and traps. The rabbits would be tasty.

I confirmed what Will had told me and I said, "I think, David, that tomorrow we can use just two men to watch here. The next time they come, it will be with a larger army to try to destroy the workings."

"You are sure, Captain?" I heard the eagerness in the knight's voice.

"Not certain, my lord, but I have met this Welsh prince and he is not one to take the building of a castle in Gwynedd without a fight. I think you and your men will get the opportunity to test your mettle against the Welsh, but I doubt that it will be Llywelyn himself. Of course, I may be wrong, in which case you and your men at arms will suffer the discomfort of a camp in a Welsh winter!"

"Captain, my uncle said that you had forgotten more about war than most men learn. I am happy to be your student!"

The site of the skirmish was sobering for the young knight. Our dead had been buried in shallow graves, but the arrows in the trunks of trees and the broken hafts of spears told their own story. I said nothing, for this was a lesson he needed to learn himself.

I watched him as he looked at the bloody ground and the broken shafts of spears and arrows. He turned to me and looked at my green clothes. His own surcoat, which covered his mail hauberk, was brightly coloured. The six yellow crosslets and yellow bar on the orange background lit up the gloomy trail like a brand in a castle passage.

"If you attacked an enemy then they would be easily seen but they would have no idea of where you were."

I nodded. "You can see the four archers who came to speak with us. There are another two somewhere but I cannot see them. The first you would know of an attack was when a goose feathered shaft suddenly sprouted from your chest!"

He looked at the hauberk's links, which were visible through the slit in his surcoat. "I have the best mail that money can buy!"

I drew a bodkin arrow from my arrow bag and placed the tip in one of the mail links. "At anything fewer than two hundred paces, most bowmen can drive this arrow through these links, your gambeson, undershirt, and into your flesh. I have seen some penetrate helmets, too, but at closer range."

"I need to have archers."

"Or light horsemen who can close with archers and are cheaper than knights or men at arms!"

He continued to question me as we rode back. He was right. He was attending school and that school was one of survival. He had read of war and he had studied battles. He was now seeing the reality of it.

We had three days of peace and I reduced the watchers to two at each of the three key areas. I had the rest of the archers fortify our camp by deepening the ditch and making an abatis of last autumn's brambles.

We fashioned a hurdle into a gate so that, at night, we were secure. I did not tell Sir Walter to do the same, but he did so anyway. He was a quick learner. He saw that we kept our horses close to us. It made for a more pungent camp and there was noise, but when I explained that the horses were as valuable to the Welsh as the man who rode the beast, he understood. We were a highly mobile army!

I also reduced the number of watchers to increase the number of night guards. The workforce for the castle had swollen to over a thousand now. A night-time attack would result in many deaths unless we were vigilant.

Sir Walter was an unusual knight, for he was happy to talk with any who might help him to be a better soldier and, as a result, was very popular. He even spoke to the castle builders, for he was keen to learn.

He reminded me of Sir John Malton, and I hoped that he would not change as Sir John had. Sir John was still one of the best knights I knew, but the Holy Land had shown that he had political aspirations. I thought that they were unnecessary, but then, I would never be a knight, and the best that I could hope for was to remain a gentleman.

There was a pleasant atmosphere in the camp, but I was

counting down the days I had left to serve. I was confident that Sir Walter had learned enough to withstand any winter attack, for he and Matthew of Tarporley got on well and I had heeded Stephen's words. I had been exacting too high a standard.

Even when I was not on watch, I was always awake before dawn. It was just habit, and my body seemed to have a will of its own. When I was at home with Mary, I often slipped from our bed to make water and to begin my work for the day.

So it was that I woke and was instantly awake. I rose and, after leaving the tent, sniffed the air. The wind was from the east and was chilly, having crossed the Dee. I was an old campaigner, and I walked the half-mile to the river to make water. I nodded to the sentries who were seated around a fire, which had been kept burning all night. All told, twenty men were guarding the camp each night. Sixteen were archers and the rest men at arms. Dotted along the Welsh side of the camp, they would give us warning of an attack.

There was a mist on the river. Here, at Flint, it was wide and slow. I peered along it but detected nothing untoward. All was as it should be.

William of Matlac was in command of the archers and I approached him. He handed me a mug of ale and a hunk of toasted bread. Stale bread always toasted well, and we had butter. As the butter dripped down my chin, I felt replete. We had a good life, even though we camped. "The night was quiet?"

He nodded and then rubbed his chin. "Aye, Captain, quiet enough, but…"

"But what?"

"The horses were restless for a while. I thought nothing of it, but as I did not hear an animal, I walked the outside defences."

"And?"

"And when I stopped, I heard nothing."

That was ominous. "Nothing at all?"

"No, Captain. Neither animal nor bird. Bats should still have been around, but none came."

I nodded. "Rouse the camp quietly and have your archers stand to."

"Aye, Captain."

I went to the four men at arms. "My nose itches – wake Sir Walter and have your men stand to."

"We heard nothing, Captain, and we walked the camp!"

"Yet we should have heard noises. There may be something out there, and I would rather look foolish and have men mock me than one stone damaged!"

"Aye, Captain!"

I went to my tent and saw that all of my men were awake and arming. I strapped on my sword and slipped my daggers into my boots. I chose my war bow and I stuffed four bodkins in my belt. My arrow bag was already full of war arrows.

By the time I had done that, the camp was awake and there was more noise from the builders than I would have liked. I noticed that the tethered horses were becoming skittish too. There was someone out there. We did have the advantage that the ground to the Welsh side of our lines sloped down and any attacker would have to ascend the slope. It was not a steep one, but it would put them at a slight disadvantage.

There was a cry to my fore and a voice shouted, "Alarum! Alarum!"

There was an attack; it was just that we had no idea of the size of it. Was it merely men on foot, seeking to cause mischief, or was it a serious attack that was intended to destroy the workings, labourers and the tools?

I nocked a war arrow and hurried forward to peer down the slope. The archers all knew their business and they had formed a skirmish line at the edge of the camp and on the top of the slope.

A Cheshire archer suddenly fell at my feet with an arrow in his head. I heard the sound of bowstrings as arrows were released. This was the worst kind of archery duel. It was being fought in the darkness, which meant the range was less than forty feet. At that range, a fully drawn arrow could go through a lightly armed archer and we would have only a moment to react to an enemy. The fastest hands would survive.

As if to prove my own point, I noticed a Welsh archer draw back and saw that he was aiming at John of Nottingham. I lifted as I drew and released. The force was so much that when the war arrow hit him in his right shoulder and neck, it knocked him from his feet and the dying man hit others who were ascending.

It bought us time. I stood next to John and found that Jack of Lincoln was to my left. Shadows were ascending and arrows flew from the dark. I aimed at a large shadow just a hundred feet from me. A cry told me that I had hit the man.

Jack suddenly cried out. He had an arrow sticking through his leg.

"Get to a healer!"

Shaking his head, he dropped his bow and took a piece of leather thong. He tied it above the arrow and then snapped off the flight and the head. He dropped them into his satchel. He was an archer through and through.

"Captain!"

John's voice made me whip my head around. John of Nottingham was nocking an arrow and a Welsh archer had advanced to within twenty feet of us. I had been distracted by Jack's wound. I released as I dropped to my knee. The Welshman's arrow struck my brigandine but a combination of my duck, the leather and one of the metal studs, meant it did not penetrate; it bounced up into the morning sky.

I heard Sir Walter shouting, "Form a shield wall and protect the archers!"

Then I detected the sound of mail in the dark as more Welshmen advanced.

Behind me, I heard the labourers as they were organised by their leaders. They had hammers and picks as well as other tools. They would defend themselves.

I nocked another arrow and this time saw four Welshmen with shields advancing up towards our line. Arrows descended from the sky as the Welsh tried blind arrows. Although they could not guarantee a hit, falling from the sky meant that any arrow landing on an unprotected head was likely to be fatal. I did not waste my arrow. I let the four Welshman advance and prayed that the arrows would fall further back than our front line. I could hear the sound of metal on metal as Sir Walter and his men advanced to engage the Welsh. I waited until the four Welshmen were just fifteen feet away and when I saw a face, I sent an arrow into the right eye of one of the two in the middle. Jack had secured his leg and his arrow went through the wooden shield of another Welshman, pinning it to his arm, while John's arrow had also been driven through a Welshman's skull. I was the first to nock an arrow as the last Welshmen pulled back his spear to skewer me. It is hard to strike with a spear and not leave a gap close to your shield, unless, of course, you strike over the top of it. He could not do that because I was above him. I saw the arrow had been stopped, not by the man's mail but the goose feathers. He fell back.

It was time to pay them back and I shouted, "Release arrows into the air!"

Those without a man to the fore sent arrow after arrow up into the air. While the Welsh arrows might be wasted, we could pick up all those that landed in the ground when the battle was over.

I was aiming into the sky when a pair of archers aimed at us. I dispatched one and Robin's arrow hit the other. I was now out of arrows.

I dropped my bow and drew my sword whilst picking up a Welsh shield. The first hint of dawn was in the sky to the east and I could make out the enemy host. In places, they had gained the high ground. It was here, around myself and my men, that they had made little impression.

"John, take command here." I knew that he would continue to win the battle of the high ground and I had to see what I could do about our left.

I ran to my left, for I saw fighting behind me. There were dead archers from both sides, but it was their spearmen who had made the most progress, for whilst we had wagonloads of arrows, they were not close to hand, and an archer without an arrow was in the gravest danger, for his short sword was no match for a spear.

"Sir Walter!"

I hurled myself into the left flank of the spearmen. They were slow to react and I managed to hack my sword across the shoulder of the nearest Welshman. As spears were turned in my direction, I blocked with my shield but did not stop. The closer I was to them, the less effective would be their spears.

I heard Captain Matthew shout, "Labourers, fetch arrows for my archers!" He had come of age, for I should have thought of that. Some labourers had no weapons but wished to fight. Fetching arrows would win the battle.

As the weak autumn sun rose, I saw that we had to have been attacked by hundreds of Welshmen. Thankfully, from the weapons I spied on the dead, they were not all warriors.

I had to put all such speculation from my mind, for I was in the midst of a dozen spearmen. Of course, they got in each other's way, but the edge of a sharpened spear could still be fatal. I blocked with my shield and slashed and hacked with my sword. I kept moving forward and then I heard a roar from behind me. I did not turn. If I was to die, then I would keep fighting those to my fore. If I turned, death was guaranteed!

I dropped to one knee as a spear was driven to where my head had been, and it was an easy kill to ram the sword under the spear and into the chest. As I rose, I smashed the edge of my shield under the chin of a spearman. The light went from his eyes as he was rendered unconscious.

Then I saw what had caused the roar. Sir Walter had led his metal-clad men at arms to charge into the Welsh spearmen. Our combined attack created a huge hole in their line and, more importantly, we were behind their other men at arms.

Sir Walter grinned. "We will deal with these, Captain; take your archers and flank the others!"

It was a sound plan and I roared, "Men of Cheshire! To me!"

Two dozen archers, including Matthew of Tarporley, ran to my side and I saw that they had arrows bags which were full.

"We will flank those men who are attacking our centre!"

The duel between my archers, the men of Cheshire and their Welsh counterparts was fierce, but my archers were, as yet, undiscovered, for we had destroyed the Welsh on this side and were approaching from their right side.

"Release." The twenty-four arrows struck almost as one, but I had already ordered a second and then a third set.

The wall of goose feathered ash slammed into the sides of the Welsh archers. Our war arrows struck them as they pulled back on their own bowstrings. Three flights destroyed them, and my archers needed no encouragement. They hurtled down the slope to get at the remaining enemy. The Welsh ran, and those that fell were shown no mercy. By the time we had reached the bottom of the slope, only the dead remained.

Sir Walter was young, but he was a quick learner and, after mounting his men at arms, they pursued the Welsh back up the Clwydan Mountains. His journey alongside me had borne fruit.

We cleared the battlefield. Their wounded had their throats cut, for we had no means to heal them. There were no prisoners taken but the dead were stripped of all that was of value. We collected every unbroken arrow and the heads and goose feathers from the damaged ones.

By the time it was noon, Sir Walter returned, driving twenty captured ponies and without any empty saddles. The Welsh had lost more than sixty bowmen as well as forty spears and swordsmen. Twelve Welsh men at arms had perished.

We had not escaped without losses. Twenty archers were slain as well as thirty-five labourers. Fortunately, none of those who were slain were specialists. They could be replaced. It was not only Jack who was wounded but also John of Nottingham, and in John's case, the wound was to his right shoulder. A plunging arrow meant he would never draw a bow again. He had been growing old and his time as an archer might have been drawing to a close, but none of us wished that fate on one of the most loyal archers who had ever served with me. Tom, Alan and Will Yew Tree suffered cuts, but they would heal. We had earned our pay!

Chapter 12

The Earl of Warwick arrived the next morning, not long before noon. We had sent a rider to tell him of the battle. We had lost one whole day of building and managed little more on the day he arrived. He walked the battlefield with his nephew and me. The ash from the Welsh bodies still smoked and was the clearest evidence of the fight that had taken place.

"Do we know where they were from?"

The question was addressed to me. "I think, my lord, that they are the men of the Clwyd Valley, but we saw no evidence of a knight with them. They relied on sheer weight of numbers."

He nodded. "It is as King Edward and I discussed. They are not yet ready to meet us in battle. The king will need you and your archers come the summer, Captain Warbow."

Sir Walter said, "You are right, uncle. I thought that horsemen could win this war alone, but I have seen myself the skill of the archer both English and Welsh. I will not underestimate them again."

I pointed to the workers. "One thing has resulted in a benefit for us. The workmen, once they get back into the swing, will have greater urgency. They need the walls to be erected."

The Earl nodded. "And when they have built this one, then they will move on to Rhuddlan and Rhuthun! We shall be like the sea and all will be swamped before us."

We turned to view the labourers as they repaired the damage done to their work and began to dig more holes for foundations.

"You remember, my lord, that soon my men's contract will end. Captain Matthew is happy to command the archers and I believe that we have torn the heart from the Welsh. They may recover, but not before the next year." As if to prove my point, I stamped the ground. "Soon frosts will come, and travel will be limited. Your master-builder promises that there will be a wall around the castle by Christmas, and by Easter you will have the lower walls built. The Welsh have gambled, and they have lost."

"Just so. We shall miss you. I will send your payment the day before you are due to leave."

I could not help smiling, for this guaranteed that he would be given more days than he paid for. It would take three days to return to Yarpole and our pay was supposed to be from door-step to doorstep. I would not complain, for we had taken more in treasure from the dead Welshmen than we had been paid. Along with the ponies, arrows and weapons, we had done well.

We probably worked more days than we needed to, but we had all grown close to the archers, men at arms and even the labourers. They felt like a family; a different one, but a family nonetheless.

We were paid and took our coin the sixty-odd miles to Yarpole. Winter was about to descend. We could travel no faster, for although the wounded men had begun to heal, it would not do to rush and risk undoing all of the work done by the healers.

We stayed in religious houses, for I still had my parchment from King Edward. It meant we were fed well and our horses cared for.

I sent Tom ahead to warn our families of our imminent arrival. The result was that everyone from the manor was there to greet us as we rode in through the gates as the afternoon sun set in the west. I saw that my wife had not given birth yet and Hamo was toddling about with more confidence than when I had left. I had missed so much.

I dismounted and James led Eleanor away. I picked up Hamo and said, "Who is this little warrior who has grown so much since I last saw him?"

He grinned and hugged me. He said something to me, but I confess that my ear was no longer attuned to the toddler's words.

Mary said, when she saw the puzzlement on my face, "He says he wants to be a warrior like you!"

I squeezed him. "First I shall be a father and then I will teach you." Still holding him, I put my arm around Mary. "I feared I had missed the birth."

"No, your child is obedient even in the womb and awaits you, but another month may have seen you arrive too late!"

It was a joyous reunion, for we had lost no one and even the wife of John of Nottingham was just pleased that her husband was alive and would go to war no more. He had sons to take his place.

I do not even remember what we ate, except that no lord ever ate finer, and I laughed so much that I thought my sides would split. Everything was perfect and made the time spent apart bearable!

When all had departed and Hamo had fallen asleep at the table, we took him to bed and then I lay down with my wife. We were happy, and yet she wept. It was strange, but the tears were not of sadness but joy. I felt like crying too but I was a warrior. We had been apart for the longest time since we had met, and I did not like it. Perhaps I would tell the king to find another captain of archers.

"You are home now?"

"The king will not need me until the spring and even by then, who knows. Perhaps the Welsh prince will see the folly of fighting such a powerful king as King Edward."

She snuggled into me. "You were lucky, husband. The wives and I prayed each day, and our prayers were answered, for none died."

"And in that the Good Lord watched over us. He must be on the side of King Edward." I thought back to the fearful fight in the night. When I had killed that archer, his arrow might so easily have split my skull. Who determined the outcome of such fights? He was as good as I was, and yet I had survived. I had my answer. I had to have been better or he would now have my sword and I would be dead. Of course, I could not rely on such an advantage forever. One day my skills would wane and, in that split second, I might be the one to be brought home, draped over a horse. I would not take life for granted.

I rose slightly later than when on campaign and that was the fault of my wife and unborn child. As she lay in my arms and I considered rising, my hand touched her belly and the bairn kicked. I could not move. This was another child of mine and I lay there, stroking her until the kicking stopped. I still did not rise but kissed her sleeping head and lay with her warm breath wafting across my face.

When I finally slipped my arm from beneath her, I went to the chamber next to ours where Hamo slept still. I would not disturb him.

Sarah and her women were in the kitchen, busy preparing food. Warriors were home and those who were not married and lived in my warrior hall would be hungry.

When we had been at the castle workings, we had not starved, but we had eaten quickly and consumed whatever was available. Sarah had little experience of a war camp, but she knew how to feed men and our manor was luckier than most. We had fowl, which produced eggs every day. We cured our own hams so that we always had plenty of meat and we had bread ovens, which could give my men fresh bread every day. Those in the village would bring their dough to cook in our ovens.

The manor was now, truly, the centre of the village. I walked through the kitchen, greeting all who were there and then, wrapping myself in the cloak I had hung over the peg on the back door, went out into the cold.

There was an early morning mist. We did not keep the gates manned but they were barred at night. We had dogs to warn us of danger. I climbed the ladder to the fighting platform. My land was still and, more importantly, seemed at peace. When we had travelled home, we had seen that the Welsh had withdrawn to their lands and homes. The raids begun by Dafydd ap Gruffydd had ceased when we had started work on the castle. It was strange, but the hostilities brought to an end the petty raiding. It was as if both sides were preparing for war.

I walked my walls and descended at the front gate before returning to the hall. In my warrior hall, I heard the noise of conversation and saw some of Sarah's women carrying wooden platters laden with food. They were hurrying, for they did not wish the hot food to cool too much.

I entered my hall and I could hear, up the stairs, the sound of Hamo and his mother. This would be a lazy and leisurely day. Sitting down at the table, I began to run through the tasks that needed to be done before Christmas. We had the animals to cull. There had been too few men left on the manor to do the job properly. The older animals had been partly reprieved. The pigs had been turned out to graze the stubble, and so the winter barley could now be planted. Alan would organise a hunt to cull the animals in the woods and we would coppice the trees for firewood and to maintain healthy woods. The bone fire would be a celebratory event marking the end of autumn and the start of winter. Mead and beer would be specially brewed. Sarah liked to make a black beer made with roasted barley for the celebration. She only made it once a year and the men enjoyed it all the more for that.

When my wife and son came into the hall, I had organised my work in my mind. The military preparations we would need to make could be delayed until after Christmas. King Edward's ambitions could wait, for there was little we could do until the days began to become longer.

I had another child due to be born. I doubted that the bairn would be born on Christmas Day as Hamo had been, and so unless the child was born on a saint's day, we would not remember their birth date.

Sarah brought in the porridge and Mary began to feed Hamo.

She saw me studying her and smiled. "What goes on in that mind of yours, husband?"

"I wondered when the next child will be born."

"I do not think it will be soon, for Mags said that the baby is not yet low enough." She frowned. "You are not planning on leaving again?"

I heard the fear in her voice, and I shook my head. "No, my love, but there are tasks that I need to undertake. We need to cull the wild animals and harvest the woods. If you say that the child will not be born in the next days, then we shall complete that task first, for the rest only need me to be close to the hall."

She looked relieved. "Good." She nodded to Hamo who was trying to feed himself, somewhat unsuccessfully, with a spoon. More of the porridge was on the table than in his mouth but he was trying. "Your son has missed you and when the new child is born, he will need you to lavish attention upon him."

"And I will do so."

We had spoken at length of my responsibilities and I took them seriously. As I had finished my porridge, I sat next to Hamo and Sarah and tried to show him how to use the spoon properly. It was then I realised that he was making a game of it. He enjoyed spreading the oatmeal on the table. I learned a lesson there. Children liked to play!

I knew just how much food he had spread on me when I left the hall to speak with Alan. The dogs followed me to lick the lumps of porridge from my breeks. Alan and his wife, along with their children, lived a mile or so from the hall but I enjoyed the walk over the frosty fields.

Alan went with me to the woods. "I intended to walk the trails today, Captain. It has been some weeks since I have done so. The rut should be over by now and I can see if any of the stags were hurt. If not, I know which one is the oldest. There are a couple of females who no longer produce young and we can cull those too."

"Wild boar?"

He shook his head. "The herd is not yet built up enough for us to hunt, but from what my wife and sons told me, there are too many rabbits. I thought to set snares and traps to thin them out. It will make for a healthier stock."

"And wood pigeon?"

"There are always too many of those. It will be good practice for the younger archers. Taking a pigeon in flight makes for a better archer."

Once I was satisfied, I headed for John of Nottingham's farm. Now that he was no longer going to war, I needed to know what he had planned for himself.

He was already up and working, one-handed, with his sons. Using billhooks, he was showing them how to make the hawthorn, which grew along the side of his fields, into a barrier and a windbreak.

"Morning, Captain. A fine crisp day, eh?"

"It is. Are you pleased that your father is home, boys?"

John, son of John, was more than a boy. He was a young man and I saw that he had been practising with the bow, for already his chest was growing. "Aye, Captain, and now that he no longer goes to war, I shall have his best bow."

His father snorted. "When you can draw to the full, but that will not be yet!"

I smiled, for this would be the encouragement that young John would need. I had been but little older when I had first served. I remembered being relegated to holding horses and disliking it! "I need to speak with your father. Can you work unattended?"

"Aye, Captain, for he has shown us what to do."

We walked over to the pond, which kept a few fish. It was

another source of food for John and his family. We had a much larger fishpond and that served not only the hall but the village in times of need.

"Have you thought what it is you wish, John?"

He nodded. "I cannot be an archer and I am content with the farm, and the money you paid me was useful. I would not take charity, but John, my son, is a fair archer."

"And you would have me take him on?"

"Aye, Captain."

"What say you we give him a trial of a month and pay him a penny a day? It will be a way to introduce him to the life of an archer and to tell if he likes it. I know that he has practised, but you and I know that our practice is harder and can often break a man."

"He will not break, Captain, but it is a fair offer. We will speak this day and I will send him to you on the morrow to give an answer one way or another."

I left. John could always do as I had done and go on the road to seek an employer. Often that meant greater pay, but then again, that usually meant greater risk. I had made the offer and now it was up to the son.

I wondered where the day had gone, for by the time I returned to my hall, it was late afternoon. A visit to Father Paul had meant passing through the village when everyone wished to speak with me. I knew why. The attack by the Welsh was still a raw wound.

My wife gave me a wry smile. "And where have you been all this long day?"

"I forget my responsibilities, but I am yours now. In three days, we hunt, but other than that I can amuse Hamo and see to your every need!"

"I was not chastising you, for I think you need to sit and enjoy this hall. We have spent much of your gold making it comfortable, and yet you barely sit in it!"

I looked around and heeded her advice.

I felt guilty as for the next two days, I did nothing except to play with Hamo, speak with Mary and eat. It helped that it poured down with rain for a day and a half, and I wondered if the hunt would go ahead. When on the day we were due to hunt the sun shone, albeit weakly, I took it as a sign that we were meant to hunt.

The hunting would take place over three or four days, but I would not be there for the whole time. It was important, as I was the landowner, that I was seen to begin the hunt.

I had sent a messenger to Baron Mortimer to inform him that I intended to hunt. He could have objected or demanded the game for himself, but Yarpole's land was a tiny portion of that available to the baron.

The first thing we did was to set snares where Alan had identified the presence of rabbits. We had not culled them for a couple of years, and this would make for fatter bunnies in the future. Setting the snares allowed us to find the game trails and that, in turn, enabled us to work out where to hunt.

Alan was the master hunter and while all of us knew how to hunt, we listened to him and his advice. The boys would be used as beaters and the rest of us left the wood to walk all the way around to where the young men would drive the herd. The beaters would be upwind. John, son of John, led the beaters. This would be the last time that he did so, for he had agreed to a trial as an archer and that would begin the day after the hunt. He had a horn, and when Alan sounded his horn, John would use his to let us know that they were beginning their beat.

As we waited with hunting arrows nocked and more ready, Alan gave us our instructions. "Old Seven Spikes was hurt in the rut. He is still game, but he cannot move as quickly, and next year he might well die in combat. It is better that we take him now so that it will be the young bucks who fight for the herd. Three older females have not given birth for a year or two. Do not kill any with young. Seven Spikes will be at the fore with the other males. They do not normally congregate together, but when the beaters come, then their natural instinct will be to herd together."

Stephen was with us and held a spear as well as three hunting javelins. "You are saying that we only take the stag and three older females? That does not sound a lot!"

Alan smiled as he explained. "We want a strong herd. Wolves are rare, but if they come, then a strong herd will not lose any young to them. We may end up hunting more than four animals. That depends upon fate. Are we ready?"

He was looking at me and I said, "Aye. Spread yourselves out. Stephen, stand by me!"

We were ten paces apart and I had a large chestnut tree close by, which I could hide behind if I needed to. Alan's horn sounded, followed a few moments later by John's. The beaters were more than a mile away, but we heard them as they banged and clanged, shouted, whistled and sounded the horn.

When we heard the noise of terrified animals ploughing through the undergrowth, then we knew they were close. This was like the night attack at the castle. The difference was that a deer could keep running even when mortally struck. It was why I had all of my archers.

When I smelled the animals and the crashing drew closer, I began to pull back on my bow. The first deer I saw was the new male. The new stag led the herd. He saw the line of men and aimed for one of the gaps between hunters. As soon as he did, we knew that the herd would follow, and we would allow the gap to be bigger so that none of us were risked.

Two other stags hurtled past and then I saw Seven Spikes, well known by the seven points in his antlers and the fact that he had a white blaze on his head. He was labouring, his wound hurting him. I drew and released. Alan and Will Yew Tree were the closest to me and they released too. Even though we all hit him, no strike was mortal, and they merely enraged him. Seven Spikes had led the herd for many years and his instinct was to defend. He came directly for me. Even as I drew and nocked another arrow, I knew that I would not be able to release it in time, and then Stephen hurled not the javelins but the broad-headed spear. It struck the animal in the chest and the speed of the beast, allied to the power of the throw, drove it deep within the stag. As it stumbled, I sent my arrow at a range of just five paces into the eye of the stag. He crumpled at my feet. And then the herd was upon us.

The females with young were not harmed. Most of the young males were also left alone, but two young males with the beginnings of antlers chose to attack us and they were both hit by eight arrows and died. The three old females lumbered along at the rear. None of them were moving well and it was a mercy when we slew them. There was silence except for the panting of the beaters as they ran up to view the kill.

I turned to Stephen. "Thank you, my friend."

He nodded. "I have never hunted before. I think that fighting the Welsh is a safer occupation!"

We all laughed, and David the Welshman said, "You have it right there, Englishman!"

We spent the rest of the afternoon gutting the animals. The heart, liver and kidneys would all be taken back to eat, but the guts and intestines were left for the animals of the woods. We hacked down some saplings with which to take the animals back.

As we headed towards the manor, I said, "The young archers and the boys can come with Alan tomorrow and thin out the pigeons. The archers can empty the snares and hunt hares."

It was all practice for war, and in addition we would all eat better for it. The animals would be hung for a month or more so that we could cook them and preserve them in time for the short days of winter. Our life was measured by such events.

When we reached the hall, our work did not cease. The animals were skinned and the offal removed. We gave it to Sarah, for she would make us a hunter's feast. We sent the boys to fetch mushrooms, wild greens and herbs to go with it. The blood we collected from the dead animals would, with wine and beer, enrich the stew. Even as we were skinning Seven Spikes, I was salivating.

Mary and Hamo came into the yard as we were attaching the hooks to hang the carcasses in the meat larder. My young son hid behind his mother's leg. It made me smile. My father had made me help him skin and gut animals from the age of three. I would do the same with Hamo.

The feast was for the hunters and the beaters. The young boys who joined us in the warrior hall when we ate were as pleased to be invited to dine as they were to partake in the food. This would be the beginning of their journey to becoming warriors. For that reason, I stayed until they had all eaten and were replete. It meant it was late when I entered my hall and Alice met me at the door.

"Captain, Anne the midwife is summoned. Mistress Mary's time has come. Her waters…"

I nodded. "Where is Hamo?"

"He is asleep."

I nodded again. "And you are needed. I will lie with my son. Tell my wife…"

Alice smiled. "She knows, Captain. She knows."

It was a week into December and that meant the child had come a few days early. I did not know if that was a good thing or signified a problem. I stroked my sleeping son's hair. He looked so peaceful and I wondered if a brother or sister might change his life. I had been an only child. I had often thought it might have been good to have someone else in the house but my father. He rarely spoke to me and it made me wary of people. My children would have no such problem, for the house was filled with noise and laughter.

I must have fallen asleep because Mags woke me and whispered, "You have a daughter, Captain. She is healthy." She nodded towards Hamo. "He will sleep now. You can come; Mistress Mary would like you to hold the child."

With the bluest eyes I had ever seen, my daughter enchanted me as soon as she opened them and stared up at me.

"I hope you are not disappointed, my husband."

"How could I be? She is beautiful. Do you have a name?"

"You could name her?"

"I am not good at such things. You name her."

"Margaret; it was my mother's name."

I saw Mags beam, for she was a Margaret too.

"Then Margaret it is." Sarah put my daughter, swaddled and cosy, into my arms. I was happy.

Chapter 13

Christmas passed and the snow came. We put old furs by the door to keep out the draughts and burned the wood we had harvested. The hunt had given the whole village plenty of food and unlike some villages, none of my people starved. No one died and that was rare, for normally, winter saw the old wither and waste, but no one did, and that caused great celebration as February drew to an end and we were able to believe that we had all survived. Father Paul spoke of God rewarding us and we all smiled. I knew that no matter what part God had to play, the whole of Yarpole and Luston had worked hard, and we had enjoyed a better winter than we might have hoped when the Welsh had raided us.

I was summoned to Wigmore in April. I had been expecting the summons and I resigned myself to spending the summer away from my family, fighting for the king.

Baron Mortimer, however, now looking old and frail, had good news for me. "King Edward is coming north, Warbow. He will be here in July. First, he will begin the building of an abbey at Nantwich and then he will inspect the work on the castle at Flint. He is less than happy with the lack of progress that has been made. You and your archers will be needed at Flint on 15 July, St Swithun's Day."

I smiled. "Then I hope the day is dry, my lord, or the king will be even unhappier."

I left Wigmore in a good mood. I had an extra two months or more at home. It also meant that I had more archers to take. John and Edward, John of Nottingham's sons, had both become archers. John would be fully paid as an archer as he had inherited his father's skill. Edward would fetch and carry arrows as well as holding the reins of the horses, but he had shown great promise. He would be paid a penny a day. Ralph, son of Jack, was also a good archer and he would come with us.

When I told my men that we had another two months at home, it did not make them lazy. If anything, knowing that we would go to war in high summer made them work even harder.

Thanks to our success, we had horses and that was rare, for I had the only company of archers who rode to war. Stephen had trained them all to use the sword and, with the swords we had taken from the Welsh, my men were better armed than any other archer.

I also paid for them to wear my livery. I had no coat of arms, but I had paid for tunics that reflected me and my skills. They were half dark green and half light green. Along with the green hose they wore, they not only looked smart and could be clearly identified as my men, but the greens also helped to disguise them a little. Additionally, we had taken to dying our goose feathers green. Every archer had a slightly different arrangement so that while they were all, generally, green, there were variations. My arrows were the exception. My goose feathers were all exclusively dark green.

When we left, we were all better warriors, and that included me. Along with the sword skills that Stephen had given us, some of us could even use a shield, although I hoped that they would never need to.

There were many tears as we left and that was only right. It was not only the families who were upset. All of the village knew and respected every single archer. It was their communal family who were leaving and whilst the villagers might not be in any danger from the Welsh, they would rather that the archers of Yarpole defended their homes.

I rode with Stephen at the head of my men. I had been persuaded to wear a helmet, although the attempts of my wife and Stephen to get me to wear mail had failed. My padded gambeson and metal studded brigandine would have to suffice. I took Lion and Eleanor. As we had half a dozen boys to act as horse holders, I was happy that Lion would be well looked after. Edward had shown that he had some skill with horses, and I had learned long ago to use whatever skills men had.

The camp outside Chester was not large. There were no more than three thousand men and that was not enough to invade Wales, but it was the start of the muster. As soon as we arrived, the Earl of Warwick sent us straight to Flint. King Edward intended to sail directly there, and so he needed his best archers, my men.

Disappointingly, the builders had not made as much progress over the winter as we might have hoped. I think that King Edward expected to see the many stones in place, but the low walls that had been mortared would not have stopped Hamo! The outline of the central part of the castle could now be seen and seemed to be part of the rock that rose above the river. There were now, however, many more workers.

Jack of Lincoln organised the camp while I rode with David the Welshman and Stephen of Frankton towards Dyserth. There were still a couple of hours of daylight left and I wished to ride to St Asaph. The bishop of St Asaph was friendly towards the English, partly due to the generosity of King Henry, who had been a benefactor of the cathedral town. Anian de Schonau had been bishop for eight years or more and he was a devout man. Although he did not know me, he had heard my name and I was invited into his hall.

"It is good that King Edward builds a castle on the river. It will give the people a sanctuary in times of trouble."

"My lord, are you troubled by Prince Llywelyn and his men?"

"Not troubled, Captain, for Prince Llywelyn does not worry about the Church. He is not a godless man, but he is not devout!"

"Have you seen him of late?"

"He came in the spring to speak with me on his way to Anglesey." He lowered his voice, although we were alone in the room. "He left men in Rhuddlan and that town is now fortified."

Rhuddlan was just a couple of miles from St Asaph and there had been neither soldiers nor any adequate defences when we had left last winter.

"Thank you, Bishop Anian. I will tell the king of your kindness."

The king arrived by ship late the next day and I had to hide my smile as he stormed around the castle site. I had seen his temper before and knew that it was like a wild storm. You could not fight it and the rage would have to be endured. The Earl of Warwick was with him and he did not escape his wrath. I was not close to him as he had other lords with him, but as he strode towards what would be the keep of the castle, eventually, he shouted over his shoulder, "Warbow!"

The lords made a path for me. They were pleased to have a barrier between them and the king's temper. "The delay in building fortifications is intolerable, Warbow." We had reached the small wall that afforded a good footing and he turned to face the Clwyd. The road that we had used in winter was now invisible, for the trees were laden with foliage. "That road, whence does it lead?"

I pointed north-west. "The coast is twelve miles in that direction. The ruins of Dyserth are close by." I pointed west. "There is no road in that direction, but it is the direct route to the Clwyd Valley and in that direction," I turned and pointed southwest, "Rhuthun."

He rubbed his beard and nodded. "I knew your local knowledge would aid us. And the river, this Clwyd, we can navigate it?"

"Aye, King Edward. There the river can be sailed as far as the old Welsh fort of Twthill."

"And yet my father did not build a castle there!"

I said nothing, for it did not do to criticise King Henry.

"Then, when my army has arrived, we head in that direction and establish another castle on the Clwyd. We will establish a line of defences along that valley. Llywelyn can have his mountain fastness! I do not want that." He turned. "Warwick, I want the land on both sides of the road clearing. I want neither tree nor vegetation within four hundred feet of the road. The timber can be used in the construction of my castles. When I bring my army, I do not want to lose a single man to ambush! That is where the Welsh excel. I want no place for them to hide, so that they have to fight a battle with me. When they lose then

Wales will be my vassal once more! See to it! I return to Chester to summon my army."

He turned on his heel and headed down to the ship, which waited for him on the river. The lords were stunned into silence. I watched as King Edward walked through sucking mud to board the small flat-bottomed boat, which ferried him across the river. He was not afraid to get dirty!

The earl broke free from the trance when King Edward stepped into the boat. "How far is it, Warbow? To the coast, I mean."

"Sixteen miles or so, my lord." I saw his face fall. "But the woods and vegetation do not extend that far. There are just a few miles to clear."

He nodded. "Then if your archers will act as guards, we will get our soldiers to hack down the trees."

That began a month of what we considered an easy duty. The four hundred men who were assigned to hew down the trees were all soldiers. Even had the Welsh wished to cause mischief, it would have been hard for them. However, we quickly developed a method that guaranteed no interference with the wood clearing. We formed a line of archers who waited in the uncut wood just four hundred paces from the tree felling. With our new archers and boys, we had a line of more than thirty pairs of eyes and ears.

Three days after the trees began to fall, we spied the Welsh as they came down the trails we had identified as their likely paths. In the three days since the work had started, we had learned how to read the land. We could stand as still as a deer sniffing the air and blend into it. King Edward was paying the men, and for that, they were prepared to stand for as long as it took.

Tom spotted the Welshmen first and he threw a small green acorn at me. I turned and he pointed down the trail. There were Welshmen two hundred paces from us, heading down the path. They had bows but their arrows were not nocked. I picked up a pebble and threw it at Jack. The message was repeated along the line, and I nocked an arrow. There were twelve of us close enough to this path and that would have to be enough to deter them. My arrow would be the signal for the others to release theirs.

I waited until the leading Welsh archer was just one hundred paces from us. Any closer and they might have seen us. The arrow slammed into his chest, the green-dyed goose feathers almost burying themselves in his body. Eleven other arrows followed. One Welshman managed to get an arrow away and it struck the tree close to my head. Then they fled. I took the hunting horn I had taken with me and blew two blasts upon it. That was the signal for my archers to follow the sound.

We found six dead or dying Welshmen. From the blood trails, they had taken their wounded with them. We discovered one more body, a mile down the path that climbed up towards the high ground. We stopped and returned to the workings.

That night we reported to the Earl of Warwick. He was not alarmed by the attack, in fact, we had all expected it, but it was a spur to prick the tree fellers to work even harder.

The next two days saw similar attempts to stop the work, but they failed. There were many paths through the trees, but we had them all covered. We gained arrows, bows and strings as well as wickedly sharp knives and even a few coins. It was the easiest work my archers had ever had.

King Edward returned in the middle of August. More and more soldiers had arrived in the month he had been away, and we now had more than ten thousand men. The widened roadway was almost finished, and the king actually smiled. The castle now looked like a castle. The ramps and cranes to enable the towers and walls to be built were in place, and wheelbarrows filled with stones and mortar trundled up them.

The king held a council of war with his leaders. I was not invited but I did not expect to be. However, Sir John Malton arrived with his small retinue and he sought me out so that I learned more than I might have expected.

I had known Sir John since he had been Lord Edward's squire and he had been with me when I had travelled to meet the Mongol khan. He looked genuinely pleased to see me and after we had exchanged news about our families, I asked him what he knew of the campaign.

He pointed south and west. "Edmund, the king's brother, has taken all of the land in the south as far as Aberystwyth. There he begins to build a castle, which will secure the mouth of that river. Prince Llywelyn has withdrawn all of his men and placed them here, to the north. This is where the battle will be fought and won!"

As with all such wars, the men who would do the actual fighting found out what they were to do last! It was Sir John who informed me that my archers were to scout out the road to Rhuddlan. King Edward had decided to begin his war immediately. It was August and the days were long. I did not know it then, but he had a clever plan, though he told no one, for he wanted the surprise.

We left before dawn and we took our sumpters with our spare arrows. As it was summer, we did not bother with tents. Edward, son of John of Nottingham, led the boys and horse holders.

We told them to follow after the vanguard, King Edward's household knights.

"Will we not be in trouble if we are too close?"

Will Yew Tree laughed. "Stay far enough to the side and you will be safe enough. Now that the way has been cleared, we have the widest road I have ever seen!"

In truth, it was a strange feeling to be riding in such an open area and I felt exposed. Having said that, we made good time to the end of the cleared way. We were just a couple of miles from Dyserth when the vegetation closed in on us, but fortunately much had been cleared when King Henry had tried to build a castle there. We had a clear enough sight of the sides to spot any ambush.

We knew the castle ruins well, for we had used them to keep watch on the Welsh in Rhuddlan and beyond. We reined in and, from the back of my mount, I could see the two miles to the wooden castle that had been thrown up next to the river. Our main army would be moving behind us and we had at least half an hour before they caught up with us. I wanted to study the defences. Before we closed with it, I was able to determine that there were many soldiers there. The fires told me that. But I could also see that there were no town walls to defend.

"Alan, ride back to the king and tell him that they have a wooden castle and many men but no wall. We will ride nearer and have a closer view."

He turned and rode off, not directly towards Rhuddlan but down one of the many streams that fed into the Clwyd. I knew them well. This was the land where I had hunted on foot. The streams were often the easier way to travel, and one who wished to remain hidden had a better chance of doing so.

David followed me but it was I who chose the stream. The folds of the land hid us from the castle and would do so until we were almost upon it. When we reached the Clwyd, I had my men dismount to make an even smaller target. We strung our bows and nocked an arrow each. Leading our horses, we made our way to the old Welsh fort of Twthill. It was two hundred paces from the outer defences of the new castle, but the hill hid us from view.

Leaving most of the men at the foot of the hill, Stephen, David and I made our way to the top. When we neared it, we crawled. There was enough wild, unkempt grass and weed to hide us. Once at the top, we saw that the Welsh were camped not only in the castle but also in the outer bailey, while their ponies were tethered and guarded beyond the walls. They were grazing close to the river. They were so close that we could hear their noise. We kept still and David tapped his ear. He could hear the sentries one hundred and fifty paces from us.

I did not wish to alarm the Welsh and we slipped down the old hill fort.

David said, "I could not hear all the words, but they know that King Edward is at the castle they call 'The Flint'. I do not think they know we are close."

That made sense to me. The Welsh had spies. The river was used by both nations and it was likely that Llywelyn knew King Edward had arrived with his army. What he could not have predicted was that King Edward would act so promptly. In that regard, the king had the chance to catch the Welsh unawares.

At the bottom, I said, "Robin, ride to the king. Ask him if he can send archers here. We can use Twthill to rain arrows into their flanks. The Welsh occupy both the castle and the ground around it." I did not need to elaborate. I knew King Edward had a sharp mind. He would know that the Welsh would not be expecting him.

He mounted his horse and walked it for half a mile before mounting it and galloping off.

"Tether your horses by the river and fetch your bows."

Stephen asked, "What is it that we intend, Captain? Are we not simply scouts?"

"There is no such thing as simply a scout. We are King Edward's archers. Those two hundred and seventy crossbowmen he is paying a fortune may think that they are the elite, but they are wrong. King Edward knows our worth. He will rely on me to use my mind. I plan on securing those ponies for us. It will deprive the Welsh of mobility and, who knows, we may be able to affect the outcome of this attack."

We moved up the slope and I smiled at the struggle enjoyed by Stephen. He had mail and a shield. Although his shield was over his back, he found it hard to climb the slippery, long grass.

Once at the top, I spread my men out and we slowly advanced to the tussocky top of Twthill. We could see the Welsh sentries and were able to move when they were distracted by a moving pony or a shout from one of the camps. That the Welsh did not expect an attack was clear to me, for the men in the camps had their arms stacked. The walls were manned, and I have no doubt the sentries there were vigilant, but they had no idea that our army was so close.

We managed to get to the last ditch on the north side of Twthill. We were above the sentries and the ponies but below the walls of Rhuddlan. The small camps, which were dotted beyond the ditch that surrounded the castle under construction, were occupied by their most deadly weapon, their archers. We could get no closer, but once we heard the sound of combat, we would be within one hundred and fifty paces of the curtain wall and forty-odd paces from the pony guards. We could hear them talking, although only David could understand them.

The horns from the castle walls told us that King Edward was here. Approaching from Dyserth would have given him cover until the last mile or so. At the same time, I heard a shout from one of the pony guards.

"Now!"

I rose and sent an arrow at the Welshman who was pointing beyond me. My men slew the other six pony guards and as I nocked another arrow, I saw what the pony guard had seen – Matthew of Tarporley was leading his forty archers to join us. I pointed to the camp and then turned to send an arrow into it.

Stephen ran to begin to herd the ponies back towards us. It was a brave thing to do as the Welsh in their camp would soon be sending their arrows at us.

We had the advantage that we had strung bows and arrows nocked. Each of us aimed at a Welsh archer. At a range of fewer than one hundred and fifty paces, we would have been embarrassed if we had not struck flesh! We also had the advantage of a ditch. We were able to release and then as we nocked another arrow, move below the top of the ditch so that when the Welsh aimed at the place from which we had sent the arrow, we had moved and their arrow was wasted.

I ducked, nocked and ran. When I rose, I saw that Stephen, his shield pricked by arrows, had started most of the pony herd and they were hurtling towards the river, away from the castle. I sent another arrow at a Welsh sergeant who was trying to rally men to come and shift us. The war arrow struck his arm. Then a horn sounded, and the Welsh archers turned to head back within the walls of the wooden castle.

"Archers! Now is our chance! Close with them!"

We left the safety of the ditch and ran after the Welsh archers. We ran, released, and as we ran again, nocked another arrow. We were closing with the Welsh all the time and sending arrows into unprotected backs. As it was the archers who were running, we knew that no arrows would be coming back in our direction.

The outer curtain wall was a wooden one and unfinished. While there was a gate for the archers to use, there was no gate-house. Tom and Martin, along with John, son of John, were my youngest archers. That meant they were the fittest and, in the case of John, the most eager. I saw a Welsh archer try to close the gate and my arrow not only slammed into his arm but pinned it to the wooden wall. The Welsh could not close the gate while he was pinned and my three youngest archers took advantage and, as the rest of our men knocked archers from the wooden wall, they wrenched open the gate and entered.

I could now hear the battle in the village as the attack began on the rest of Rhuddlan's walls. My arms were burning with the effort of pulling back the bowstring, but I put the pain from my mind. I sent another arrow towards the walls and knocked a spearman from the fighting platform. With the outer gate opened and in our possession, we poured through it. The men on the walls tried to flee across the outer bailey, but the gate to the inner bailey was closing. John, son of John, Tom and Martin were the closest and they sent arrow after arrow into the men who tried to close the gate. The Welsh were defeating themselves, for none wanted to be left outside and were unwilling to sacrifice themselves.

Stephen de Frankton burst through the gate we had used, with the rest of Matthew of Tarporley's archers, and he saw the half-closed inner bailey gate. Holding his shield before him, he ran at the gate. Every Welsh bow and spear that was close enough was aimed at the man at arms. It was my archers, with their green flighted arrows, who protected him. He was not an archer, but he was of our company and we kept his passage clear. A Welsh warrior had almost managed to close the gate when he hurled himself at it and the weight of his armour, weapons and shield, burst it asunder. I joined my three youngest archers, and we were through the gate moments after Stephen.

We were just in time. We all had an arrow nocked and the seven men who were attacking my brave man at arms suddenly found themselves under attack from the machine-like arms of my three youngest archers. I had loosed all of my arrows, and so I dropped my bow and drew my sword. I ran to Stephen's side and as I blocked one axe, which was aimed at his head, with my sword, I drew my bodkin blade and rammed it through the eye of the axeman.

We had broken through to their last line of defence, but we were now vulnerable. The men in the keep had barred the door, sacrificing the hundreds who were in the inner bailey. Their archers on the top began to hit our archers. I had run out of arrows and soon the others would run out too. We had to close with the men stranded in the inner bailey to make it hard for the defenders in the keep to hit us.

As Stephen and I killed the last of his attackers, I shouted, "Jack of Lincoln, take my men and open the main gate for the king!"

"Aye, Captain! Come on, you heard him!"

As they ran off, I saw that Matthew's men had clambered onto the fighting platform, and they began to pick off the Welsh who were close to us.

Stephen was the expert here and he said, "Let us get close to the stairs leading to the keep. Their archers will struggle to hit us there."

I nodded, but we had an awesome task ahead of us as there were twenty or so Welshmen between us and the keep. Most, however, just had spears or short swords. I tucked in behind Stephen's right side so that I had some protection from his shield and mail. Arrows slammed into his shield and I heard an arrow ping off his helmet. Had the arrow been deflected just a little, then I would have been a dead man, but the missile careered off the metal. I was a fair swordsman, but Stephen was as good as any knight I had seen in the Holy Land. I had the easier task as I used my sword to block the spears that were thrust at my invitingly naked head. My sword deflected them, and I rammed my bodkin into any flesh that I saw.

When I heard a roar from my right, then I knew that Jack had succeeded and the gate had been opened. Stephen and I were still in a perilous predicament, but the brotherhood of archery came to my aid. Matthew's men saw that we were surrounded and rallied to hit those who threatened us.

As soon as I realised what they were doing, I said, "Stephen, do not move your feet. Let our archers aid us!"

He nodded. This was an exercise in trust. Good swordsmen know how to fight well by using their feet. We now had to fight and use a slight sway of our bodies. The skill of the archers was ably demonstrated as I blocked one spear and saw a second coming towards my head. I felt the wind from the white fletched

211

arrow as it struck the skull of the man who thought he had me. That appeared to be the turning point, for I heard horses as Otto de Grandson led King Edward's knights to charge into the Welshmen stranded in the inner bailey.

I shouted, "Fetch fire!"

This was a wooden castle, and we need not batter down the gate. We could set fire to it. The Welsh camps beyond the outer bailey still had campfires burning and, while Stephen and I finished off those around us, some of the Cheshire archers fetched burning bands, and others, kindling.

The only Welshmen left in the inner bailey were the dead, so we ran to the gate of the keep and, after piling the kindling around the stairs, set light to it. As I had expected, they had a sally port, which led down to the river, and once flames began to lick up the sides of the keep, I heard a shout from the walls as men began to race towards the river.

Had we had more arrows, then the slaughter would have been greater, but the heart of the Welsh army was broken that day. They lost knights, but even more disastrously for them, they lost archers. As the newly built walls began to burn, my men collected the arrows both broken and whole and then, as we heard screams from within the walls as those on the upper floors burned, they searched the dead. We moved away from the searing heat of the fire as bodies began to fall from the top. The Welsh had lost the Clwyd Valley and in one fell swoop, Prince Llywelyn had lost any advantage he might have had.

Chapter 14

The archers all used the Welsh camp beyond the curtain wall. Our boys arrived with our horses and we chose the better tents. We found plenty of food and we ate well. We gathered the ponies and divided them equitably between ourselves.

Camping there meant we avoided the rape and drunken pillaging of Rhuddlan. Bishop Anian was so angered that he wrote to the Archbishop of Canterbury to complain. I do not think King Edward was in the slightest bit concerned. The Welsh were beaten enemies. Had their prince paid homage, then there would have been no war.

King Edward sent for me two days later. He and his knights had scoured the land as far as the Conwy River and he was in good humour when he returned. "Warbow, you did well again! I take it you reaped a reward from the dead?"

"Yes, Your Majesty."

"Good. We will be staying here until work can be started on a better castle than this one erected by the Welsh, but you and your men are needed for another task."

"Another task, King Edward?"

"You will accompany Lord Otto de Grandson and Sir John de Vesci and their men. They will join you at Deganwy. All will be explained." He smiled. "Do not worry, for the work is well suited to you and your men!"

With that, we were dismissed. I was intrigued, but as we rode the sixteen miles to the coast, David of Wales gave me an explanation. "He is going for Môn mam Cymru, the place you call Anglesey. In Welsh, it means the mother of Wales and is well named, for all of the wheat and cereal that provides bread for the Welsh people is grown there. It is harvest time and the fields are full."

Stephen asked, "Will the Welsh not dispute it?"

David gave a sardonic laugh. "Have you not yet realised, de Frankton, that we Welsh do not build castles or if we do, then a strong wind can blow them over? Môn mam Cymru is flat and open. There are no forests where we can be ambushed. Only at the far tip is there a mountain and if the Welsh retreat there then they can be left, for they will starve to death."

David proved to be correct in every detail. When we reached the ruined fortifications at Deganwy, we found ships of the Cinque Ports waiting for us at the jetty that King Henry had built and the Welsh had, conveniently, left in place.

Lord Otto was already loading the ships. He was pleased to see us. "Good, you have horses and ponies. There are three ships over there for you to use. You will land on the island first and ensure that we can land unchallenged. We will ferry our army across. The captains assure me that the voyage will take just a few hours. There is a small port where he will land you. Do not ask me to pronounce it. When I try, I end up spitting at everyone. Your men will hold the port until we bring more

214

substantial numbers to your aid. Once we have all landed, we drive across the island, eliminating all the opposition and harvesting their grain. We have one hundred and fifty scythes aboard one ship just for that purpose!"

I was stunned, for this was planning on an unprecedented scale. King Edward must have had this planned before we left Flint, perhaps when he was still in Windsor! I thought I knew just how clever he was, but I did not know the half of it.

Loading the boats was easier than I had expected. The horses were walked from the jetty over crudely nailed planks. The voyage was not across the open sea but the short six-mile crossing to the island.

The captain of the boat that would take my men was a Kentish man, and his ruddy complexion told its own story. He smiled. "We will soon have you ashore, Captain. We will land at a place they call Porth y Wygyr." He shrugged. "Funny sort of name."

David said, "It means port of the Vikings. They used to land there and raid the island."

The captain seemed happy to have garnered that information. "Well that explains much. If you would have your riders keep hold of the bridles on their horses when we sail. I believe that singing can soothe them. We want to turn around quickly, and so when you have taken the village, we shall get your horses off."

"You seem remarkably sanguine about this, Captain."

He smiled. "If I thought there was danger, then I might be worried, but I know there aren't any warriors there. I have heard of you, Captain Warbow. I remember when you scoured the Weald of the rebels. The archers of the Weald have a good reputation, but they still speak of you as the master. We shall be all right! Now be ready. Cast off forrard! Hoist the mainsail! Cast off aft!"

I held on to the reins of Eleanor. I had left Lion with Sir John Malton at Rhuddlan. I knew that he would be cared for. I had seen horses become so distraught with the experience of being at sea that they had kicked holes in the sides of the ship. Eleanor was quieter and she had been at sea before.

Being below the level of the gunwale meant I could see little of the island, but Snowdon, Wyddfa to the Welsh, towered above us to the east. It would be to that holiest of Welsh mountains that the Welsh would be gathered to lick their wounds and plan for the war. I only knew we were close to the port when the Captain ordered the sail reefed and boys were sent to prepare to jump ashore and tie us up.

The other ship would follow us. I saw, at that moment, the mistake we had made. If we were opposed, we could not do anything because every one of my archers was holding a horse by the bridle. Luckily, there was no opposition. We bumped next to the jetty and the wooden planks were put into place.

I was the captain and I led Eleanor to the jetty first. She was a placid horse and she obeyed me. That set the mood for the others and they dutifully followed us ashore. I nocked an arrow but there was no sign of a Welshman, let alone a weapon. My men each nocked an arrow, and I waved an arm to lead them towards the road that led from Porth y Wygyr.

When we reached the edge of the village, we waited. It was eerie, for there was no one to be seen. It was a peaceful summer's morning and sea birds swooped down to the sea. I kept my eyes pointing inland to look out for danger. If this had been England, then someone would have sought the help of the local landowner and he and his men would be coming to dispute our landing. There was nothing.

Richard of Culcheth joined me. "We have all landed, Captain, and the ships are heading back to Deganwy."

"Have the boys search the houses for food and treasure. The ships with the men at arms and knights will be along shortly. We wait!"

Stephen de Frankton said, "Where are the Welsh? If this is the mother of Wales, then surely they will defend it?"

David the Welshman dismounted to adjust his girth. He shook his head. "I heard a story... it may be like the stories of dragons, but when the Romans came, it is said, the Druids and the Welsh who lived here taunted their enemies and dared them to risk the straits. The story is that the Romans made their horses enter the straits and they swam across. That was the first great slaughter of the Welsh. I fear, Stephen de Frankton, that we set too much store by the power of this island. We expect it to be safe and therefore need no defence!"

Even though we had landed unopposed, I did not relax our vigilance. The farmers fled at our approach, which was so rapid that we found food and ale in the farms as well as oats for the horses. The boys fetched the food they had found in the houses and my archers managed to discover where the Welsh had buried their treasure. We would all share in it.

I was relieved when Alan shouted that he could see the ships returning. The two that had brought us were joined by another seven and I knew that we had a bridgehead on the island. With archers and knights, we could hold the island once we had conquered it.

Lord Otto landed first, and he sent us to ride as far as we could and then return. I knew why he did so. We were archers and if we found an enemy, we could escape and report it. We were expendable. His men at arms and knights were not!

We reached Llangefni, which David the Welshman told me was an important place, in the centre of the island. Even though there were fewer than thirty of us, we encountered no opposition. I had yet to see a sword or a spear. We returned to Porth y Wygyr and reached it before dark.

My news brought a huge smile from Otto de Grandson. He put his huge mitt around my shoulder. "We will take this island in days. I have one hundred and fifty men come to take the entire harvest. We shall be well fed, and the Welsh will starve! I like the way King Edward wages war. We are well fed, well paid, and the men we fight are nothing!"

It did not prove quite as easy as Lord Otto predicted. Although there were few men on the island and no places that would provide a defensive obstacle, we had to fight, and the first place that they defended was the old royal palace at Aberffraw, in the west of the island. Although more of a hunting palace, the warriors and lords who had fled when we had arrived sought refuge there.

King Edward's planning astounded me, for even while we were in the west of the island, the eastern corner, where we had evicted the farmers when we arrived, was having their wheat harvested and taken by the ships from the Cinque Ports back to Chester. King Edward was fighting the Welsh by withholding food. The effects would not be seen until the depths of winter, but they were as inevitable as a January freeze.

As captain of the archers, I was summoned with Sir John Vesci to view the walls of Aberffraw. "My men have examined the ditch. It is not well maintained but it will be an obstacle. Can you burn the wooden walls with fire arrows, Warbow?"

I shook my head. "It would take a couple of days to make the number we would require, and we have too few archers. You wish a quick victory?" He nodded. "My men can clear the walls for an assault by your men." I pointed to the gate. "The wood of that gate does not look new."

Lord Otto said, "You mean make a ram? That would work, and we could tear down the walls of some of those fishermen's houses and make them into bridges for the ditches. Get your men into position, Warbow, and we will hew a tree."

I had no intention of standing my men where the defenders could rain arrows upon us. I sent the boys to fetch the hurdles that were used to gather the sheep. By putting three together and binding them, they made an effective man-sized shield that could be propped before us. The Welsh knew what we were doing, and they tried to disrupt our work as we advanced the hurdle shields into position. They failed and wasted arrows.

We were ready when Lord Otto's squire, protected by his own shield, ran to us. "Lord Otto is ready."

"Tell him he can move his men forward. Archers, let us show these Welsh that we are now the masters of the bow!"

I nocked an arrow and then stepped to the side of the shield. I had identified the man I would hit when the Welsh had attempted to stop us closing with them. We were duelling with their archers. The men at arms and knights could be dealt with by Lord Otto.

I had the advantage that although the archer on the gate-house might be expecting me to aim at him, he did not know from which side of the shield I would emerge. I knew exactly where he stood, protected by the wooden wall, and I stepped out and released within moments. The archer had those moments only to aim and draw. Such are the margins between life and death. My arrow slammed into his head and threw him from the gate.

I stepped back behind the shield and nocked another arrow. I was now gambling, but the odds were increasingly in our favour as our arrows hit the archers on the walls. The ones who saw where we emerged, died, and when the knights and men at arms moved forward, then they became the more obvious target.

When I stepped out with my second arrow, I had to scan along the wall to find an archer. As I saw a bow move around to aim at me, I released and stepped back behind the wooden hurdle. The Welsh arrow smacked into the hawthorn. I gambled that the archer would expect me to step out of the other side of the hurdle. I stepped out the same side and released. This time I watched, for I saw that the arrow was still being drawn, and I would have time to step back. My arrow hit the hand holding the bow and careered into his head. He tumbled from the wall.

I saw the Welsh archers had been thinned by my men. The wrecked houses were now bridging the ditch and I saw men at arms carrying the tree to be used as a ram.

I nocked another arrow and, seeing neither archer nor crossbow, sent it into the shoulder of a man about to hurl a spear. As I was nocking another arrow, I saw a crossbow rise from behind the wall, but William of Matlac's arrow threw him from the wall.

Our concentration on the gatehouse had reaped its reward. As the Welsh sent more archers from other parts of the walls, they were hit by my men before they could identify where we were.

As the mighty tree slammed into the gate, I heard an ominous crack. I sent an arrow to strike the shield of a Welsh knight exhorting his men to greater efforts. It struck so hard that he was rocked. He moved behind one of the roof supports for the gatehouse, but Jack of Lincoln was then afforded a better view and his arrow hit him in the side of the head. It was a war arrow, but it hurt him, and the head disappeared.

Then there was a mighty crack and the gate burst open. Dropping the tree, the men at arms drew their swords and, whilst swinging their shields from around their backs, they raced into the king's palace.

We nocked arrows and ran forward. The defenders had to expose themselves when they tried to send arrows or spears at the men at arms and knights who flooded in, and when they did so they were an easy target for my men. Once we were inside the walls, we slung our bows and drew our swords as we ran to winkle out the last of the Welsh defenders.

By the early afternoon, it was all over and the last of the defenders had surrendered. Lord Otto was ruthless. All of the Welsh archers had their drawing fingers removed. We took every weapon and sent the men at arms and archers from the palace, bootless and bleeding. They might get to the mountain fastness that was Wyddfa, but as warriors, they were broken. Only two knights surrendered, and they were sent back to Porth y Wygyr and thence to Chester. They would be ransomed.

We joined the others in ransacking the palace. The knights did not bother but my men and I were experts, and we knew where to look. By the time darkness had fallen, we had taken everything of value, and we had found some sumpters so that we could take back our treasures.

Lord Otto wasted no time. Anglesey is not a big island. It is twenty-two miles from east to west and eighteen miles from north to south. The last stronghold of the Welsh was the old three-sided Roman fort at Caer Gybi, on the Irish side of the island. We headed there, knowing that it was stone and a ram would not work. We reached it in less than half a day, for we were a mounted chevauchée. The Welsh had manned their walls, but our advance had been so swift that few of the islanders had managed to make the safety of its stone walls. We set fire to the town, and the billowing smoke convinced the defenders to surrender. Some managed to flee in ships from the harbour, but the half dozen boats that left carried fewer than forty warriors.

As we watched them go, Lord Otto turned to David the Welshman. "You are a Welshman – where will they go?"

David shrugged. "Where can they go? Captain Gerald has told me that we hold Aberystwyth and the south. King Edward holds the Conwy. That leaves just the land of the Penrhyn Llŷn, the Llŷn Peninsula."

Lord Otto nodded. "South of here and north of Aberystwyth. Good, then we have the Welsh penned in the mountains. Our job is almost done. We take every animal we can find and when the harvest is in, we return to the mainland. King Edward will need us to take the Welsh prince!"

It did not take us long to empty the island of all the food. There were no soldiers to stop us and the one hundred and fifty men with their scythes worked their way across the island. We guarded wagons laden with wheat as well as barley and oats. The halls of the nobles who had died or fled were burned to the ground and we unearthed the coins buried in their homes. We were amongst the first to leave and we reached the royal camp on the Conwy by the start of September.

We escorted the wagons to King Edward, and I noticed that most of the mounted men had gone. Lion was being cared for by King Edward's men, for John of Malton had been sent home without even drawing a sword. Even as we arrived, I saw more men at arms being paid off. King Edward knew he had won the war and now awaited a formal surrender. That it would come was clear to us all, for men had to have reached Llywelyn from Anglesey. He now had neither money nor food and we had defeated his best warriors.

My men made camp and I wondered what the future held for us. Unlike many of the men, we would not mind being paid off. We had families and homes. It was as I was tending to Lion that I spoke with the king. It was two days after our return and followed the return of John de Vesci.

He deliberately sought me out rather than sending a man to speak with me and that was significant. "Warbow, once again you have done me great service and I am in your debt." I knew then that he had another task for me. I merely nodded. "The war is over; it is just that the Welsh prince is stubborn. You went to him once for me and sought a peaceful end to the conflict. I think he may be more amenable now. I have a specific offer to make to him and you will deliver the ultimatum to him."

"Where will I find him, King Edward? Winter is coming and I cannot spend all winter seeking an elusive prey."

He frowned, for he liked me to acquiesce without argument. "I believe he is in the castle built by Llywelyn the Great, Kaerinarfon, opposite Anglesey. I wish you to go there and ask for his surrender. In return, I will leave him Gwynedd and Anglesey, although he will pay me one thousand marks a year for the privilege of that island."

"And if he refuses your offer?"

"I do not think he will. Rhufoniog and Dyffryn Clwyd will be ruled by his brother and all the rest will be ruled by me!" There was little point in arguing and I nodded. "I have a document for you to speak on my behalf, but the formal negotiations will be at Deganwy. Bishop Anian will attend. You are to bring him there. It goes without saying that he must first disband his armies. You may assure Prince Llywelyn that I guarantee his safety. His brothers, Dafydd and Owain, are my guests. Owain in Carmarthen and Dafydd in Flint. Dafydd will be present when I speak with him."

"And when do I leave?"

"You may wait until the morning if you wish! It is not far to travel. I will furnish you with a pursuivant to accompany you, but you shall negotiate. His presence is merely to identify you as my man!"

A pursuivant was just one level below a herald and wore the king's livery. It was a clever move by the king, for the regalia would help to reassure the prince that there was no treachery involved. Of course, it also meant that we would have to have a couple of servants travelling with us. Such officials rarely travelled alone.

I went to choose my men. I knew that the sooner I completed my task, the sooner we would be paid off and able to return home. That was incentive enough.

Chapter 15

It was obvious that I should take David, and as Tom and Martin had been with me the first time, then they were easy choices. I remembered how well Tom and Martin had worked with John, son of John of Nottingham, and I chose him too. The last archer I would take would be Alan; his hunting skills might be useful.

They all looked up expectantly when I returned. They could see that the camp was emptier. "Do we pack our gear, Captain, and prepare to head back to Yarpole?"

I shook my head. "That day will not be long in coming but the king has asked us to perform one more task."

Jack shook his head and grumbled. "When he needs something dangerous doing, then we are the ones who have to do it."

"Jack," I said mildly, "I am Lord Edward's archer, and he commands me to do anything he chooses. Each of you chose to follow me, for good or for ill."

He looked shamefaced. "Sorry, Captain, but it is annoying that others are rewarded more for doing less."

I laughed, for Jack had his pile of weapons and coins before him. "You do not seem to do too badly out of it,

Jack." They all laughed. "I am sent to find Llywelyn again and this time return with him to face King Edward." They were silent, for they all understood the implications. "David, Tom, Martin, Alan and John, you shall be with me, and we have a pursuivant and, I do not doubt, his servant. We leave on the morrow."

John looked delighted to be chosen while the ones who had been told they would have to stay behind looked slighted, including Jack of Lincoln!

"Where do we look for him, Captain?"

"Kaerinarfon."

David shook his head. "The old name is y gaer yn Arfon, the fortress in Arfon."

"And is it a fortress?" I was curious.

David laughed. "It is a small wooden castle on the banks of the river. Llywelyn the Great thought to build a castle from behind whose walls he could defy England. The dream did not last long."

The king was already up when we walked our horses to his camp. The pursuivant and his servant were speaking with him. I was surprised that the king was up and ready. While we waited, I examined the pursuivant's horse. It was a courser, and his servant had a good horse. I saw that both men had swords strapped to their baldrics.

The king waved for me to enter his tent. "Captain Warbow, this is Godfrey Landvielle and his servant, Walter. Godfrey has written information for Prince Llywelyn, but we would rather you spoke to him. I believe that he will respect a warrior rather than a courtier, and he knows you. He knows that you can be trusted. God speed."

We bowed and left. Godfrey said, "I expect you anticipated some courtier who did not know one end of a sword from another." I smiled, for it was as though he was reading my mind. "I was a knight, but a fall from a horse at the Battle of Lewes means that I cannot grip with my left hand. I chose to serve King Edward this way. Walter here was my squire, and he is handy with a weapon, but I believe that if we have to resort to force of arms, then we have failed. You know this place we seek?"

I nodded. "We will save time if we use the ferry across the Conwy, and then it is just sixteen or so miles along the coast."

We mounted and I saw that Godfrey, despite the use of only one hand, managed to mount easier than some men who had two. "I am surprised that Prince Llywelyn risks being this close to our army!" he said.

David spoke. "It is simple enough for him to disappear south to the Llŷn Peninsula or lose himself in Wyddfa. This way he can take advantage of any slip that the king might make."

Godfrey laughed as we headed towards the flat-bottomed ferry, which would take us from the land we had taken to the land held by our foe. "I do not think King Edward is the man to make such obvious errors!"

Once on the other side, I had Tom ride fifty paces ahead of us and Martin fifty paces behind. My bow was in a case and I did not think that I would need it. There might be places where we would be in danger, but they would be beyond Llanfairfechan. This would be about my ability to persuade the prince that his life was safe. I did not trust Dafydd. He was a treacherous man but since we had begun this war, he had stayed close to King Edward and he had been rewarded with two Welsh cantrefs. I knew he wanted more, but he now had his own fiefdom.

I spoke of these matters to Godfrey as we rode the narrow piece of land between the sea and the scree-covered cliffs that bordered it. "I think that the two cantrefs will not be enough for Dafydd. He seems more ambitious than that!" I was still suspicious of Dafydd.

Godfrey showed me that he was a clever man who was close to the king. His words were those of a man near to the heart of the politics. "Oh, he is. I have spent these last months with him and Gruffydd ap Gwenwynwyn. You are right, but King Edward has been astute. The third brother, Owain, is to be given the Cantref of Llŷn. That is part of Llywelyn's land. Gruffydd ap Gwenwynwyn has been the best advised but his wife and his son are the two clever ones. He has given up his claims for Powys in return for land in the Marches. The foolish knight still seems to be a thrall of Dafydd, but Lady Hawise has negotiated with the king."

That fitted in with my understanding of the nature of the man. I put all the brothers into place in my head and then saw the whole picture. King Edward was giving them land and surrounding them with Marcher lords. They were being placed in a prison! Would Llywelyn agree to give up half of his country?

Once we had passed Llanfairfechan, we kept a good watch, although the brightly coloured pursuivant should have told even the most rustic of Welshmen that we were not here for war. We met the first Welsh warriors when we neared Bangor. There was a defensive wall around the town, but we were passing more than half a mile from the port. Riders left Bangor to speak with us. A knight, his squire and ten men at arms surrounded us. I knew that John was nervous, for he kept looking around. His horse became fidgety too, for animals are very sensitive to the mood of their rider.

"John, all is well. These men just wish to discover our intentions."

The knight took off his helmet. "I am Madog ap Owain ap Fychan, and I guard Bangor. What brings a pursuivant and archers here? Do you wish to take ship somewhere?"

He looked at Godfrey and seemed surprised when I spoke. "I am Captain Warbow and I command the king's archers. We have a message to take to your prince."

He nodded. "Ah, I wondered how long it would take. We saw your ships as they sailed Môn mam Cymru, laden with our wheat. You have a clever king. He uses starvation to defeat us."

I said nothing, for the king's action would save many men from a violent death. If the prince agreed to the peace plan, then the Welsh would be fed... at a cost.

"My men and I will escort you, for it would not do to have some of the hotheads decide to punish you for your victories."

As we neared the Welsh town of Kaerinarfon, it was clear how few men the prince had. It was an armed camp that surrounded the castle, but King Edward had already released more Englishmen than Welshmen remained to fight us.

The stares and even some of the growled comments were reserved for Godfrey. Now I saw why King Edward had chosen him. He had been a warrior and he was not worried by the glares and remarks.

My men and Walter had to stay in the outer bailey with their horses, but Godfrey and I were allowed to keep our swords and were taken inside the wooden keep. It was there I saw Maredudd ap Iago. His face now had a long scar running from his eye to his chin. It was red and angry. He had fought in the war. His eyes narrowed and his hand went to his sword.

Prince Llywelyn snapped something in Welsh and Lord Maredudd stormed out. The prince shook his head. "Archer, you seem to bring out the worst in my men. Is that why King Edward sends you?"

I said, "No, Prince, it is because he thinks you will trust the words that I speak, for I am an honest warrior and not a noble. I do not lie."

He nodded. "And if I had come with you to meet King Edward at Chester, then I would have been safe?"

"Your brother, with respect, Prince Llywelyn, is a self-serving snake. We would have protected you."

He smiled. "You are right, archer, and King Edward has chosen well. Come, you and this brightly coloured bird can tell me the conditions of peace which the victor wishes to impose upon me."

There was resignation in his voice and I actually felt sorry for him. We followed him into the hall. It was not a large one and it reflected Prince Llywelyn's position. He might have been able to outwit King Henry, but the son was a different proposition. The prince sat on a raised dais. Four warriors, lords, I had no doubt, flanked him, and a bishop stood behind him.

"We are ready to hear King Edward's words."

I took a deep breath. I would have preferred that Godfrey do the speaking, for he would have chosen better words. I just spoke the words King Edward had spoken to me. "You will return with us to the River Conwy and formally surrender to King Edward. Bishop Anian will be there to see that all is done well. You will do King Edward homage and, in return, the king will leave you Gwynedd and Anglesey. You will pay the crown one thousand marks a year for the privilege of that island." I saw the lords look at one another. They were weighing up if this was good for them or not. I saw, in Llywelyn's eyes, that he thought it was a better offer than he had expected.

"And my brothers? What of them?"

"Rhufoniog and Dyffryn Clwyd will be ruled by Dafydd ap Gruffydd and Owain ap Gruffydd will be given the Cantref of Llŷn."

"Poor Owain hoped for so much more than that but I fear that Dafydd will be even unhappier." He glanced up at the bishop, who shrugged. "And how long do we have to make our decision?"

"There was no time limit, Prince Llywelyn, but King Edward is not a patient man." I paused and then took a deep breath. "You cannot win, Prince Llywelyn, and all that Welsh pride will bring will be death and starvation. Your granary is emptied. Your army will just live off fresh air, but your women, your children, your old? What will they do?"

"You make a compelling argument, but we will sleep on it." He gave me a sad smile. "As you say, we have little food. There will be no feast tonight but there is some good cheese, rye bread and ale."

I nodded. "I am a soldier and I have boiled leather before now to make a stew. We will survive. With your permission, I would eat and sleep wherever my men are housed."

He stood. "And that shows that you are a soldier. However, I would not be able to vouch for your safety. You and your men will have to sleep in this keep. Lord Maredudd is not the only noble who wishes to see this war continue and to see your

231

life ended. We may be crowded, but this will be your sleeping quarters tonight."

"I have had worse!"

It felt strange to be sleeping on the floor of the hall with the throne of the Prince of Wales a few feet away, but we were together. The prince put a guard on the door and after we had eaten, my men and I sat and spoke.

Godfrey was a little bemused. "You have all the makings of a courtier, Captain. I know not if it was instinct or luck, but your words were perfectly chosen, and I cannot think of any other who could have plotted such a successful course."

"He has not answered yet!"

"He is saving a little face but as soon as you made the offer, he was happy to accept. He keeps the most valuable part of Wales and his brother will have to bend the knee to him."

David the Welshman lay down on his cloak and said, "We have an implacable enemy, Captain. Each time you meet him, you humiliate Lord Maredudd. I know not what he plans but we had better sleep with swords in our hands, for he means us harm."

"When we have finished the work for King Edward, then we will be back at Yarpole, and this time there will be English knights between us and this Welsh hothead." I had spoken with Godfrey and he had given me the names of some of the lords who would be castellans of Flint and Rhuddlan. He had told me that Rhuthun and Hawarden would also be made into strongholds and the king was choosing the castellans carefully. If men like Lord Maredudd decided to cause trouble, they would have to reduce our castles. It looked like peace was finally coming to the frontier.

We rose early and vacated the hall, for the prince would need to address his lords. His decision, whilst inevitable, would not be popular. Prince Llywelyn summoned his senior nobles and clerics to the inner bailey, where he would make his announcement. I had our men wait there, and I asked David to translate for me. We stood to one side and endured the stares of the nobles. Godfrey seemed confident that the prince would go along with the surrender, and so it proved.

"My nobles and my bishops, we have fought a valiant fight, but the war machine that is England has proved too strong. King Edward will allow me to rule Gwynedd, and that means our people will not starve this winter. I propose to travel with Captain Gerald Warbow and Godfrey Landvielle to the River Conwy, where we shall sign the treaty which will bring peace to this land."

That was as far as he got, for many knights, led by Lord Maredudd, began screaming and shouting so loudly that Prince Llywelyn's bodyguards had to physically place themselves before the prince. Even David could not translate.

The ten angry lords, still led by Lord Maredudd, left us, and Prince Llywelyn smiled. "Not all, it seems, support me. Let us not waste another moment, Captain Warbow. Let us ride while we may!"

Despite the fact that many unhappy Welshmen had ridden away, there were still enough who were loyal to the prince for me to be confident about making the short journey to the Conwy without fear of attack. Lord Maredudd and the others were dangerous, but not yet. If they wished to rouse the populace, they needed a leader behind them whom they could rally. If it was not Llywelyn, then it had to be one of the other brothers, Owain or Dafydd, and both were guests of King Edward.

When we reached the river, I saw that the king had invested Aberconwy. I guessed that the king had used Captain Matthew's men to keep watch and they had alerted the king. It showed the Welsh nobility how efficient King Edward was.

King Edward was there to greet us, and I saw the contrast in the two men immediately. It was not just that King Edward was both younger and taller – he looked more confident. The two rulers greeted each other courteously. I saw Llywelyn's brother Dafydd. He was in the background and had a look of victory on his face.

When the introductions had been made, the king said, "Thank you, Warbow. Your work here is done. You may return to your farm, having served England."

Prince Llywelyn shook his head. "King Edward, I would like the archer to attend the talks. He is an honest man, and I am unsure of where I may find allies." It was a barb aimed at his brother.

The king nodded. "When all of your men are gathered, we shall begin the talks, for there will be no discussion, Prince Llywelyn. Bishop Anian is here as a guarantor of fairness."

"And he supports you, King Edward. In this real-life game of chess, I am left with few pieces at my disposal."

I was included in the talks. That I was in unknown territory was clear. The Treaty of Aberconwy, as it was known, merely put on parchment the words I had spoken to the prince in his castle. Godfrey was next to me and when some Latin phrase was used, he explained it. Thanks to his words I saw that Prince Llywelyn's hands were tied. England effectively ruled Wales.

The only parts that could raise their own taxes were Gwynedd, Rhufoniog and Dyffryn Clwyd. Anglesey was the only place that could raise serious money and Llywelyn had to pay a thousand marks a year for that privilege.

When the treaty was signed and witnessed, Llywelyn knelt before King Edward. He placed his hands between the king's and bowed his head. It was the symbolic gesture that he would be a dutiful prince. Llywelyn was resigned to his fate. His attempts at becoming the ruler of a united Wales were ended, and he was a minor prince once more. However, he still held some power, and I believed he hoped that the king would allow him to marry Eleanor de Montfort.

He turned to me. "Farewell, archer, I hope we do not meet again, for if we do, then it will be war and I am tired of war. I hope you prosper."

I felt sorry for him and I nodded. "And I hope you find peace too, Prince Llywelyn. I am a man of war, but I now hope that the only time I get to use my bow is at the butts, where I try to outdo my men, rather than to slay farmers."

The king gave me a sharp look, for he knew my meaning. English knights had suffered no losses, and few had even been forced to draw a sword. John Malton had gone home richer, having done nothing. It had been the spearmen and archers who had died at Rhuddlan. He said, "Aye, Gerald Warbow, we are pleased. Baron Mortimer will reward you in due course."

I bowed and returned to my men. We wasted no time in packing up and heading home. We would have a three-day journey.

Before we left, I did two things: I spoke with Godfrey, for I had seen that pretty clothes do not mean a soft man. The man had been faced with unenviable choices and yet had made a success of his life. "Farewell, Godfrey. If you pass my farm, there will be a welcome."

He smiled. "And farewell, archer. If ever I saw an archer who should be a knight, it is you."

Our last call was to the Earl of Warwick, who was still our paymaster. With coffers filled with the ransom he had taken, he was more than happy to pay us off. We headed home and I wondered if my days of war were over.

Chapter 16

It was almost November by the time we reached home. We had not come the direct route across Powys, for I was uncertain where Lord Maredudd and his rebels were to be found, so we took a longer, safer route. We had lost not a man and I wished to keep it that way, and so we came through Chester and then Nantwich before heading for Shrewsbury and Wigmore. It cost us more, for we had gained ponies and horses and stabling was not cheap. I was being prudent. I did not fear Lord Maredudd, but I would not lose a man for my pride.

Yarpole was warm and welcoming. As I stepped through the door, Hamo ran to greet me and my daughter squealed with laughter when I smiled at her. "I am home, and the war is over!"

Mary's eyes widened. "You are home to stay? The king will not ask for you next year?"

"I think that the king's eyes will now turn to securing Wales." I had been privy to many conversations about Wales after the conquest and I explained it to my wife. "The castles that the king has built will be just the start. He is encouraging English settlers to move to those castles and has his men building new towns to house them. Indeed, he is changing the course of the Clwyd to make better farms. Then there are all the castles from which the Welsh lords have been evicted. They are being rebuilt and improved. He is bringing English law and courts to Wales. He will not need to war against the Welsh, for he is ringing it with castles and fettering it with English law. He has brought over the master builder from Savoy, Master James of St George. I do not think that the threat from the Welsh is over, but I will be at home and we shall live in peace for at least a year, and that is more than we have enjoyed hitherto."

Some of my archers announced that they wished to marry and to raise families. They had the money to make comfortable lives.

Stephen de Frankton was the only one who appeared unhappy. He came to see me in the new year when the grass was beginning to grow. "Captain Warbow, I need to speak with you."

I had sensed his unhappiness since the Welsh campaign. He had fought as hard as any, but I knew that he had not yet rid himself of the need for vengeance for his lost family. The lords and the prince who had slain his family still lived and prospered.

"Of course, Stephen, for I know that something troubles you. In the months since we have been back, you are restless."

"The Welsh war is over and my sword sleeps in my scabbard. I still feel the need to atone. With your permission, I would take the cross and join a crusade. Acre needs warriors. I have spoken to you as well as Robin and know that while it is a hopeless cause and we are doomed to lose it, perhaps I may, in my small way, slow the end." He shrugged. "I just feel that I need to do this."

"Then go with my blessing but I fear you will be disappointed. Know that there will always be a place for you here. I know that Robin and Peter will be sad."

"I have spoken to my shield brothers and they understand."

It was a sad parting, for Stephen was popular. As with all such partings, the gap was soon filled, for my archers were becoming fathers. Mary became pregnant again and I had the joy of watching Hamo and his sister grow. In fact, life was peaceful for a further two years. My second daughter, Joan, was born, and all was well in my house. Hamo played with the sons of my archers and enjoyed the rough and tumble, not to mention the bloody injuries, of young boys learning the skills that they would need when they were older, for all would be warriors. Only John of Nottingham was truly a farmer, and that had been imposed on him by a wound. We saw little of Baron Mortimer, save for the times when we took his taxes to him or one of his messengers informed us of a change in the law. We simply got on with life.

We had more years of peace than I had predicted. New castellans were placed in the castles at Hawarden, Dinefwr, Llandovery and Carreg Cennen. In fact, so prosperous were the Marches that our income increased year on year. Yarpole and Luston grew, and some of the woods were cleared to make new farms.

It was April, and more than two years had passed since peace had descended upon Powys. Baron Mortimer now had three castles that had belonged to the lord there, Lord Rhys Wyndod. Baron Mortimer had used the king's stonemason to improve them and garrisoned them with his men. Sir Roger had done well out of the war and was now one of the richest of the Marcher lords.

Early one April morning, he came to visit and was accompanied by twenty men at arms as well as his squire and three knights. The baron now looked his age. He was one of the oldest of King Edward's advisers and, as far as I knew, had not been to war for some time. Now he rode mailed and ready to fight, I feared the worst.

"Is this war, my lord? Does the king summon us?"

He dismounted. "Not the king but your feudal lord: me. I have not called upon you for the past two years but now I need you."

"Will you enter my hall and take refreshment, my lord?"

"We have no time for that. A rider reached me last night and told me that there is trouble close to my castle at Llandovery. The former lord is causing mischief. John of Reading is my castellan and eight of his men were attacked and murdered. Animals were taken and houses were burned. I need you and your men to hunt them down."

I could not refuse but I did not want to go. Llandovery was almost sixty miles away. "How many men will you need, lord?"

"You have more than twenty now; leave ten here and fetch the rest."

I nodded and waved over Peter. He was in command of my men and knew them better than any. "Peter, I need ten of my archers." I lowered my voice. "Choose the younger ones and those who are unmarried."

"Aye, Captain. And which horse?"

"Better make it Lion; Eleanor is getting old." As he went off to obey my orders, I said, "My lord, if you wish to start down the road, my men will catch you before you have gone five miles."

He nodded. "Damned Welsh! The only one you can really trust is a dead one! Do not tarry, Warbow; I need your archers!"

The visit had been so brief that Mary only reached the door, having made herself presentable, as the men at arms headed down the road. "That was a brief visit."

"And I fear it does not bode well for us. My archers and I are to help capture some rebels. I know not how long I shall be away."

She gave me a sad smile. "I suppose we should be grateful for the two years you have been at home. You will take care."

"Of course."

It was Tom and Martin who were now the mainstays of my archers. The rest who accompanied me were all young archers. Only John, son of John of Nottingham, had experience of war, but this would be the chance to blood them. I saw the older ones, like Robin, Will Yew Tree and William Matlac, were watching the young archers as they mounted their horses. I was leaving them behind, and they saw the new generation taking over.

Peter had packed four ponies with spare arrows and tents. The tents would be for four of us and the others would make hovels. I assumed that we would be housed in Llandovery Castle while we hunted the rebels.

Tom asked, "Peter said we hunt rebels – do we know how many?"

"No, and the land in which we seek them is rocky and affords many places to hide. I fear this will not be a quick campaign. The Welsh will close ranks against us."

Martin said, "Aye, and there is no David the Welshman to help us."

"David has done enough, and he has married late. His wife is expecting a child. Baron Mortimer can use one of his men to translate. This time we are here to help and not to lead."

As far as I could recall, the baron had done little fighting when we had ended the revolt. He had taken men to Carreg Cennen, but that stronghold had surrendered when Llywelyn

241

had been defeated. He had enjoyed an easy war and gained castles as a result.

We caught up with the slower moving men at arms by the time we had ridden three miles. The baron nodded to me and I joined his men at arms, and I rode next to their captain, John Giffard. I learned as we headed towards Builth Castle that he was a landless knight, which was why he did not use his title. He was, as I came to know, a truly professional soldier. He seemed to be another like Godfrey Landvielle. He had suffered ill luck but thanks to an indomitable spirit and self-belief, he had carved out a career for himself. He led the men at arms from Wigmore Castle and, as I came to realise, had trained them to his own exacting standard. He and Stephen de Frankton would have got on well.

It was he who told me the issue. "There are too few men garrisoning the castles. Many lords have taken their men to Gascony to fight in King Edward's wars there. Otto de Grandson was in high favour after Anglesey, and he and Robert Burnell were sent to Gascony to impose the king's will on the rebellious lords there. Builth Castle, where we will spend this night, has but three heavy horsemen, three light horsemen, twenty crossbowmen and forty archers. Builth is one of the king's fortresses. Llandovery is even worse off. Before the attack, there were four heavy horse, six light horse, ten crossbowmen and ten archers. Two of those who were killed were men at arms, while the others were crossbowmen and archers. John of Reading has barred the gates."

I read much into that. For the men to have been taken unawares and murdered was careless in the extreme. Locking the gate after the attack also reflected badly on the castellan. Baron Mortimer was learning the folly of choosing poor leaders.

Builth Castle was imposing and had been improved, but the garrison would soon have to withdraw to the keep if they were attacked. They simply did not have enough men to man the walls. The king's castellan, James of Tewkesbury, did not inspire me with confidence.

If Builth was imposing, then Llandovery was a shadow of that fortress. It was a smaller, meaner castle and Baron Mortimer had done little to improve it. However, there was potential. The round keep was built on a large mound and the ditch ensured that an attacker would struggle to assault it without ladders. The lord, John of Reading, was a mouse who looked afraid of his own shadow.

There was plenty of room for us in the castle, and we made ourselves comfortable while John of Reading bore the wrath of the baron. The three knights kept apart from John Giffard and me. It did not bother us. We were warriors for hire and knew our own worth. We had fought in the same battles but had not come across each other before. That was not unusual, for most times archers fought on foot and, when they could, men at arms fought on horseback.

John was what was known as heavy horse. It was not the horse that was heavy, just the weight of the armour the rider wore. John wore a mail hauberk, although he did not wear the chausse. With his coif and helmet, he would be a formidable sight riding towards Welsh spearmen. The danger to all of our mounted and mailed men would be the Welsh archers, and that was why we had been brought along.

When the baron returned, John of Reading followed sheepishly behind. The baron did not choose his words to alleviate the embarrassment of the castellan. "This could have been avoided. The men were allowed to drink in the small town, and they were attacked when they left. They were drunk and easy to kill."

"And the sheep, Baron?"

"That, Warbow, appears to have been the main reason for their attack. The flock is mine and allowed to graze on the hillsides close to the castle."

John of Reading ventured, "All the local farmers leave their animals to graze, Baron!"

The baron's head whipped around. "The Welsh will not steal Welsh sheep, but mine are English! You have cost me money."

While the baron was apportioning blame, I was trying to solve the problem of how to find the thieves. "I assume that they would not simply slaughter them." The baron's anger turned to me and I explained as he glared. "What I mean, my lord, is that they cannot have got far. It has been, what? Three days?"

John of Reading nodded. "Tomorrow will be the fourth."

"Then they must be within twenty miles of here. Castellan, where do you think they would go?"

"Up the Towy valley. There are many side valleys where they could shelter and slaughter the animals they do not need."

The baron rubbed his beard. "This is a flouting of my authority."

John Giffard said, "It may be more than that, my lord; it may be an attempt to ambush you. If this castellan knows where they have gone, and we find their trail, then I would suspect it to be an attempt to capture you. A Marcher Lord would fetch a fine ransom."

"Reading, what do you think, if you are capable of such action?"

The man coloured. "There is resentment to your presence here, my lord. The people were all supporters of Lord Wyndod."

"And where is he?"

"I believe he is with Dafydd ap Gruffydd in Rhufoniog."

My heart sank. Dafydd ap Gruffydd kept appearing just where we did not want him. I saw him as the only weakness in King Edward's strategy.

"I will deal with him when we have dealt with these sheep stealers." Ignoring his knights, who had remained silent throughout, he said to us, "You two plan a way to avoid being ambushed, capture the sheep stealers and retrieve my sheep!" He turned to the castellan. "And let us see if you are able to furnish food that is edible. When we leave, on the morrow, you will ride at the fore. If anyone is going to die in an ambush, it might as well be you!"

I did not feel sorry for the man. He had brought about his own ruin, but whatever position and influence he had enjoyed were now gone. Llandovery was one of the smaller castles belonging to Baron Mortimer. Had John of Reading done well, he might have moved on to Chirk, Montgomery or even Wigmore. Now, when the sheep were returned, he would have to seek another employer.

The man at arms picked up the jug of wine and two goblets. "Come, let us sit by the light. Wine will help my thoughts."

I poured us two goblets. They were made of pewter and were a little battered, but they were serviceable. "My men and I can move faster than the baron and your men. I would suggest that we leave before dawn and pick up the trail of these murderers."

"Do you think it is a trap for the baron?"

"If Dafydd ap Gruffydd is involved, then aye! It makes perfect sense. Would Baron Mortimer have come if his men were not murdered? More, would John of Reading even tell the baron if it had just been sheep that were stolen?"

"Probably not. And you will walk into the trap?"

"No, for I am no fool. A flock of sheep and the men who took them will leave a trail and we will find them. I will send a man to fetch you and we will ensure that the murderers do not escape. The sheep are immaterial. They will not run."

"And if there are more of them than us?"

I laughed. "I can guarantee that there will be, but the only weapon to worry about is the warbow." I rose.

"Where are you going?"

"The castellan strikes me as a fool. I will speak with his men. As archers, they may well speak with me rather than their master. If I am any judge, they will wish vengeance on the men who slew their friends."

I slipped from the hall unnoticed. The food would soon arrive. I headed for the small gatehouse, which overlooked the settlement. As I peered down, I saw it was more of a large village than a town. I saw that there were two men on duty. Both were archers and had the broad barrel chest of the typical Welsh archer.

"A pleasant afternoon, Captain?"

"It would be if I had not been dragged sixty miles from my hall to apprehend murderers."

My blunt words had an obvious effect. One of them, a red-haired and bearded archer, said angrily, "They were fools and liked their drink too much, but they did not deserve to be murdered!"

I nodded. "And tomorrow I will hunt the killers down and catch them." There was steel in my voice. "But I need a place to look. You are archers and that makes you both clever and observant. You saw the direction they took."

They looked at each other and nodded. "As clear as the nose on your face, Captain. They headed for Rhandirmwyn. It is six miles up the road."

"Six miles? Surely they would go further than that! That is almost within spitting distance of here."

The archer smiled. "Captain, my name is Madog ap Davy and I grew up in that village. My da was a lead miner. He died young and I swore I would do anything rather than go down the mines. That is all that there is in Rhandirmwyn, and since the baron came, no one has mined it." He shrugged. "He may not know the worth of it. The man who ran the mine for him was close to Lord Wyndod and still lives there. Captain, I have heard of you and your reputation. I believe that this is a trap. They wish to draw you and the baron there. The miners are hard men. How else do you think they were able to murder the men at arms and our friends? There were at least thirty of them, and there are other Welsh warriors who did not flee to Rhufoniog with Lord Wyndod. They will be waiting."

The other archer had said nothing. "And what is your opinion?" I asked him.

"Madog is right, Captain, and there is a wood through which the road passes. If I wanted to ambush horsemen, then I would do it there."

"And is there any other way to get to the mine without going through the wood?"

Madog grinned. "The Towy is just eleven paces wide and not very deep. If you are a confident horseman then you could walk up the river and ambush the ambushers. There is a wood and trees for cover." He frowned. "You are good riders, are you not? That is what we have heard. The men with the green arrows ride to war on horses and not ponies!"

"Aye, we ride, and I fear that the rest of the garrison will be called upon to fight tomorrow."

"We are ready. We were made to look fools and it was not our fault. We are archers and good ones."

I nodded. "And soon you will have a new castellan, of that I am certain."

Madog brightened. "You, Captain?"

I laughed. "I have a manor and I have no desire to be the keeper of any castle."

I headed back to the hall and saw that the food had arrived.

"You almost missed it, Warbow! Let us hope it is edible." The baron was already eating.

"I believe I know where they will ambush us!"

Every eye turned to me. "Are you a magician?" The baron was smiling.

I smiled. "No, but I talked to the archers, who are angry about losing their friends. There is a mining village six miles or so from here: Rhandirmwyn."

The baron looked at John of Reading, who nodded. "And why do I not earn an income from the lead mining?"

"I have enough to do here, Baron Mortimer, without managing a mine. I thought you had another who acted for you there."

The look on the man's face told me that it was clearly a lie and the baron knew it, but I saw that he was more concerned with the ambush. "And this ambush, where will it be?"

"The road passes through a wood, a mile or so from the village. There, many miners await; they are the ones who killed your men, and there are also disaffected warriors who served in the castle."

"Why did you not discover this?"

John of Reading's silence told everyone that he had not the wit to do so.

I carried on. "I plan on using the river to get beyond their ambush. If you leave with the garrison and the men you brought, just after dawn, then we can spring their ambush prematurely, and my men can take them out while they are distracted by your arrival. You know how good my men are."

John of Reading could not help himself. "You cannot leave the castle without a garrison! I will stay here with ten chosen men."

The baron laughed. "You will lead the column of men, Reading, and you had better pray that you have good mail and that Captain Gerald strikes before the Welsh do! We empty the castle and end this!"

We were up in the middle of the night and we slipped from the castle to head to the river. We walked our horses through the village to the river. There might have been spies but there were no other horses in the settlement, and that meant none could get ahead of us.

We entered the water and mounted our horses. Madog had been quite right; it was neither wide nor deep and the trees overhung the narrow stream – we were invisible. John of Reading should have spoken to his own men. From what I had seen of this castellan, he was as inefficient as they came, and I knew that the baron was regretting his choice.

I rode at the fore. We had our bows strung and over our backs. We each had a bag of arrows at our waist and two more bundles on our saddles. The splashing of our hooves in the water was masked by the sound of the mountain river as it tumbled south. There were bats, which swooped over the water, catching moths. In the distance, we heard the sound of an owl and not long before dawn, we heard the squeal of a vixen. Other than that, we appeared to be alone.

The river headed roughly north, and I was aware of the sky becoming lighter in the east. Madog had said that the wood came to within a few hundred paces of the river when it was close to where he thought we might be ambushed. The trouble was, we had no idea where that was as there was a wall of vegetation on both sides. When I deemed we had come far enough, although it was a guess, we left the river and headed in the direction of the road. When we found no open space, then I knew we were at the right place and I dismounted. We tied our horses to trees and began to head up to where we thought was the road.

We heard and smelled the ambushers long before we saw them. They had lit fires for warmth and, although the fires had long died, the smell still lingered. We smelled sweat and we smelled mutton fat.

I held up my hand and we stopped. Baron Mortimer and the bait would not be coming from Llandovery until the sun rose, and it would take them an hour to get to the ambush. That was deliberate as we wanted them to be nervous. They would be expecting the baron and awaiting his attack. Nervous men make mistakes.

I waved my hand to spread us out and we headed up the slope. We had plenty of time and we moved silently. Tom and Martin were at the two extreme ends of the line while the others, the young archers, were closer to me. As soon as I heard Welsh being spoken, then I stopped close to a tree and dropped to one knee. The others copied me. We would now wait for daylight.

I knew that this would be the hardest for the ones who had never sent an arrow in anger.

Dawn began to break. Birds sang and the sky behind us began to grow lighter. I did not move my head but instead flicked my eyes until I saw the Welsh. They were three hundred paces from us, on either side of the road, and that was lucky. Had we advanced any closer, then we might have been spotted. I saw one man leave the camp. He was not a warrior, but he had the broad chest and diminutive stature of a miner. I feared he might walk all the way down to the river, but he merely walked forty paces, dropped his breeks, and the stink told us what he was doing. He appeared to be looking directly at me, but I knew it was an illusion. We were still, and as long as we remained so, we were safe. When he finished, he used some of the large weedy leaves to clean himself and ascended the slope. We heard a cheer as he neared the others.

Now was the time to move and I waved my hand for my men to come a little closer. I risked another one hundred paces. I could smell the fires as they were relit and food prepared. It would be mutton. I held my hand up, and we all stopped and each chose a tree. We would wait for the sign of alarm amongst the ambushers.

Although there were warriors above us, they had been the garrison of Lord Wyndod. They could fight but they had to be told what to do. The miners were used to obeying orders but did not understand about sentries and silence.

We knew when the baron was heading towards the trap, for men began to shout in the camp and they raced to their positions. Of course, we could only see the half who were on our side of the road, but that would be enough. As all eyes were looking down the road, I signalled my men and we moved slowly through the trees until we were within one hundred paces of the ambushers. I saw the variety of weapons, from the archers with the bows to the miners with the hammers and chisels they used to hew the lead from the rock. I drew back and aimed at an archer who was further back than the others. I released, and the arrows struck him hard in the back and pinned him to a tree. He had no time to call out.

Tom, Martin and John had the experience to release when they knew they could hit a target and not alert the others. We had spoken of this when we had tethered our horses. The others would wait for my low whistle. The next three men were silently slain, the range too close for men to survive the war arrows that penetrated the clothes they wore, tearing through flesh, cracking bones and finding vital organs.

It was when I saw the rebel bowmen pull back on bows that I whistled, and then we showed the rebels the difference between one who can draw a bow and one who practises every day. We drew back and released so quickly that it seemed as though a swarm of wasps was around. The Welsh arrows were sent, but few from our side of the road.

When the last two Welsh archers were slain, we switched to the men who posed less danger to men at arms – those armed with hammers, swords and spears. When the first of them was hit, their leader realised the trap had been sprung and he shouted something. By then it was too late for the men on the other side of the road.

Whilst they had been able to send their arrows towards the horsemen, the effect had been thwarted by the shields the men at arms and knights bore on their left arms. Madog and his archers had dismounted, and they would be almost as deadly as we.

The Welsh raced towards us, down the slope and through the trees. It was a mistake, for we were not tired, and the Welsh wore no mail. Few had leather, and the closer that they came to us, the easier it was to hit them, for they were a bigger target. None came closer than twenty paces to us.

By then the battle on the road was over, and the ones who remained alive surrendered. I sent four of my archers for the horses and we advanced up through the woods. Any who were badly wounded were given a merciful death. We had no healers with us.

The Welsh had little we wanted, and so we kept our arrows nocked until we reached the road. I spied Madog and his garrison archers descending from the woods on the other side of the road. Three horses wandered disconsolately along the road. That meant three of our men had been hit. I did not recognise the horses and deduced that they belonged to men from Llandovery.

We had recovered the bodies and begun the pyre by the time that the baron and the others returned from the mine. They had with them eight men. All were bloody and had needed to be subdued. I saw that John Giffard and his men were whole. There was also a wagon.

The baron dismounted and took off his helmet. I saw his sword was still sheathed. He had not needed to use it. "A good plan, Warbow, and it worked, although Reading and two of his men died."

I knew that it had been deliberate. It would have been impossible to guarantee no casualties, and the baron was ruthless enough to have the castellan and his men at the fore. "Not much treasure, but we took a wagon-load of the lead they had mined. You and your men shall have a share of the proceeds. Now let us get back to Llandovery. This fighting has given me an appetite."

We rode down the road and I was able to see why Madog had been able to identify the ambush site so readily. The road rose steeply so that men and horses riding along it would be tired, and the trees along the side gave good cover. I would speak to the baron about Madog, for he needed a reward.

It was just after the sun had reached its zenith when we stopped at the castle. Ropes were thrown over the battlements and the miners were dragged kicking and screaming until the last of them became still and they died.

"Tomorrow morning, Giffard, take down the bodies, remove the heads and put them on spikes. That will show the Welsh that the wind has changed and blows now from England!"

Thus, I discovered that Giffard was to be rewarded with the castle. Half of the men we had taken were left with him, and I advised him to make Madog the captain of his archers. Even as we left with the wagonload of lead, I saw that my new friend was making the castle more secure. The Welsh would not take him so easily. It would take treachery and not a force of arms!

Chapter 17

The attack at Llandovery should have been a warning that the Welsh pot of rebellion stew was not cold and still simmered. I think that the baron knew that, for I was elevated on the way home to ride at his side. "I will visit with the king and tell him of this. I know that he has plans for Gascony, but these new castles all need garrisons."

"What worried me, my lord, was the news that the rebel Wyndod has sought sanctuary with ap Gruffydd. I do not trust him. I met the two brothers and I believe that Llywelyn is more trustworthy."

The baron nodded. "Lady Maud and I share your opinion. We could not wait to rid ourselves of his presence, but he has his fiefdom now and perhaps that will suffice. But I will keep watch."

I shook my head. "Lord, I come from the Clwyd; the king could not have given Dafydd ap Gruffydd a more dangerous home. We have new castles at Flint, Rhuddlan and now at Rhuthun, not to mention the one that has been rebuilt at Hawarden, but as you discovered at Llandovery, where are the knights with strong hands to control them? Men like John Giffard are rare."

"You are right, and I will make that case to the king."

Once at home I put such military matters from my mind. When the likes of Lord Maredudd had lived close to me, then I might have feared for my home, but since then we had increased the men who could fight and we had strengthened our defences. I entered a hall with a welcome as warm as a fire on a winter's day.

It was the next year when one of the boys watching the sheep raced into the manor. "Captain! Captain! There is a mounted warrior, and he is heading this way!"

There was a small hill around which the road from the south passed. The shepherd had come the short way.

From the way he shouted, one would have thought that it was a horde of wild Welshmen, but I knew that one man meant a visitor. "Thank you, Chad." I flipped him a farthing. "Here is for your trouble – now back to your sheep."

I went to the gate and saw the weary warrior. It was Stephen de Frankton, and he led a horse, which was laden with war gear.

Peter of Beverley joined me. "The prodigal son returns, Captain. He still wears the cross of the crusader."

I nodded. Peter had not been on a crusade. "A wise move, for it guarantees him shelter at every monastery and nunnery on the way home. If I am any judge, he will discard it soon."

My former man at arms reined in and dismounted. "Is your offer of a bed still there, Captain Warbow?"

I held out my arm and we clasped. "Of course. And you survived the heat and the Turks?" I waved over two of the younger archers who had been at the butts. "Put these horses in the stable and the war gear in the warrior hall."

Stephen was not wearing mail beneath his surcoat and I saw that he had the inevitably darkened skin of one who has been in the Holy Land. It would fade.

"You were right in every case, Captain, and the war can never be won, but I am glad that I went, for I feel that I have atoned. I did my duty and slew many Turks, but there were always more, and the men who fight them are led by leaders who spend more time fighting amongst themselves. I have come back a rich man."

We entered my hall and I saw Hamo's eyes widen when he saw the cross.

Mary smiled. "Welcome, Stephen; we have missed you and I look forward to your tales when we dine this night. Hamo, come with me. You can fetch your father and his guest wine and food while they talk."

I was no knight, but I liked the way that the sons of knights were used as servants in their halls and we had begun to do so with Hamo. Now six summers old, he took his duties seriously, for he saw it as a sign that I would soon begin to train him with a bow and wooden sword.

"I was offered the chance to fight for King Edward in Gascony, but I have had enough of those kinds of war. I would have a home."

"And there is one here for you."

"I may not stay long, Captain. Seeing Hamo and your daughters reminds me that I have yet to leave my mark on the world. I am the last of my family and I wish the de Frankton name to live on. I have money and I would buy a piece of land."

"Then when you are settled, we will speak with the baron."

I told him of the incident the previous year and he frowned. "I knew that the Welsh problem was not resolved."

"Yet it is not Llywelyn who is the source of the intrigue but his brother."

He shook his head. "It is all one. Until that line is extinguished, Wales can never be under civilised control and I can never be free from the memory of what they did to my family."

I thought he might have learned to forgive but I was wrong.

He had brought gifts for my family. Mary was given a beautiful dress, which looked expensive. Stephen told me that he had taken it during a chevauchée. I realised that things had not changed since my time there. Hamo was given a Turkish dagger in a scabbard. It endeared the man at arms to my son.

I had invited Peter and Robin, along with their families, to dine, and we all enjoyed Stephen's stories. The presence of women and children sanitised the content, but I could read between the lines. I knew the violence that underpinned them.

We left for Montgomery just three days later. The baron was making that castle even stronger.

He saw the cross and was eager to hear Stephen's words. "De Frankton, how was the crusade?"

"Hot, bloody and ultimately doomed, my lord, but I am pleased that I went."

"And if you are here with Warbow, then it is not just to tell me that you have returned."

"No, my lord, you are as sharp as ever. I wish to buy some land and settle. I would raise a family. I am no farmer, but I can afford to pay someone to manage a farm for me."

The baron rubbed his beard and I saw his eyes sparkle. "This may be fortuitous. Since I appointed Giffard to Llandovery, I am keenly aware that I need someone to lead the Shropshire levy. Giffard used to train them for me. Warbow here will tell you that this Welsh problem is not solved. The Bishop of Hereford has complained to me that his castle, Bishop's Castle, and the church and the village, are so close to the border that they are in danger of being raided. Like me, he is still suspicious of the Welsh. There is a manor there, on the English side of the border. The owner was killed almost twenty years ago when John Fitzalan raided. It has been left empty ever since. If you would lead and train the Shropshire levy, then it is yours, and the title of Gentleman. What say you?"

We all knew the dangers, but the temptation of the title and a manor was too great. "I will accept, my lord, and I am your man!"

"Good, but I want the Shropshire levy to be as efficient as Captain Warbow's archers!"

"Then I have a Herculean task ahead of me."

We rode back together. "This could be a poisoned chalice, Stephen. The Bishopric of Durham, the Palatinate, they man their castles with the best of warriors and castellans, but the Bishop of Hereford seems to have little idea of what is involved."

Stephen shrugged. "We all start somewhere. You made something of Yarpole. I will have to select men to serve me. If the manor has been derelict for twenty years, then I can do as I wish."

I nodded. "I will send James with you to assess the property. Heed his advice, for he knows farms. He has made mine prosperous. Let him do the same for you. I would advise you to find a local that you can use – one you can trust."

"Aye, that is the trick, is it not? That close to the old border there could be spies and traitors who know the right thing to say."

"Trust in yourself and trust in God. That is all that any man can do."

My men and Mary were delighted with Stephen's good fortune and Mary, who was a rock of kindness, provided him with all manner of furniture and supplies. When I cocked an eye, she said, "It is Christian kindness and, besides, we need new!"

For the first six months, we were in regular contact. James spent more time at the manor than he did at mine, but I did not mind. When he returned after the last visit, not long before Christmas, it was with the news that not only had Stephen made the house habitable and defensible, he had also begun to court the widow of a farmer who had been killed in the Welsh war. All seemed well.

As usual, the peace only worked so long as men wished it to be peaceful. Being where we were meant we saw travellers who passed to Chester and back. It was their stories that told us of the increasingly chilly wind blowing across north-east Wales. Prince Llywelyn made his usual plea to King Edward when he returned to England from Gascony. He wished the return of the land of Arwystl from England. The land the Welsh prince wanted belonged to Llywelyn's old enemy, Gruffydd ap Gwenwynwyn, now a lord with lands further south, which merely antagonised Llywelyn. I believe, for I knew him better than most men, that the fact that Gascony had not gone as well as it might, made the king react the way he did. King Edward appointed Reginald de Grey as justiciar in Chester. This was a bone of contention for the Welsh. It meant that England, through Chester, was the final arbiter of court decisions. As this meant, effectively, control of the Welsh courts, it did not bode well, and de Grey's judgments meant that the Welsh lost the cases they brought. De Grey hated the Welsh! King Edward also appointed a castellan for Hawarden Castle. It was one of his closest friends, Roger de

Clifford, and that guaranteed that any disputes with the lands of Dafydd ap Gruffydd would be settled in favour of the English.

For us in Yarpole and, indeed, for Stephen at Bishop's Castle, life was peaceful and there were no disputes. So, it came as a shock when the rebellion flared up again. The castle at Hawarden was unfinished; Roger de Clifford had held it for less than a year. On the Eve of Palm Sunday, Dafydd ap Gruffydd and an armed band of men stormed and took the castle. De Clifford was made prisoner and members of his family were killed. The castle was destroyed. That this was treachery and clearly planned could be seen when large bands of armed men stormed and took both Aberystwyth and Rhuddlan Castles while their garrisons were at church celebrating Palm Sunday. Even John Giffard lost Llandovery when Rhys Wyndod rose and seized it while the new castellan attended church. Dafydd ap Gruffydd had planned his treachery well. He had coordinated his men across the borders.

Ironically, it soon became clear that Prince Llywelyn knew nothing about this. If he had, then the effect of the rebellion would have been greater.

All along the border, the English market towns, which Edward had built and filled with colonists, were destroyed and there was a great slaughter. These rebels were not lords who revolted but the ordinary Welsh who were denied the right to live in these towns. Oswestry and the other market towns in the east of Wales were destroyed and law and order broke down.

It was then that we were affected. The king was in London and we had no standing army. The attacks along the border took the castles and the garrisons. With many soldiers still in Gascony, Baron Mortimer raised the levy and told every land-owner to look to their own defence. That message alone told me how serious this rebellion was. It was as though the whole of the eastern Welsh border was afire.

Those in the southern part of the Welsh March were not initially attacked, but the Welsh spirit of rebellion meant that they had to prepare their own defence. There would be no help for us. I sent word to Luston and the village decamped to my hall. This time there was no need to rush into my walls, and people brought their livestock and whatever food they had. We would be able to live behind my walls for at least two months. We had maintained our defences and actually improved some. Most had lived through the Maredudd raid and our success at that time engendered a calm atmosphere within our walls.

It was the end of April when the warbands descended upon our lands. We saw the fires burning to the west in Lucton, Kingsland and Yatton. A few survivors made their way to my hall and when they were identified as from those places, they were admitted. Unlike us, they had not built defences and the Welsh had simply appeared and stormed the villages.

The attacks saved us, for we were forewarned, and I had half of the men standing to on the walls so that when the brand-bearing mob appeared from the west, we were ready! That first attack was unplanned. It was a mob that saw the chance to steal, cause mischief and make merry at the expense of hard-working Englishmen. Those from Lucton, Kingsland and Yatton told us that what the mob could not steal they destroyed, regardless of purpose. When the same mob saw my walls, they assumed that I was rich. The five hundred or so men simply charged through the early morning light, thinking that they had another Yatton at their mercy.

Every one of the men in my manor could use a bow and had been well taught by my men. Every boy could use a sling and for the rest, we had darts and javelins. My people waited for my command before they released. I waited until the mob was just one hundred and fifty paces from us. Some of the Welsh archers had released and wasted their arrows when they were two hundred paces away. Our wooden walls, and the fact we could track their solitary arrows, meant no damage to any of my people.

When I shouted, "Release!" and our arrows soared and then descended, it was as though someone had taken a scythe to the Welshmen. When a further four flights followed almost on top of the first one, then the few survivors simply turned and fled. By the end of the afternoon, there was not a living Welshman to be seen.

I went with my archers and we left the walls. We took the arrows and the bows, as well as the weapons, from the dead, and they were taken within my walls. While half of my men made pyres of the bodies, I went with my mounted archers to see if the Welsh had camped close by. It was clear they had not. We returned to my hall, and the bodies, with the wind blowing from the east, were burned. The pall of smoke would be seen for miles and the survivors would know that they had met their match.

I was tempted to send a rider to Wigmore, but Peter pointed out that the attack had not been organised. "Captain, Dafydd ap Gruffydd could be out there with an army. We know he has taken three castles. That happened within a few days. Who is to say that Wigmore has not fallen? Better we wait until we see a standard that is English."

His advice was sage. A week later we saw a standard approach, but it was not English. It was Maredudd ap Iago. My nemesis had returned and this time he would know what to expect. He had with him a few heavy horsemen, but most of his horsemen were the Welsh light horse. The bulk of his army was made up of ordinary Welshmen similar to the ones we had slaughtered. The difference now was that they were led, and Lord Maredudd would not make such a simple attack.

He surrounded us with his men, and they lit fires. That was deliberate and intended to intimidate us. It was only those who were refugees from Lucton, Kingsland and Yatton who were affected. It was my old campaigners who reassured them that we had strong walls and even stronger warriors than the Welsh. The Welsh had learned to respect our bows and they were camped beyond the range of our arrows. We used that to our advantage.

The first night that the Welsh camped, my archers, not the levy nor the villagers, crept from the gate on the barn wall and with a pot filled with fire, we crossed small bridges that our boys carried to cross our ditches. We stopped just two hundred paces from the large camp on that side of the wall and we released sixty fire arrows into the night. None of us expected even half of them to ignite anything, but when we saw tents flaring and heard men crying as they tried to beat out the flames in their clothes, we knew we had enjoyed success. We were back inside the walls before the Welsh could even react.

The next day they began digging their own ditches and placing their own sentries to watch for us at night. Not a single animal lay within three miles of my hall, and soon the Welsh would have to either head east to forage or starve. Instead, they chose to make their first assault on my walls. They had banged nails into crudely made split timber and used those to advance towards the walls. They came on every side at the same time and I could see that they hoped to weaken us. I had my best archers, Warbow's Men, scattered amongst ordinary archers. The Welsh would have a hot reception.

The sheer weight of numbers meant that some of the Welsh would manage to get close to us. A few made it to the ditch, but the accuracy of Warbow's Men, added to the arrows that had struck the improvised shields they carried, blunted their attack, and those who arrived at the ditch were forced to flee.

That night they kept a good watch, while I only used one in four of my men to watch. The fire arrows had made them wary. I knew that was a trick you could only play once!

The next day they tried another assault but this time they only attacked one wall, the south wall, between the barn and the stable. That suited us, for I was able to put my best men along that wall once it became clear that it would be their only attack. We still had a watcher on the roof. It was Alfred, Harold of Luston's grandson.

"Captain, I see banners!"

Cupping my hands, I shouted, "Where away?"

"From the south, Leominster."

The last we had heard, Leominster was still held by the English but that did not mean much. "What is the banner?"

"A blue diagonal line with a yellow box and another yellow box with four small white boxes."

It did not sound like a Welsh banner. "Are there knights with them? Can you see banners on lances?"

"Aye, Captain, at least ten of them!"

"Alan, mount a dozen horses and fetch Lion. If these are friends, then I intend to end the mischief of Lord Maredudd once and for all."

I returned to the southern wall. The attack had slowed, for although we had hit fewer in this attack, it was still a larger number than the Welsh wished. When I heard the horn sound and the Welsh begin to break camp, I knew the identity of the mailed men; they were English. I might not have recognised the banner, but the Welsh had!

I mounted Lion and shouted, "Fetch me a shield!" I dropped the bow and the arrows. We had taken Welsh shields after the last attack and I had painted them a simple green. "Peter, take command. Those who ride with me, we seek Lord Maredudd. Do not charge off alone. Stay together and stay with me." When my shield was brought, I shouted, "Open the main gate and close it behind us."

Since the last attack, we had made a bridge we could draw up and secure with ropes. I heard it lowered and then the gates swung open. We galloped across the recently made timbers as the Welsh horses fled north and west. I spied Lord Maredudd. He was with another four mailed men. I saw no spurs, and so I assumed that they were not knights. The ordinary Welshmen, some mounted on ponies and some afoot, were also fleeing. I used the flat of my sword to smack into the backs of the heads of those on foot and render them immobile as I passed them. The men on ponies had to feel the edge of my sword and they perished. We could not afford to be merciful. My men rode with me as they fought alongside me, closely. We were like the point of an arrow and I saw that Alan and Robin were right behind me. Like me, they had drawn their swords, and both had taken small shields too.

Lion began to stretch his legs and to open a lead. Although I wanted my men close behind me, I could not afford for Lord

Maredudd to escape again. I might have to face four or five enemies alone. However, I would be approaching from their rear and I could choose the side from which I would attack. I was gaining on the five men and we had overtaken the others who had fled first. Lord Maredudd had the best horse, and the five men were strung out. I heard hooves and saw that Robin and Alan had managed to urge their horses to either side of Lion's rump. We were not mailed, and the five Welshmen's horses were labouring.

As I neared the rear of the last Welshman in the line, I lowered my arm so that my sword was hidden. Thanks to Stephen de Frankton I could use a sword and use one well. He had even taught me how to wield one from the back of a horse, and Lion was a warhorse! The Welsh rider kept glancing over his shoulder, a sure sign that he lacked confidence. I rode on the right side of his horse with my shield before me. He saw where I was and as soon as he looked ahead again, I dug my heels into Lion's flanks and jerked his reins to the left. The burst of speed allowed me to use my archer's strength and swing my sword into the centre of his back. I heard his spine crack and he fell from his horse.

When the horse of the third Welshman in the line stumbled and threw him, it forced the fourth one to veer sharply to the right, and there Alan used not only his archer's strength but his hunter's skill to hack into the right shoulder of the man. Even if it was not a mortal wound, it would incapacitate him. The last two men at arms were already slowing, and the rest of my men were almost upon us and I would not be alone.

I wanted Maredudd to myself and I shouted, "Maredudd is mine!"

It made him turn and he saw how close I was. His horse was

lathered and struggling. He saw my warhorse and he had no choice. He could either surrender or fight me. I did not think he would surrender to a mere archer nor would he wish to pay a ransom. I prepared to fight.

He reined in and shouted, "I yield! I yield!"

I had not offered him surrender and I confess that I was taken aback. I thought of all the deaths he had caused and how his treachery had ruined lives. "I do not accept it. Fight or I will slay you where you are."

He could go no further and so we fought. He had little choice other than to try to fight whilst his horse was still, for the beast was done. I rode at his shield side and stood in my stirrups to bring down my sword towards his head. Stephen would have berated me for such an obvious strike, and he easily blocked it with his shield whilst swinging his sword at head height. I had neither helmet nor coif and while such a blow aimed at him would hurt, if it connected with me, it would be fatal.

I urged Lion on and tried to get around the rear of the knight. His horse could not gallop, but it was able to turn, and Lord Maredudd brought around his horse's head so that he was facing me, and he realised my weakness. He stood in his stirrups to bring his sword down towards my head. I raised the shield to block the blow. I managed to do so, but the shield was a cheaply made one. There were just two layers of wood and no leather. It was split in twain and my arm briefly numbed.

I would have died but for Lion. My warhorse saved my life. It snapped and bit at the horse of Lord Maredudd and his weary and weaker horse stepped back so that the Welsh sword struck fresh air. Without a shield, I dragged Lion's head around, and while the Welsh knight tried to finish the job, raising his sword again to do so, I swung my sword backhanded towards his chest. The blade cracked into mail, and while the gambeson might have absorbed some of the power, the blow was strong enough to hurt. I suspect I cracked ribs.

He grunted and I saw the pain in his eyes. More importantly, his sword dropped a little and I pulled back my arm and lunged. It was a strike intended to make him back away, but I must have hurt him more than I knew, for he did not react. His sword did not come up to block the blow, and my sword slid into his left orb and I punched hard. I am not a cruel man and I ended the treacherous knight's life quickly. His body fell from my sword and he landed heavily on the ground.

I turned as I heard horses. I saw an English knight riding towards me, surrounded by men at arms. I recognised John Giffard as one of them.

The knight said, "I am Roger Lestrange and Giffard here tells me that you are Captain Warbow, King Edward's man. I am sorry that we did not arrive more swiftly, but I see that you did not need our aid. It is an impressive feat of arms for an archer to defeat a knight, especially on horseback!"

"I was lucky, my lord."

"I am on my way to Wigmore. King Edward has sent me to relieve the border and join him at Chester. You and your archers are needed."

"But the Welsh, lord? What of my people?"

"The Earl of Gloucester is driving from the south and Builth is relieved. I believe they will be safe, but I am charged with fetching you. We will head to Wigmore. Follow within the hour. Leave your manor defended, but I need you and fifteen of your archers!"

"Yes, my lord."

He led off the column of men and John Giffard rode up to me. "I was caught in church. Can you believe that! Treacherous Welsh. The knight is quite correct, Warbow; it is the lands closer to Chester that remain in Welsh hands. This Maredudd was an opportunist who sought to wreak revenge on you. Yarpole is unimportant. We seek Baron Mortimer's men from Wigmore and then we can strike!"

He rode after his new superior. Sheathing my bloody sword, I said, "Tom, Martin, I need you two and the archers we took to Llandovery. I am to lead fifteen archers to give aid to Baron Mortimer and King Edward. The rest may recover what they can from here. We need our war gear!"

Inside Yarpole there was celebration already, and those from within my walls were stripping the Welsh dead.

When Mary saw my face, her hand went to the cross around her neck. "This is not over."

I shook my head and waved over Peter of Beverley. "Peter, I have to take fifteen men to Chester. I am told that the manor is safe. Keep the people within its walls for as long as you can. I will send a rider when I know more."

"Aye, Captain. You did well to defeat Lord Maredudd."

I shook my head. "You and I know how lucky I was." I turned to Mary and hugged her. "I am sorry, but this must be ended."

"I thought it ended the last time."

"This time it will be ended, not in a treaty but blood. There will be executions. King Edward will not be so treacherously attacked again."

She kissed me. "Come home safe, my husband! We need you."

"And I need you."

Chapter 18

We headed for Wigmore and I wondered why Baron Mortimer had not given us succour. When we reached the castle, I discovered the reason; the old warrior was dying. He was in his bed and his sons, Edmund and Roger, were in command.

Lady Maud was a shadow of the woman I knew. She took me to Baron Mortimer's chamber, and I thought, at first, that he was dead, but as I neared him, he opened his eyes.

"I heard you finished off that snake Maredudd. I should have made you a knight."

I smiled and took his proffered hand. It was cold. "You have given me more reward than I could ever have expected. You will be well again."

I saw Lady Maud give a shake of her head.

Baron Mortimer's eyes were closed but he said, "I shall not stir from this bed, but I will fight whatever ague attacks me. Go with God. I am tired."

Lady Maud took my hand and led me from the bedchamber. "The doctors say that there is no ague. He is simply old, yet he has seen just fifty-one summers. He always thought well of you and told me that you were the one man upon whom he knew he could rely. Be safe, Warbow." She kissed me on the cheek and returned inside to her bedchamber.

I joined the baron's sons, Sir Roger and John Giffard in the Great Hall. I saw that they had waited for me.

Sir Roger said, "You know this Stephen de Frankton, Warbow?"

I nodded. "He is a good man."

"Then I will send a rider to him. I wish him to raise the Shropshire levy. I will leave the baron's sons here to keep this land safe and the levy can guard the border. We will ride to King Edward. Cheshire must be kept safe."

That night we ate a sombre meal in the Great Hall. Lady Maud was a gracious hostess, and her husband was not yet dead, but we spoke quietly while we ate. I learned that the Earl of Gloucester was driving north and that Lord Luke de Tany, with a fleet of ships from London and the Cinque Ports, was on his way to Anglesey. King Edward had acted swiftly. It seemed that Prince Llywelyn had used his powers to take command of the Welsh from his brother, who had instigated the fighting and was planning to take his war into Cheshire. We would have a hard fight to recover the castles we had lost.

King Edward was already in Chester when we arrived, and he was his usual ebullient self. He had called up the levy and summoned knights from across the land. He had been betrayed, and the Welsh had made the mistake of attacking his castles. This was now a personal fight.

I was too lowly to be involved in the planning and I was housed by the river with the rest of the gentlemen and archers. I was sought out, however, by Godfrey, the pursuivant, two days after I had arrived. The urgency with which we had been summoned had made me think that action was imminent, but it was not so. Godfrey took me to the king. As we went, I learned that the fleet of ships had landed men on Anglesey. It explained our delay, for the king had wanted to wait until his ships were in position. I also learned that King Edward had been apprised of news in the Welsh camps. He knew that Llywelyn had the bit between his teeth, but the one thing that the Welsh prince could not plan, however, was an act of God, and while King Edward had allowed Prince Llywelyn to marry Eleanor de Montfort, any hopes of an heir for whom the prince could fight were dashed when his queen died in childbirth. He had begun the revolt for his unborn child, but any victory he might have would now benefit his brother, the treacherous Dafydd.

Godfrey smiled. "A man needs children if he is to have any lasting legacy. Llywelyn's heart will not be in this. That is why the king is striking now."

"Why has King Edward sent you, Godfrey? You are a courtier?"

He smiled. "When I was sent with you, it was not just as a courtier. I was, I am, a warrior, and King Edward needed me to spy upon the Welsh. You took the attention away from me. They thought me a painted bird. I was assessing the strengths and weaknesses of the Welsh. There are divisions amongst their leaders and that is why the Earl of Gloucester holds them in the south, Lord de Tany threatens them in the west, and we will drive south and west to trap Llywelyn and his brothers in their mountain stronghold!"

I looked at Godfrey in a new light. I had been used, but I understood why.

King Edward was surrounded by papers and courtiers, but Godfrey whisked me to the king's side.

"Warbow, I need you and your men. De Grey has forty of my household knights and I want you to guide him to Rhuddlan. You are to retake that castle. Hawarden has been burned and abandoned. We will retake Rhuddlan and I can use it as a base. We destroy Dafydd before I seek Llywelyn and end his life. You and your men will be scouts. It is de Grey who will assault the castle."

I was just about to leave when a messenger raced in and threw himself to the floor. "King Edward, there has been a disaster. The Earl of Gloucester has been defeated at Carreg Cennen by Prince Llywelyn. There has been great loss of life, including William, son of William de Valence!"

That was the king's cousin and I saw the anger in his eyes. I was close enough to hear him whisper, "Foolish Gloucester." He recovered his composure and said to the gathered men, "We will see to Llywelyn in the fullness of time. First, we secure the northeast!"

I had not fought alongside Sir Reginald before, but the king held him in high esteem, and as he commanded the household knights, his loyalty and his skill were never in doubt. Unlike many nobles, he did not look down on humble archers.

He took me to one side the night before we were to leave. "You, I believe, know this valley well?"

"Yes, my lord; I was born here, and I was here when we took the valley from the Welsh."

"You were there when the foundations of Rhuddlan were laid."

"Yes, my lord."

"Good. I do not intend to bleed upon its walls. I plan on a night attack. Your men, so I hear, are good with knives and swords as well as bows?"

274

I knew that many called them bandits and cutthroats. It did not worry us, for we knew our skills and our worth. "Aye, my lord."

"Can you gain us entry to Rhuddlan, unseen and at night?"

"Only a fool would say yes, my lord, without having seen the Welsh dispositions."

"A good answer. Then we will get there in the late afternoon and you and I can ride and see what awaits us."

"Yes, my lord." I hesitated. "If you could wear a good cloak that would hide you, then we would have less chance of discovery."

"The king said that you were forthright. Of course. In this, I will bow to your expertise."

It was then that I saw young Sir Walter. He had matured and was now one of King Edward's household knights. "It is good that I fight alongside you again, Warbow. I hope I have learned well!"

I nodded. "If you are now a household knight, then you have."

I knew the approach to take. We headed for Dyserth, and we would use the route my men and I had taken before and use Twthill for cover. I saw that Sir Reginald had heeded my advice and all his knights wore dark cloaks. It went against their nature to cover their colourful liveries and reflected the king's need to restore his power.

I think that Sir Reginald wondered where we were going when we left Dyserth and used the trees and the waterways to reach the Clwyd, but after leaving the horses and the bulk of the men at the river, he followed Tom, Martin and me up the hill. It seemed like yesterday that we had done this, when we had taken the wooden walls of the Welsh prince's castle. Now we were trying to take a stone castle I had yet to see!

This time there were no sheep and we peered over an empty pasture. I saw that the new town built by the king was a blackened ruin and that when the Welsh had taken Rhuddlan, they had done much damage. The castle had been unfinished indeed; the outer wall was still just made of timber. I suspected that was how the Welsh had gained entry. The stone towers and gatehouse were in place, but the catapults employed by the Welsh had not only damaged the stonework but also the gates. I saw that the gate that led to Twthill had been hastily repaired. It was late afternoon and just four men watched the gate. I saw few men on the fighting platform of the castle, and that may have been because the castle was incomplete and the fighting platform did not extend all the way around. The partly finished towers – there were six of them – were manned. I did not say anything until the knight had spoken.

"The gatehouse, it seems, is the most likely place for us to gain entry."

"Aye, lord. When it is dark, we will head across this open ground and gain you the gate. When we signal, then bring your knights across."

"Why not follow you across and be there when you have the gatehouse?"

"With respect, my lord, even though these are the finest knights in England, they cannot help but make a noise. Mail and swords jangle. You will need to be swift, but we can hold the gate for the time it will take you."

"How can you be so sure?"

"I know how long it takes the man at arms, Stephen de Frankton, to cover the ground."

"Then we will do so even quicker."

I stayed at the top with Tom while Martin fetched my bow and the rest of the men. We did not move and watched the sun slowly set in the west. The nights would soon be the same length as the day but, for now, the sun held sway.

I watched the sentries change and was reassured that just two men were on each tower and two on the gate. I had no idea of overall numbers, but I had confidence in our knights. They were only vulnerable to arrows, and in the confines of a castle at night, they would win!

"Ned, go and tell Sir Reginald that we are leaving and he can bring his men here."

Ned was the son of James, my steward, and one of the most reliable archers I had ever known. While he could not send an arrow as far as John, son of John, he could keep going long after my other archers tired.

When he returned, we each nocked an arrow and silently descended the slope. There was still a hint of light in the west but as we were approaching from the darkness of the east, we were invisible. We used the wooden palisade for cover.

Tom led half my men from the side furthest from the river. The two night guards had a brazier. It was not cold now, but it might be in the middle of the watch. It would ruin their night vision. I waved for John and Martin to move to my right and crawl up the slope. They would use their bows to slay the two sentries, but Tom and I were waiting next to the wooden wall in case they failed. I saw them rise as one and their arrows thudded into the two men. Seated on barrels and with their backs to the wall, they were an easy target, and at a range of just twenty paces, my men could not miss. I ran around the end of the wooden palisade. The two men were pinned to the wall. Both arrows had penetrated the bodies and embedded themselves in the new mortar! I stood in the gateway and waved my bow. Behind me, my men began to silently dismantle the improvised gate. I heard a noise from inside and realised that the garrison was eating in the hall.

Sir Reginald and his men were swift, but I could hear the occasional jingle as a loose piece of metal found another. We had the gateway, and my men were inside, making a protective circle. They faced an empty inner bailey. The castle was still far from finished. The hall had a roof, but the rest of the buildings were half-completed walls. I had to work out where the garrison was, and that was evidenced by the light I saw from the largest completed building and the noise that emanated from within.

Sir Reginald joined me, and I pointed to the building. He nodded and, drawing his sword, led his forty killers. We followed. Some of my archers watched the top of the walls while others kept looking for danger at ground level. It was Edward, son of John, who saw the sentry on the finished part of the fighting platform. The man looked down and we all raised our bows, but Edward was the fastest, and even as Sir Reginald threw open the door to the hall, Edward's arrow smacked into the sentry and he tumbled, screaming to the bailey below.

That alerted the other sentries on the walls, but we knew where they were and had the element of surprise. As swords clashed in the hall and men screamed as they were slain, we sent our arrows towards the sentries. We knew how many there were, and all but two were slain.

I pointed to Tom and John. "Go and find them and secure the main gate!" They ran off and I led my men towards the hall.

Inside it was like a scene from hell. There looked to be more than one hundred Welshmen in the hall, but the knights were immune to their blows. Where they had been eating, there were no Welshmen with bows. At best they had swords.

I sent four arrows at the nearest Welshmen and then realised that knights could accidentally walk into an arrow, and so I said, "Put your bows away and use swords."

The slaughter did not last long, for there was another door and that led to the kitchen. They ran through it to escape to the main gate, but John and Tom were there. After six men had been killed, the Welsh began to throw down their weapons. Sir Reginald stopped the slaughter, for we had done what we intended. We had retaken Rhuddlan. The recovery of Wales was well on the way!

King Edward was delighted when he arrived, two days later, and a week later we had more good news. Anglesey had been taken and de Tany was in a position to invade across the straits and take on Llywelyn, who was at Penmaenmawr.

The king had ships bring more timber and stone up the Clwyd to repair the castle, and we were sent to escort builders to Rhuthun. As well as conquest, the king intended to secure his gains with even stronger castles. The setback in the south could be minimised with a swift strike from the island of Anglesey. Reginald de Grey recaptured Caergwrle and drove Dafydd deeper into Gwynedd and closer to his brother.

It was not an easy campaign, and we were used to help the king (who arrived from Chester), de Grey and the Cheshire knights. We had to fight our way past narrow passes, which suited the ambusher. Although I lost no men and no knights died, many of the Cheshire archers and levy paid the price for each yard we took.

The Archbishop of Canterbury arrived to try to bring a peaceful solution to the problem. I was there when the archbishop, the king and de Grey spoke. We had suffered attacks from hidden archers, and so my men and I had been assigned as bodyguards to the king and his guests. We scanned the land for danger, and it meant that we were privy to the conversation.

"The prince is at Penmaenmawr, King Edward, and I believe that we can speak with him there."

Reginald de Grey, I had come to learn, was a hard man who would not bend in the slightest. "Better, my liege, if we were to negotiate from a position of strength. De Tany will soon be able to launch an attack over a bridge of boats from Anglesey. Even if Llywelyn were to escape, we would have him trapped in his mountains. With winter approaching he would starve!"

I saw the king weighing up the two options. The treachery of both brothers was what swayed him. He wanted them punished and humiliated. His friends had been hurt. "When de Tany has trounced the Welsh, then send your men to speak to him, Archbishop!"

It was November when the straits were crossed, and it was an unprecedented disaster. The Welsh were waiting, and they fell upon de Tany. Sixteen knights, including de Tany, were killed. The tide turned and trapped many of those on foot. Otto de Grandson recalled from Gascony, swam the straits on his horse, but even though he and some other knights survived, the successful ambush put heart into the Welsh and meant that we could not attempt the same again until the new year.

The king was apoplectic with rage. That it was his decision was forgotten and the unfortunate de Tany was blamed. The good news, as far as I was concerned, was that it changed the strategy of the king. The Clwyd became a holding campaign, and he had to send soldiers to Shropshire to counter the threat there. Since Gloucester had been defeated and withdrawn, the only men left to defend the land west of my home were the Shropshire levy and the Mortimer men. Roger Lestrange was tasked with organising the defence of that part of Wales. That he would have to do it with few knights was not even a consideration for the king. He had given a command and it would be done. My men and I were sent with the dozen or so knights who accompanied the Lord of Wilton, Roger Lestrange. I felt happier defending my home. John Giffard was with us and he was keen for vengeance. The three of us rode at the fore and I wondered at the wisdom of King Edward. If the land around Builth was now devoid of English defenders, then the numbers he had sent were not enough. Were we being sacrificed?

At Wigmore, we learned that Baron Mortimer was now asleep more than he was awake, but I had no opportunity to see him. I was given command of the Shropshire archers. Stephen de Frankton was there with the rest of the levy. He had far more men under his command than did I, but the archers would be a more potent force. The knights of the Mortimer brothers added another twenty to our number, but we were still woefully inadequate.

The six of us had a council of war. I knew the Mortimer brothers, but they were both shadows of their father. They had served with him, but it had always been the baron who made the decisions. The presence of Giffard, myself and de Frankton ensured that they listened to us and heeded our advice.

Sir Roger had once been Lord of Builth and knew the area well. "We will need to watch every road and stifle any attempt by the Welsh to move east. The problem will be one of mobility. Warbow, it is your mounted archers who will hold the key. We need all of your mounted archers."

I shook my head. "If there is a danger to my family, then the ones I left at home will do more good there. Do not worry, Sir Roger; my men will not let you down."

He sighed. "Then this is what I propose. I will base myself at Builth with the Sirs Roger and Edmund Mortimer as well as the other knights. Captain Giffard, you will command the men at arms you lead as well as de Frankton and Warbow's archers. There are two roads from the north-west, one from Pontnewydd ar Wy and one from Llanafan-fechan. Those will need to be guarded."

It was John Giffard who shook his head. He knew the land better than any. "The road from Pontnewydd ar Wy has to cross the bridge which is east of Builth. The bridge can be seen from the castle. We would waste men by placing them there. Your horsemen could reach the bridge before any Welshman."

I saw the knight rub his chin. This was a test of his leadership. Would he listen to the man at arms or would his pride get in the way?"

"You are right, Giffard, and I had forgotten. Then place yourselves at Cilmeri and guard the road from Llanafan-fechan."

It was November and we would have to endure the cold. Once the snows came, then we could return to our homes, but the really bad weather was four weeks away. It seemed ominous when, as we were about to set off, a rider arrived to tell the Mortimer brothers that their father was dead. I think I was affected as much as they. Since I had come to England and fought for King Henry and then his son, my life and that of Roger Mortimer were intertwined. I had no time to mourn, for we had to leave. Every moment we delayed increased the chance of Llywelyn coming down the road and laying waste to the heart of the Marches!

We were camped by a hamlet called Cilmeri. There was an old farmer and his wife who remained there. The rest had been tired of the upheaval and moved. The old man, Idris, was too tired to move. I got the impression that he and his wife were just waiting to die. Their animals were not properly cared for. We treated the couple well and our cooks took them food.

We were just five hundred paces from the Irfon, although we had a small unnamed stream, which passed below our camp. It acted as our toilet. As we had some empty houses, John and Stephen de Frankton, along with some of their men at arms, took one each. I used a tent with my men. It was my way, and I did not blame the others for having a roof over their heads.

The first afternoon, while the others were making our camp defensible, I took my men to ride along the road. Llanafan-fechan was bigger than Cilmeri – and occupied. I got the impression we were not welcome. We left the road to ride in a loop to the northern river, the Chewfri. It meant we could see the other road. I knew that the Welsh could ford it, and so I decided that I would make our camp where we could watch the ford I found. On the way back we found half a dozen sheep and I had no misgivings about taking them for food.

That evening I sat and ate with John and Stephen.

Stephen was quite cynical. "It is all right for the levy to sleep rough, but lords and knights must have a roof and a real bed."

I laughed. "And that is the way of the world, my friend. Did you not learn that in the Holy Land?"

He smiled and spat out a piece of mutton gristle. "I hoped that the crusader cross would bring some benefits in this country, but it seems that I was wrong."

I leaned back and put my hands beneath my head. The sky above was clear and I could see the stars. Were these the same stars I had seen when I had met Mary? "Stephen, we have both done well from this land; all three of us have. When you were a prisoner of the Welsh, working in their mines, did you see yourself with a manor? Baron Mortimer was good to us and I shall say a prayer for his soul each night until I return to my home and church. I will remember him there."

John laughed. "You are quite a philosopher, Gerald, and there is more to you than meets the eye." I sat up and rested on my elbows. "Tell me, you who have the ear of the king and know him better than any commoner, can we win this war? Do we wish to?"

I reflected on his words and then spoke. "We have endured setbacks. The king has made mistakes. He trusted Dafydd and when he had him, he should have incarcerated him with his brother Owain. You are right, John; I do know him, and he has the beating of the Welsh. It may take a year or two, but when all of his castles are built, he will have a ring of stone around Wyddfa that no Welshman can break."

"I pray that you are right."

Stephen said grimly, "Put Llywelyn within striking distance of my sword and that old man will never cause King Edward any more trouble. He has no son for me to punish and I will have my vengeance on him."

I was not surprised by the venom in his voice, but I was not sure that King Edward would see it that way. He would want a rebel he could punish through his courts and show the Welsh the power of England.

I left my friends to return to my men on the other side of the road, where we could watch the ford. I had two of my men on watch all night, but they heard nothing. We rode, each day, up the road to the belligerent village and then across to the ford. We were looking for signs. We saw none for five days and then on the sixth day, we woke to thick fog. Everyone in the camp, all fifteen hundred of us, knew that this meant danger. An enemy could sneak up easily. Leaving my men to make their way to the ford and watch it, I headed for John and Stephen. They were both awake.

John Giffard took charge. "I do not like this. We will make a defensive line across the road. Gerald, you keep your men on the flank closest to the Chewfri. If they come, then sound the horn three times."

I nodded. Each of us had a horn and by their very nature, each one was unique. We would know where lay the danger.

I donned my helmet when I reached our empty camp. I spread my archers out – there were too few of them for my liking – along the line of spearmen. John Giffard had spread his men at arms out amongst Stephen's Shropshire levy. Our task was just to hold the Welsh, if they came, until Lestrange could bring help. The fact that we had seen no sign of any Welsh scouts had me worried.

By the time I reached my men, the fog was beginning to lift a little and I wondered if our precautions had been premature.

Ned was not just a steady and dependable archer; he had good hearing too. It was he who heard the jingle from the Chewfri. "Captain, someone comes."

"Nock an arrow." I took the horn and readied it in my left hand. In my right, I held my bow with an arrow nocked. I could hear something but there was little point in sounding the horn too soon. We had to know if it was the enemy or some other cause. A combination of the fog dissipating and the noise becoming clearer showed me that while it was mailed men, it was not the knights of Lestrange. I sounded the horn three times and, as I did so, my men drew back on their bows. It was then we saw that the Welsh archers and spearmen were fewer than two hundred paces from us, for the horses and those with mail were further back.

"Release!" I dropped the horn to hang from my waist, nocked an arrow and released. We hit some fifteen men and when we released a second shower, a Welsh voice shouted a command. The Welsh riders, their knights and their mailed men dismounted for the ground, which we had discovered was very rough, and while the fog was lifting, it still hid treacherous ground.

"Fall back but slowly! The men behind will need to readjust their line." Our main line of defence faced Llanafan-fechan and the forty or so archers I had with me were the only ones opposing the Welsh. Perhaps I should have brought all of my archers. Most of the archers I led were the Shropshire levy, and already I could see that Warbow's Men were the ones releasing more frequently and hitting the enemy.

I heard a shout behind me. I did not allow it to distract me. I nocked a bodkin and sent it at the Welsh warrior with a mail vest. He looked surprised when the green fletched arrow blossomed from his chest.

"Shropshire! With me!"

It was Stephen de Frankton and he had taken it upon himself to wheel his men and come to our aid. Of course, if the Welsh were advancing down the road as well, then we would be in trouble. But we had to fight one battle at a time.

We had slowed down the enemy and they were reorganising, with spearmen protecting their archers. Soon we would have to endure their arrows. Stephen had anticipated the problem, and already the first of those of his men with spears was racing to stand before us. The fog was rapidly clearing, and I saw that we were equally matched.

Then I saw Llywelyn. He wore mail and a helmet, but I had met him several times.

I shouted, "It is Prince Llywelyn."

I sent a bodkin at the knight next to Llywelyn. It hit his helmet and stuck there. I knew that I had not penetrated the metal to hit the skull, for the knight reached up to break off the shaft. It angered him and he came directly for me. Tom was more accurate, and his arrow hit one of the knights in the left shoulder. His shield dropped a little and John, son of John, killed his first knight.

Some of the Shropshire archers were dying, for the levy did not wear brigandines. We were struck, but none of the arrows sent by the Welsh impaired my men's ability to fight. We used war arrows and they used hunting arrows.

I heard Stephen shout, "I am coming for you, Llywelyn, and either you or I will stay upon this field of battle."

When the Welsh prince raised his sword to accept the challenge, then I knew that the Welshman had chosen death or glory. Up until that point, he could have fallen back and let others bear the brunt of the fighting, but he did not. He came on with his men at arms and knights around him.

"Warbow's Men! Take out the men at arms!" There was little point in expecting the levy to send arrows at mailed men.

Stephen had two men at arms with him as well as men from the levy. They had raw courage, but would that be enough?

We did all that we could, but we were hampered when the men on either side of Stephen and his vanguard fell back. I sent every arrow that I had at the Welsh and when I ran out of arrows, I slung my bow and drew my sword.

"Tom, keep releasing. I go to the aid of my friend." I drew one of my daggers instead of a shield and advanced.

Even as I took the decision, I saw one of the two mailed men left defending Stephen fall, leaving no one on Stephen's right. My former man at arms was having the better of the fight with the old prince, but the men around him were falling, and the Welsh were defending their leader with their lives. One of the last knights remaining, the one whose helmet I had dented, raised his sword to hack down on Stephen's exposed right side. I threw, underhand, my dagger. It was a lucky throw, but I had good coordination. The blade struck his left cheek, and he whipped his head around, his sword mid-strike.

"You!" He turned to face me and advanced. I had saved my friend but put my own life in harm's way. I reached down and drew a second dagger from my buskin. This one was a bodkin; good for stabbing but less useful when it came to blocking a sword. Even as the Welshman came, I saw that Stephen had drawn first blood. My archers were trying to keep him safe.

I heard, behind me, John Gifford's voice. "For England and King Edward!"

The battle was finely balanced. I was too close to my opponent now for my men to aid me. If I survived, then it would be down to me, and the Welshman had vengeance on his mind. Seeing that I had neither shield nor coif, he strode towards me, slashing with his sword as he punched with his shield. I was nimbler and I danced out of the way. The uneven ground came to my aid and he stumbled. I feinted with my sword, and my left hand darted out to stab him in the right shoulder with my bodkin.

I saw Stephen had the upper hand in his own fight, for Llywelyn's left arm had been hurt and his shield hung down.

"Trickster!" The Welsh knight was angry, for he was being humiliated. Regaining his feet, he swung his sword wildly and the ground punished me. I fell. With a roar of triumph, he brought his sword down. I did the only thing I could; I rolled, and, as I did so, I saw Stephen de Frankton lunge and plunge his sword into the face of the Welsh prince.

As Llywelyn died, I thought I had escaped, but the knight's sword hit my back. I was saved by my bow; although it was sliced in two, it allowed me to roll and as I did, I hacked across the knight's leg above his buskin. I tore through his breeks and his muscle before ripping through his tendons. His leg crumpled and I leapt upon him before he could recover. I drove the bodkin through his eye and into his brain.

His sword had not only broken my bow; it had also torn my brigandine and sliced a line across my back, but I was alive, and I struggled to my feet. The Welsh were fleeing, and I heard a horn as Roger Lestrange brought his knights to end the rebellion.

I walked over to de Frankton. "Are the ghosts laid to rest?"

He nodded. "They are, and now I can enjoy my manor. He was a brave old man!"

"He had nothing left to live for. His wife is dead, and she bore him a daughter. He has a treacherous brother and land surrounded by enemies. Look, he has a smile upon his face."

I looked down at the last native Prince of Wales and gazed upon the end of an independent country. We had helped King Edward do that which none of his predecessors had managed. We had given him Wales!

Epilogue

Lestrange took Llywelyn's head back to King Edward and the rest of us returned to Wigmore. Lady Maud had waited for our return to bury her husband. She had paid stonemasons to make his tomb and to put upon it his epitaph. It matched the man.

Here lies buried, glittering with praise, Roger the pure, Roger Mortimer the second, called Lord of Wigmore by those who held him dear. While he lived all Wales feared his power and given as a gift to him all Wales remained his. It knew his campaigns, he subjected it to torment.

I did not wish to intrude upon the feast that was held after he had been interred and I was about to leave when Lady Maud sent Edmund, her eldest son, after me.

I was brought before her like a naughty child. "And where are you going, Gerald Warbow?"

"I was leaving you and your family to mourn a great man."

She took my arm. "You may be a commoner, Warbow, but you were as much, are as much, a part of our family as any. My husband thought highly of you. So much, that he has left to you the manor of Caynham. It was a special place for him as it was one of the first manors his Norman ancestors were given. I know that he always intended to give you your spurs, but fate intervened. Now come back to the feast and then we will let you get home to your family!"

The manor was a good one, but I did not move there. I was content at Yarpole. My wife was delighted, for we had an even greater income but more importantly, even more security, for it showed how much the Mortimers thought of us.

The Welsh war did not end properly for a year after my friend killed Prince Llywelyn. His brother managed to evade capture for many months, but he was caught, for his treachery was too much for even the most patriotic Welshman. He was tried at Rhuddlan. He was found guilty, of course, and brought to Shrewsbury. For his treason, he was dragged through Shrewsbury by a horse's tail. For his homicides, he was hanged alive. For his murders during Holy Week, he was disembowelled and his intestines burned, and for the plotting of the king's death, he was quartered and his parts despatched to the four corners of the kingdom. Llywelyn had fared better; his head had been sent to adorn the gate of the Tower of London.

Historical Note

My story is the story of Gerald War Bow, the archer. The kings and lords are incidental. It is the archers of England and Wales that I celebrate in this series of books. Porth y Wygyr is Beaumaris. The taking of Anglesey was as fast as I describe. In military terms, it was pure genius and, effectively, ended the war. Flint and Rhuddlan castles were the first to be built by Edward. They were not huge fortresses like Conwy and Caernarfon but cost more than £5,000 to build, in modern-day values, millions. 1,500 labourers were needed for Flint castle. King Edward was making a statement.

Books used in the research:

The Normans, David Nicolle
The Knight in History, Francis Gies
The Norman Achievement, Richard F. Cassady
Knights, Constance Brittain Bouchard
Feudal England: Historical Studies on the Eleventh and Twelfth Centuries, J. H. Round

Peveril Castle, English Heritage
The Castles of Edward in Wales 1277–1307, Gravett and Hook
The Longbow, Mike Loades
Norman Knight AD 950–1204, Christopher Gravett
English Medieval Knight 1200–1300, Christopher Gravett
English Medieval Knight 1300–1400, Christopher Gravett
The Scottish and Welsh Wars 1250–1400, Christopher Rothero
English Longbowman 1330–1515, Bartlett and Embleton
Lewes and Evesham 1264–65, Richard Brooks
A Great and Terrible King – Edward 1, Marc Morris
The Mammoth Book of British Kings and Queens, Mike Ashley

Griff Hosker, *October 2020*

Glossary

Battle – a medieval formation of soldiers.

Burghers – Ordinary citizens of a town.

Chevauchée – A raid by mounted horsemen.

Gammer – Mother, used as a term of affection for any older woman.

Garderobe – Toilet (basically, a seat above a hole which led outside a castle).

Pursuivant – The rank below a herald.